ROB WILLIAMS

Third Edition

Three Days in Brandon Springs

First novel of the Brandon Springs series

**In memory of my father and mother,
Bob & Jewel**

Rob Williams

Three Days in Brandon Springs
Third Edition Published by Winged
Publications
http://wingedpublications.com/
Copyright © 2007/**2023 by Rob Williams**

**Printed in the United States of America
First Printing: July 2008
Second Edition: January 2016
Third Edition: 2023**

ISBN: 978-1-0881-5618-6

Special thanks to Connie Dunham
for editorial help

Forward

    This fictional Christian novel is the first of the Brandon Springs series. It is about the life changing events, both real and imagined, encountered by a young man. Ryan Walker, a thirty-year-old career minded Boston professional, returns to a small town in the southern Appalachians after receiving a letter from a probate judge requesting his presence. Hating this small town since childhood, he views himself to be superior to those living there. The main character thinks Brandon Springs to be a clean and dull little village, but there he experiences emotional and mental turns which cause him to doubt his sanity. Ryan is haunted by a mysterious fellow even in his dreams. There are elements of mystery and unexpected twists as the story progresses to a revealing conclusion.

Chapter 1

RYAN WALKER COULD BARELY SEE. The continual pounding of water on the windshield distorted visibility so that details of the world outside his protective shell were almost indistinguishable. Shallow streams rising across the pavement were sliced apart by the moving vehicle. Water gushed from tires as they struggled to maintain contact with the asphalt surface.

Ryan had forgotten what spring thunderstorms were like in the South, for several years had passed since he made a new life for himself in Boston. His journey became slowed by the crippling power of the rain. Even with the wipers set to maximum, he was unable to see the road if his speed exceeded forty miles per hour. Under the shadow of intensely dark and heavily saturated clouds, Ryan felt the powerful winds and rain violently shake his car. Fear surged through his body as though he had been attacked by a powerful adversary. Death flooded his mind. He thought about his parents, who had been murdered while their home was being robbed. Ryan was away at college when he received the news of their death. Now, his own mortality was foremost in his mind.

Something is wrong. I can't put my finger on it, but something isn't right. Maybe I shouldn't have come. Maybe this storm is an omen.

1

Ryan didn't really believe in the supernatural, but his nerves were on edge. His heart pounded and he clasped the steering wheel with a death grip.

When the rain first began, he had the advantage of using the red taillights of the vehicle ahead as a beacon. He couldn't remember the point at which he lost sight of them, but now he was left on his own to navigate through the torrential downpour. This normally confident man felt vulnerable. Though protected from the punishing elements by his vehicle, Ryan felt an unsettling rise from deep within.

As he exited the main artery onto an old country road, the rain eased to a steady but gentle shower. Ryan was so relieved for the storm to loosen its hold, that for a moment, he ignored the condition of the pavement. The neglected rural tar and gravel road caused his luxury sedan to produce vibrations similar to what a child would experience while riding down a sidewalk in a toy wagon. His upscale car usually offered a ride that was gracious in handling, very quiet, and as smooth as a lone canoe on a small still lake at first morn. As the rain became a mist, he became more mindful of the surface on which he traveled. After only a few moments he found himself irritated.

Why must my expensive car have to endure this pitiful excuse for a road?

Ryan's irritation was the type of thing that could grow into a powerful force, but he had learned how to not allow his anger to erupt into violent behavior. Most of the time, he was able to channel anger into an energy that drove his career. Ryan managed to burn off his anger and stress by immersing himself in problem solving and working additional hours for the company. It was advantageous for him to always have access to his work. He normally carried his laptop with him when he traveled, but he had neglected to bring it this time. Realization of his lack of focus ate at him even more than the lousy road. If allowed to mature, the growing anger could move him into a state where he found no satisfaction. If left unchecked, it could become a malignant illness that murdered a good day. Today, he was separated from his drug – his work. He felt fortunate that his growing foul mood was stopped in its infancy, as his mind was redirected by the vaguely familiar sights before him.

Brandon Springs was a clean and dull little village that sat between two mountains in the southern Appalachians. He was coming to the outskirts of the boring little town he had visited as a child. Childhood memories flashed through his mind. *I've always pictured this place as a small piece of toilet paper stuck between deformed butt cheeks of an enormous giant.*

Ryan didn't completely hate the place; it was more of an irritant. His mother and father had taken him there as a child to visit his uncle Andrew. Andrew was old, and the town was old. Everything in it was old, quiet, and somewhat stuck in a motionless state. There were no other children, and his uncle had no television. People just sat around the kitchen table, or on the front porch, and talked. Even the talking was quiet and slow. He remembered lying on the couch in the main room of Andrew's small house listening to the steady slow murmur that seemed to gently roll through the cracks in the wall. It was a lot like white noise, but not quite as continuous. There would be moments of total quietness, and he would wonder briefly whether people were still on the porch. Eventually, the vibrations of Uncle Andrew's deep throated utterances would end the silence. Ryan would be able to understand about two thirds of the spoken words, but the other third was just a meaningless soft rumble of muffled sound.

Today, he was back -- back in the crack of the imaginary giant's rump. As he pulled the car into an inviting parking space directly in front of the ancient courthouse on the square, a small boy whizzed down the sidewalk before him on a skateboard. Reflections of his bored childhood visits rushed into his mind, and he began to feel sorry for the child. *How lonely he must be in this place. At least the kid has a skateboard; at least he has some form of entertainment.*

As Ryan stepped out of his car, he heard a variety of high-pitched voices in the direction the boy was skating. *Something terrible must have happened; perhaps an elderly woman has fallen on the sidewalk and broken a hip.*

As he moved onto the sidewalk to view the commotion, his mouth dropped, and he found himself standing motionless. He gazed upon a group of children with skateboards shouting to each other and laughing.

Here he was, standing in front of the courthouse. He had arrived at his destination, the sole purpose of returning to this hamlet, but the group of children had stolen his attention. He found himself walking at an increased pace towards the flock of noise makers.

Why are they there; and where are their parents?

As he approached, he noticed the absence of Miller's Feed Store. It was no longer where it had been for the last million years. In its place was a large skateboard park, filled with as many as fifty children. The sound of scratching wheels against the concrete course, mixed with the laughter and shouts of children, was almost deafening. The feed store and the storage building behind it, had once occupied this large area. Where these two buildings once stood were three skateboard courses.

Surrounding the courses were outdoor benches and tables, where parents talked and kept a watchful eye and ear for children. Spotting an empty bench, he made his way to it. The warm scene of parents watching over energetic children, while enjoying conversation among adults, reminded him of his own family.

Much had changed in Brandon Springs; and the most surprising was the fact that so many younger adults with children were now making this place home. He remembered being the lone child in a town of middle aged and elderly people. This time, he found himself enjoying the happy atmosphere of the place and was intrigued by the current mystery.

What an idea! Who had invested the money to build such a place? Someone had seen the need for children and parents to have a common gathering place for social recreation. But, I don't understand. What caused these people to be here? What in the world could have brought them to Brandon Springs?

He glanced at his watch and was shocked to see that he had been sitting on the bench for two hours. In fact, only twenty minutes remained before the courthouse closed. He jumped to his feet and hurried back down the street to the courthouse. He entered and approached an attractive young woman seated behind a desk. She was busily trying to finish the day's work and was rapidly typing on a computer. As he waited for a response, Ryan noted how quickly her small slender fingers lightly danced across the keyboard. Her hazel eyes peered diligently with purpose from a freckled face, which was cradled by evenly parted red hair that curled uniformly inward beneath each cheek.

After being ignored for a couple of minutes, he quietly said "I'm here to see Judge Peacock."

She stopped, peered directly into his eyes, and questioned, "Are you Mr. Ryan Walker?"

He nodded with affirmation. Standing, she motioned for him to follow her. The young woman pulled open a tall oak door and led him into a large room with a very high ceiling. In the center of it was a neatly arranged assortment of file cabinets, printers, facsimile machines, and copiers. Several doors lined the walls of the room. Each door was similar, a large solid oak door that stood eight feet in height. Their destination was the one wearing a brass plate that read, "Judge Ira Peacock - Probate Judge."

She opened the door slightly and slipped her head inside. She mumbled something, but he could only distinguish the use of his name, "Mr. Walker."

"He will see you," she promptly stated.

With that, the woman quickly retreated in the direction from which they had come. The door now fully opened; Ryan spotted an older man seated behind a desk. Judge Peacock was busy at work, his head bowed displaying his bald top ringed with white fluffs of hair.

"Come on in, Mr. Walker," he stated in a distinguished voice.

Ryan stood before him, watching the judge deliberately

place his signature on a document.

"Have a seat, please" the older man said. Still not looking up, the judge carefully placed the document in a folder.

Ryan seated himself in a wooden chair just to his right. As he looked up from his position, he caught his first glimpse of Judge Peacock's clear blue eyes.

"I expected you earlier," stated the judge. "Were you slowed by the rain?"

The old man's polished voice would have been the most noticeable feature for a man his age, but it was the fixed gaze that caught Ryan's attention. Those bright clear blue eyes should have belonged to a much younger man, or perhaps a young woman. Yet the heavy brow and eyelids that sagged at the edges spoke of miles of experience and maturity.

"The rain slowed travel, but I was also distracted by something in town and lost track of the time," Ryan apologized.

"What could have captured your attention in this village?" asked Peacock.

Here was a man from a large Northeastern city who had allowed the existence of a skateboard park in a very small town to steal him away from the purpose that had caused him to drive hundreds of miles.

How can I explain this without sounding ridiculous?

He disliked this place; it had always caused him boredom or embarrassment. As he searched for the right explanation, he was saved by the next statement from Peacock.

"The only thing remotely exciting around here is the new skateboard park, unless you find the plant interesting."

With relief in his voice, Ryan responded.

"What plant?"

The judge silently stared at him for a moment. He then explained how the board of a large computer firm in California found it difficult to pass up such cheap land in the Brandon Springs area; land which happened to be within two miles of a major interstate highway. It was this company that had invested in the skateboard park and promised to pave the tar and gravel highway which led to the interstate. Construction of the asphalt paving was to start the following month.

"With the plant came a new housing subdivision, built just a mile west of the plant," Peacock continued. "Finding land so inexpensive, many of the new residents requested one acre lots. New inhabitants created the demand for a new shopping center across the road from the facility."

"I had no clue about the plant," Ryan admitted.

"I thought you knew about the changes around here," Peacock quietly spoke. "I thought that was why you so readily agreed to meet regarding your uncle's property."

"Property?" asked Ryan.

Ryan was puzzled. Uncle Andrew had died two months previously, but Ryan had not come for the funeral.

Uncle Andrew must have died leaving outstanding debts on the property, but why would they be calling on me to settle it? What about Aunt Sally, Andrew's sister? Why hadn't they contacted her to handle it? She should be the closest relative, since my father's older brother never had children.

"I wasn't informed about property in the letter," Ryan coldly stated.

I've worked hard to be where I am in my life, and I have no intention of letting the mismanagement of a backwoods relative threaten my finances.

His hardened stare told the judge that it was time to get to the point.

"Your Uncle Andrew left his money to his sister, but he left his land to you," said Peacock. "I thought you knew that the land had appreciated in value, and this was why you agreed so quickly to come. From what I have been told, you were a child when you were last in Brandon Springs."

"How much did he owe on the property?" snapped Ryan.

"He owed nothing" Peacock firmly stated.

Ira Peacock had little patience with arrogant individuals, especially those who quickly jumped to conclusions before hearing a matter.

"He owed no one, young man. Didn't you hear me say that Andrew left his money to his sister, and his land to you?

I thought you to be a bit sharper than that. Why would a man make payments with interest on land, with this kind of cash on hand?"

Peacock's face had gone from welcoming gentleness to disappointment and slight disgust. He was a learned man, both of books and of life. In one short conversation he had sized Ryan up. The judge perceived that the 30-year-old was trying to be someone he wanted to be, instead of a man comfortable with himself. In Ryan's angry eyes, he saw immature arrogance substituting for quiet self-confidence.

"The real estate office across the street can give you an appraisal in the morning, if you want," spoke Peacock. "Or you can visit the county tax office down the street; take your pick."

"I'm still a little in the dark," said Ryan.

"Andrew knew he was dying, and before his death he paid the taxes in advance to cover the next two years," explained the judge.

"Why did he leave the land to me?' stammered Ryan. "I really can't think of a reason. Did he say?"

Peacock's eyes softened.

"I wouldn't know. I don't pry into family matters. His sister didn't seem to be surprised at the reading of the will, so I didn't expect you to be."

"Does she still live in that old rundown farmhouse just east of town?" Ryan asked.

"No, she bought a home in the new subdivision with some of the money her brother left," said Peacock. "You may want to pay her a visit while you're in town. Sounds like you may have the basis for an interesting conversation. It's time for me to go home for the day."

Peacock retrieved a package out of the top right desk drawer and handed it to the young man. The judge motioned toward the door. Ryan immediately obeyed.

"I want to thank you for handling the affairs of my Uncle Andrew," said Ryan.

Peacock nodded, and then reached back into his office to turn out the light.

"It may interest you to know that there is someone interested in the pastureland," the judge casually stated. "He approached your Aunt Sally regarding the possibility of farming the property, but she told him he would have to discuss the matter with her nephew. You'll find everything contained in your package to be in order. Should you require further assistance, you may contact Jennifer at the front desk to make an appointment."

Ryan thanked him. Peacock turned purposefully and locked the office door. The young man quickly made his way to the front door of the building, where Jennifer was waiting to lock up.

"Good evening, Mr. Walker," she spoke as he moved through the doorway into the red glow of a heavy sun.

He turned to reply, but the door was already closed. Glancing at his watch, Ryan noticed he had caused her to stay twenty-five minutes past the normal closing time. He was a little surprised the judge had given him so much attention, but his arrogance caused him to reconsider.

But then again, why shouldn't he? After all, I traveled all the way from Boston because of a letter from the judge requesting my presence. It's the least he could do. I wonder if the tax office is still open. If not, I can stay the night and go to that office in the morning to verify payment of the taxes on the land. I'm curious to find out the cost of future taxes. Property tax rates in the Boston area are enormous, and I need to determine how quickly I should sell this recently inherited land."

Ryan made his way down the sidewalk in the direction of the tax office. At the end of the block, a man rounded the corner of the courthouse and stepped directly in front of him. Startled by his presence, Ryan was halted in his tracks. The intense eye contact captivated Ryan.

"Excuse me, sir," the figure stated.

"Excuse me," Ryan replied, in return.

The man's gaze shifted away, and he continued down the sidewalk. However, Ryan found himself still fixed on him.

That man definitely has to be from out of town. I'm unsure if it was the look in those eyes or the subtle tone of his voice. Possibly, it was both.

He can't be a local. Who is that guy?

Ryan intently watched until the fellow rounded the block. He noted there was elegance in the man's stride. There was an inner quality which seemed out of place for a man from this common small town.

Possibly in a large city that man would not have been noticed, but there is something very different about him. Those eyes. It's as if he has the ability to stare into a person's soul.

Chapter 2

RYAN WAS NOT IMPRESSED with the hotel room he found at the Wythington Inn. The sun had already dropped below the mountain to the west when he spotted the establishment. The interior walls were painted a shade of beige which masked the actual amount of smudge left by former occupants. A small bar of soap was provided, but no complimentary shampoo or conditioner.

Man, I'm so glad I brought my own toiletries from Boston. Still, being only one block down from the tax office, it should be convenient for the morning visit. I just hope I don't find bed bugs.

Ryan had become hungry, and the open café next door was the second asset that drew him to the hotel. After the quick assessment of the room, he immediately went to the café for supper. About half the tables were filled, and it was obvious that it still contained a smoking section. A hazy cloud of smoke slightly dimmed the view of the occupants of the booths in the right rear corner of the dining area. A sign posted near the un-manned register stated, "Please wait to be seated." As he glanced to his left, he spotted a portly middle-aged woman approaching.

"Smoking or no smoking?" she asked with a forced smile. She looked tired and appeared to be the only waitress for the evening.

"Non-Smoking, please," he answered.

She motioned for him to follow her, and then moved toward the booths that lined the front windows. The apron tied tightly around her waist emphasized the volume of her build. As the two made their way to an empty booth, he couldn't help but notice how each full hip alternately rode up and down with each step. They reminded him of the pumping of pistons within an engine, alternately rising and falling with each compressed explosion. He forced his eyes to the booths ahead, but the mesmerizing vision of those moving hips was locked in this mind.

"It's amazing how easily people can become fixated on repetition. Some people can watch the horses slide up and down on a merry-go-round pole and find it relaxing. Almost anyone can feel at peace watching the flames of a fireplace dance up and down. We rock in rocking chairs, swing as children in swings, and find ourselves swaying to a repetitive beat in music. I think it's something that is almost spiritual, as deeply natural as the repetitive beating of our heart."

"Will this be alright?" she asked, offering him the third booth at the window.

"This is fine" he replied, as he sat down.

She laid an ample menu on the table before him and turned back toward the kitchen area. He watched as the waitress gracefully grasped a pot of coffee in mid-stride and hastened to a booth in the smoking section. She must have said something humorous while refilling the cups of those seated there, because all three men at the booth chuckled at the same time. Ryan saw a faint smile invade her tired face as she walked away.

The menu contained breakfast, lunch, and dinner selections. Though the breakfast section caught his eye, he decided on a hamburger and fries. He wasn't sure about the quality of the food in this establishment, but he determined it would be difficult to make a poor hamburger. Just as he finalized his decision, she returned to his booth with the coffee pot.

"Would you care for coffee?" she asked politely.

"No, I'll just have a Coke" Ryan said. "I'm ready to order."

"OK, what will you have?" the waitress asked.

"I'll take the 'Hungry Man Burger' with fries," he said.

"Do you want everything on it, or would you like to have the fixin's on a separate side dish?" she asked.

"That sounds good" Ryan stated. "Bring the toppings on a side dish. Thank you."

"I'll be right back with your drink," she said, turning away.

Ryan picked up the menu again, for the breakfast items still held his interest. The entrees were much different than those found in restaurants in Boston. Not a single bagel was offered, but everything appeared to be extremely enticing. Most dishes came with heaps of bacon or sausage, and the biscuits were large. His arrogance exploded in judgmental thought.

No wonder the waitress is so plump! Not exactly a menu for a health-conscious public. She is pretty large, but her fat seems to be of the denser variety. I'm certain some of the bulk has to be muscle. The fat on some people seem to droop and wiggle like Jell-O as the person walks. Another type of fat seems to be made of dense round mounds that appear to be firmer. The dense fat seems to have a tendency to ride up and down, rather than sag and wiggle. It's my guess the sagging type belongs to couch potatoes, who do little physical work.

She returned with his soft drink and placed a straw and a couple of napkins beside the glass. He noticed the glass contained more ice than was offered in New England.

"It will be up in a few minutes" she said before going her way.

Leaving his analysis on types of fat, he returned to the menu again. The lure of the breakfast items surprised him. He always avoided a heavy breakfast, as he feared it would cause him to become drowsy during morning meetings. A coffee and bagel was all that he normally required.

Why would I even consider these artery-clogging heavy feasts?

Soon the 'Hungry Man' burger arrived. She placed the burger and fries before him on one large oval plate.

"Are these freshly made fries?' he asked in amazement. The fries were large thick strips of potato with some of the peel still attached.

"Yes, we wash and cut potatoes just before they're fried," she responded with a slight smile. "I hope you enjoy them."

He could not believe the size of the patty and bun. It was obvious the patty was handmade, not a frozen one. It was thick and the edges were uneven. She unloaded her tray. Beside the large plate of burger and fries, she placed a smaller plate containing lettuce, sliced tomato, pickles, and onion. Ryan quickly prepared the burger with everything but the onions and took a bite.

Wow! This is unbelievable.

He was away from his Boston acquaintances, and no one would know of his sinful indulgence. The waitress returned to refill his glass each time it was within an inch of being empty. At last, she brought the bill showing $6.50. He handed her fifteen dollars in cash and told her to keep the change.

"Are you sure?" she asked.

"Yes, please keep the change" he replied. "Both you and the meal were great."

"Thank you, so much!" she said. A broad smile puffed her cheeks.

Ryan was full and satisfied. He arose from the booth and headed out the door of the café. As he made his way to the car, he remembered the genuine smile his gesture had brought to the face of the waitress, and he found himself bathed in a warm peace which charity often brings. As he brought his bag up to the third-floor room, he began to feel very tired.

This has been an eventful day.

Entering the room, he dropped his bag in front of the nightstand and sat wearily on the bed. He began laughing as he turned on the television and found the hotel provided cable with pay per view channels.

As he lay down on the bed and stared at the high ceiling, it occurred to him this should not be the only hotel or motel in the town.

With the recent addition of the large plant, a newer motel has to be nearby. The Board of Directors for the plant would not have built a skateboard park and promised to pave the highway without first making sure there were adequate accommodations for business guests. This is not a primo hotel, but at least it isn't Uncle Andrew's house with no TV. There must be a new motel near the plant, probably part of a chain. Well, I have this room for tonight ... it's only for one night. I'll be on my way back to New England tomorrow.

He closed his eyes for a moment and tried to remember Uncle Andrew's land. The house sat far off the highway, behind what seemed like an eternity of pasture. The long gravel drive was lined on each side with barbed wire fence which led back to the small wood frame house with a broad front porch. The porch had been a gathering place for relatives and friends, having two porch swings and several rocking chairs. About 100 yards behind the house ran a small spring fed stream, which contained some of the coldest water he had ever wadded. The stream was the only interesting part of his visits, and it marked the end of the pasture. For just on the other side of the stream, the land was wooded and immediately rose up the side of a mountain. As a boy Ryan had crossed the stream, but never entered the woods beyond. He found the thickly wooded area leading up the mountain to be very foreboding. Just the thought of the ancient and gnarled oaks with their twisted limbs frightened him.

HE OPENED HIS EYES and found the early morning sun shining directly in his face. He must have been far more exhausted the night before than he had thought. He had not even undressed, climbed between the sheets, or even closed the blinds on the window. He sat up, dropped his chin down upon his chest, took a deep breath, and realized the worst of it. Before falling asleep he had not bothered to brush his teeth! They felt as if they were wearing mittens; and remnants of the previous night's café supper were wedged between two molars.

Gag! This has to be taken care of immediately.

He dropped to one knee beside his bag, and quickly unzipped it. Inside were very neatly organized items, which were now shoved aside in disrespect as he made way for his toiletry bag within. With staggered motion he gathered the toothbrush and toothpaste in his right hand and discarded the bag with his left.

He brushed for almost five minutes. When the task was done, he felt great sense of relief and accomplishment. He took the second deep breath of the morning and began to feel normal. Most people have some little something that really sets them off. For Ryan, it was dental hygiene. He had worn braces as a teen, and during the ordeal suffered depravation of self-esteem to the point that he had almost forgotten how to smile by the year the metal contraptions came off during the summer after graduating from high school. To his surprise his teeth were unbelievably perfect, both in spacing and in whiteness. From that point on, he was a different person. The students at college had never seen him with the hideous metal mess that had ripped away at the inside of his lips.

After showering, he quickly dressed and packed his bag. Ryan scanned the room for personal items, for he had no intention of leaving anything in this drab room. Confident that all was packed, he grabbed the bag and made his way to the door. Just as he reached out for the doorknob, he was suddenly aware of the strongest desire to eat breakfast at the nearby café. He had reviewed the breakfast menu while eating supper the night before. A picture of the "Sunriser" special lay dormant all night, but it was now vividly displayed on the walls of his consciousness. This awakened image consumed him and spread into portions of his brain which controlled other senses.

I can almost smell the fresh biscuits, bacon, hash browns, eggs, and fig preserves. This deal came with a tall glass of orange juice and free coffee. The price was incredible. I haven't tasted fig preserves since childhood.

Back in Boston he normally had a couple of bagels in a coffee shop before heading to work. He had sworn off eating bacon, but he felt an overwhelming urge for the fried pork slices. He knew this to be a conscious betrayal of his vows to health. With reckless abandon, he entertained the thoughts of it until it was too late. He completely surrendered himself to a consuming lust for biscuits and pig flesh.

He tossed the bag onto the bed. Ryan knew he would have to dedicate himself to vigorous flossing and brushing after indulging in such a meal.

Checkout is at 11:00 AM, and it's only 8:00 AM. I have plenty of time to consume the meal, savor it over a relaxing cup of coffee, walk over to the tax office, and then check out. There's no need to rush back to Boston. After all, I've taken vacation time to make the trip. This is Friday morning, and I have ample time to make it back to New England.

He purchased a local newspaper from a stand in front of the café. As he entered the café, the thick intoxicating smell of frying bacon filled his nostrils. A waitress of a much different appearance approached him with a smile.

"How many?" she asked.

Her slow and smooth southern Appalachian voice seemed to soothe his soul. Her healthy brown hair was neatly pulled back into a ponytail.

"I wonder how she looks with her hair down," he thought. *"I think it would probably be longer than shoulder length."*

Ryan had taken too long to reply, for when his eyes moved back to hers, he realized she had taken note of his admiration. Her eyes spelled an invitation for words other than a direct answer to the question.

"Just myself," he softly spoke. "And I want to be seated in the non-smoking area, please."

"Come this way," she said lightly, as she led him to the same booth by the front window. "Would you like a cup of coffee?"

"I'm ready for the 'Sunriser' special, and I believe it includes coffee.

"So you've been here before. I'll be right back with your coffee, sir," she chirped.

His eyes followed the waitress as she made her way back to the kitchen. Before she made it back behind the counter, he had taken note of her walk, her shape, her height, and guessed her approximate weight. Ryan watched as she stood on her toes in order to look into the kitchen window to relay the order to the cook. She quickly lowered herself and gracefully disappeared behind a wall.

He had almost forgotten the local newspaper, until he glanced down and caught a glimpse of it still neatly tucked under his arm. He unfolded it and read the section on *Community Services*. Ryan smiled and shook his head, as he noted how unprofessional it was in comparison to the papers of the Northeast.

His evaluation of the paper was interrupted by the waitress's soft voice, "Your coffee, Sir." He glanced up as she slid the cup and saucer beside the paper. "Did you find anything interesting?" she asked.

Her voice seemed so strangely familiar. Ryan knew he had never met her, because he had never met any other children while visiting Brandon Springs as a child. Nevertheless, the cadence of her words seemed to bathe his soul in quiet peaceful warmth.

Remembering himself, he answered, "It's nothing like the Boston Globe."

"Boston? Are you from there?" she asked.

"Yes. I'll be leaving for the return trip this afternoon," he quickly revealed without thinking.

Ryan grimaced. He thought of word spreading across town that a big city man was in their midst. By the contents he had observed in the local paper, his visit would probably be a feature article.

This mental picture of the gossip commentary was halted when she gently patted him on the shoulder and said, "Well, I hope you had a nice stay. I've never been to Boston, but you don't sound much like Ted Kennedy. I thought maybe you were from California or the mid-west, like most of the out-of-towners working at the plant. Have a safe trip back home."

She turned and headed back to another table to collect a tip. He prepared his coffee with sweetener, and his attention then turned back to the local paper. His eyes wandered above the top portion of the page, and then to the window near the booth. Ryan spotted a solitary man walking up the quiet sidewalk outside.

That's the same person that I almost bumped into yesterday!

The man stopped at the front of the restaurant, stared at the front door for a moment, then dropped his head and continued to walk. Ryan was about to return to his bored assessment of the paper, but was startled to see his waitress bolting out the front door of the café and moving quickly toward the man on the sidewalk. She caught him by the arm, and he turned to her. They talked for a moment. The fellow said something which made the waitress whirl about abruptly and retreat back into the restaurant. Ryan's eyes darted back and forth between the waitress and the man who stood on the sidewalk.

"*He must have really upset her*," he thought, as he caught her wiping her eyes with her hands as she entered the women's restroom. "*They must be lovers, caught up in an argument.*"

A few minutes later the waitress emerged from the restroom, her eyes red and a bit puffy. She marched over to where a couple of newly filled plates sat in the cook's window, and read the tickets clipped to a line which hung directly overhead. She gathered the two tickets and placed them on a clipboard just to her left. She seemed to stare at the two plates for a moment, then quickly took them and headed into the seating area. Ryan watched her place one plate in front of a gentleman seated three tables back, and without a word to the fellow she approached Ryan with the other.

"Here is your "Sunriser" special," she quietly said as she placed it on Ryan's table.

"May I ask you a personal question?" he asked her.

She nodded in affirmation. She then shrugged her shoulders and tilted her head to one side, as if to say that it didn't matter. "Who was the man you met outside a few minutes ago?" Ryan whispered.

She looked directly into his eyes with a glare indicating he had pried into a matter that was much too private to discuss with a stranger. The look then softened into sadness.

"His name is Jerry Prescott. For a couple of years, he and old Andrew Walker had coffee and breakfast here each morning."

There couldn't be but one old Andrew Walker in a place like Brandon Springs.

"Are you talking about the Andrew Walker who died recently and lived just outside town at the base of the mountain?" he asked.

"Yeah, did you know him?" inquired the waitress, somewhat bewildered. "I can't imagine how you would know about him."

Ryan hesitated to say more, but replied in almost a whisper, "He was my uncle. Uncle Andrew was my father's brother."

Without asking for permission, the waitress dropped down into the seat in the booth opposite Ryan.

"I knew that there was something familiar about you. There is something about your eyes that resembles that old man. Not the color, there is something else."

"Thanks a lot," Ryan stated sarcastically.

He had been told by older relatives that he had his grandfather's eyes, but he had never been compared to Uncle Andrew. Andrew did not have the look that Ryan wanted. He was missing two of his lower front teeth, and Andrew frequently used the opening to expel tobacco juice. He would place his right forefinger to his lower lip and could emit a squirt of the brown substance several feet. Ryan had always been embarrassed when Andrew performed his marksmanship with the stream of tobacco juice.

"He had really nice eyes for an older man; I would have thought you'd take that as a compliment," she said. "Are you visiting your aunt?"

Ryan felt a sudden sense of shame envelope him. He had not come to visit his aunt. In fact, if it hadn't been for the letter from the judge, he probably would have never returned to Brandon Springs. Here was an unrelated waitress who seemed to have greater fondness for his uncle than he. He began to see a vague picture of a self-absorbed successful young man who cared nothing for family. He had kept company with career minded individuals whose primary focus was to position themselves for success. A desire for true personal relationships was absent. Ryan's focus was to form relationships with those who offered benefit of success. If the time spent with them proved to be enjoyable, that would be an added bonus. For the first time, he smelled a slight whiff of how vain this life was becoming. The scent was not a pleasant one.

"I plan to see her this afternoon," he said.

The words had slipped from his mouth before he had time to think it through. He had committed himself. Ryan was vain, but the only old-fashioned trait he possessed was that of honesty. He was a man of his word. He had contemplated paying his aunt a visit to obtain information about his recent inheritance. However, in this verbal commitment to a waitress, he found himself wanting to pay his aunt a more personal visit.

"I'm sorry," the waitress apologized as she slid from the seat and stood beside the booth. "I just, sort of, plopped down here and made myself at home. I don't usually sit with customers, and I have plenty to do before my shift is over. I've kept you from eating your breakfast. I'm sorry." She looked a little concerned.

"I started the conversation, with my question about the fellow outside" Ryan stated. "I probably shouldn't have. I see by your name tag that your name is Julie. My name is Ryan Walker, but I'm sure you already understood my last name to be Walker. I hope I haven't caused you trouble."

"No, things have slowed down a little by now," she said. "But I do need to take care of some things. It was nice to meet you, and I hope you have a good visit with your aunt. I'll come back with your check in a few minutes. I hope your food is not cold." With that, she hurried back to the other customer to ask if everything was alright; and then disappeared behind the wall again.

Ryan found himself warmed by the thoughts of visiting

his Aunt Sally. He pictured her living alone. He thought about the fact that she had just lost her remaining brother. This was right. He was going to visit her for the right reason, and he felt at peace with himself.

His food had cooled a little, but it was still very delicious. Ryan savored every bite. Occasionally, he glanced out the window in hopes of seeing this man, Jerry Prescott. He now knew something of this mysterious man. He had learned the man's name, and that he was an acquaintance of his Uncle Andrew. Still, he had not learned much regarding his original reason for questioning the waitress.

What is the relationship between this Mr. Prescott and the waitress?

Chapter 3

THOUGHTS OF THE WAITRESS filled
his mind as Ryan left the café for the tax office. By observation,
he sensed she had an emotional relationship with this man on
the sidewalk, who seemed to have ties with his Uncle Andrew.

*Small towns must be like this, everyone having ties with everyone else
in the community. I couldn't live like that. It would drive me crazy to not
have more privacy.*

The warmth of the conversation with her began to leave
him; the coolness of his big city mentality began to settle back
in.

*Why did I have this conversation with her? I don't even know her,
and now she may be spreading small town talk among half the people in
the area. She works in a very public place. She has a real gift of gab. I've
never seen anything like that; a waitress sitting at the table of a stranger
to have a conversation after bringing a meal! A waitress in Boston would
be fired for being so unprofessional while on the job.*

He was still deep in thought when he reached the tax
office. The sign above the door read "Courthouse Annex -
Tax Office." This was a newer building than the main
courthouse. It appeared to have been built in the 1940s and
looked as if it had once been a small store. There was just one
room. A counter ran across the width of it to separate the
customer area from the employee area. In the customer area
there were eight simple, but sturdy, wooden chairs. Behind the

counter were rows of filing cabinets. Directly behind the counter sat a round-faced man on a stool reading a copy of the local newspaper.

"Excuse me, I would like to see the records regarding a piece of property," Ryan stated as he approached the counter.

The man looked up from his paper, folded it neatly, and placed it to one side on the counter.

"What piece of property, and what name would it be under?" the man replied.

Ryan handed him the papers given to him by the judge and firmly stated, "It belonged to Andrew Walker, and now it appears I own it."

The man read through the first page very diligently, and then scanned the rest. He turned each page with purpose, and when finished said, "I need to see a picture ID, and I will need your social security number."

Ryan presented the man with his Massachusetts driver's license. The fellow intently looked over the picture on the license and compared it to the face before him. He then reached under the counter, pulled out a form and began filling out the required information. Ryan noticed the precise handwriting of the man. The lettering was small and each character seemed almost perfect. Each small "e" was the same in size and shape of the others, each smaller case "t" was the same height as each smaller case "l," and each capital letter had its own unique elegance. Ryan rattled off his social security number when the man came to that field on the form.

When the form was completed, the man asked for a signature. Ryan made a conscious effort to be as professional as possible in the scripting of his signature. A signature of average elegance would appear awkward and sloppy in comparison to the lettering done by this fellow behind the counter.

With the signature made, the man slid off the stool and said, "I'll have the information shortly."

It was then that Ryan noticed the stature of the person.

He couldn't have been more than 5'2" and he walked with a pronounced limp due to his slightly twisted right leg. Ryan observed that the records must be stored alphabetically by the names of property owners.

The name 'Walker' should be near the last. In elementary school, I detested Billy Aaron. Billy was always first in line for everything. How could anyone beat that last name? Everything in life seems to be ordered alphabetically.

Within a few minutes the man lumbered back up to the counter, placed a folder on it, and climbed back upon the stool. He pulled out a second form.

"I will fill out the paperwork to change the name on the property deed to your name, and send the updated information to the state office," the small fellow explained. "You will be interested to know that the property taxes will not be due for twenty-two months. The previous owner was very prompt in paying taxes and has recently paid two years in advance. Once this form is completed, I will need your signature again."

Ryan nodded affirmatively, and the man proceeded to detail the deed transfer information onto the form.

"That will be $10.00 for the transfer, please," the man said.

He accepted cash from Ryan, pulled out a little receipt pad, and neatly filled the required spaces.

"I will need your signature again," he said as he handed the receipt and the transfer form to Ryan. "Right here," the man coached as he pointed to the signature space on the transfer form.

"Can you tell me how much I should expect to pay in property tax annually?" asked Ryan.

"I can't tell you what it will be in two years, but I can give you the annual tax amount that is currently being paid," he said. "If you want copies, they will be ten cents each."

"That will be fine," Ryan expressed. "What other kind of information can be accessed regarding the property?"

"Oh, the state has a computer program that can even give you a small map," the man proudly stated. "Now, the map won't indicate the exact border, but it will indicate the greatest extent of the metes and bounds. I can enter those figures based on the property description. Are you interested?"

"Yes, that would be great," Ryan replied. "I would like to have the tax information first."

Once the laptop had established a connection with the state database, the man nimbly typed on the keyboard. He handed the printout to Ryan.

"There must be a mistake!" exclaimed Ryan. How can unimproved property in this part of the state be so much? How is it possible for the tax to be $14,528.00 annually?"

Ryan felt a sense of anger begin to devour his peaceful morning.

"Let's see," the man said. "Yes, that should be about right. Out of the 400 acres, the 120 farmable acres are taxed at $46.40 per acre. The rest is noted as timber land, and it is taxed at $32.00 per acre."

"400 acres?" Ryan whispered, somewhat bewildered. "I had no idea my uncle had so much land."

"Well, the records indicate he originally had 500 acres" the man said. "Last year, he sold 100 acres to a Sally Thompson. Before selling that portion, Andrew Walker had paid over $19,000 in taxes for the property during the previous year."

"Apparently, he sold the other 100 acres to his sister," Ryan explained.

"I know," stated the man. "I knew Andrew Walker, and I processed the deed for him when he sold it to her."

"Where did Aunt Sally get that kind of money, to buy 100 acres?" Ryan mumbled.

"Are you still interested in the map?" the man asked.

"Yes," Ryan replied.

The man typed away on the keyboard, glancing up from time to time to make sure that he correctly entered the metes and bounds. The printer began to offer up another printout. This time the printing was very slow, as processing the data for the map was more time consuming. At last, the printing was finished, and man produced the copy.

"You can see the boxed outline of the greatest metes and bounds," the man said. "Would you like for me to estimate the rough area based on the property description?"

"Yes, that would be helpful," said Ryan quietly.

Where had Aunt Sally gotten the money to buy that property? Her husband died when I was just a kid. They had no children, and she never married again. She and her husband had been very poor, and they owned very little. I remember when she moved in with her brother Andrew after her husband's death.

He vaguely remembered Sally's husband and small house they rented. For most of Ryan's visits to Brandon Springs, the brother and sister shared the old farmhouse.

"OK, this should be fairly close," the little man announced.

Ryan looked over the map. Judging by the elevation lines, it showed that about a third of the property was made up of the home and pasture at the base of the mountain, and the rest rose up the side of it. The land was much deeper than it was wide, so that the property line extended just beyond the crest. There was a very small portion of land on the other side of the mountain.

Ryan paid the man for the copies and thanked him for his help. As he walked down the sidewalk in the direction of the hotel, his mind raced over the events of the morning. He tried to imagine where Aunt Sally could have obtained money, but he was getting nowhere. When had promised the waitress that he would visit his aunt in the afternoon, he instantly regretted it. Now he couldn't wait to see her. His visit was initially inspired by guilt, but now it was based on personal curiosity and stone-cold sense of business. He pondered the dilemma of coming up with the tax money, but quieted himself with the assurance that he had twenty-two months before he would have to deal with it.

It's now 10:30 AM and the hotel checkout is 11:00 AM. I have just enough time to pack and be in the lobby for checkout.

He went into the lobby and made his way to the elevator.

As he was about to press the elevator button, he heard a voice behind him call, "Mr. Walker? Mr. Ryan Walker?" He turned to see a young woman, a hotel desk clerk, approach him with a piece of paper.

"*Now, what?*" he thought to himself.

"Are you Mr. Ryan Walker, the nephew of Andrew Walker?" the clerk asked.

As she approached him, his demeanor soured with the thoughts of free loaders and of strangers prying into the details of his life.

What did that waitress spread around town? Perhaps this hotel employee heard about my generosity last night with the plump waitress. Maybe this clerk thinks she can flirt her way to a similar tip.

As he was accustomed, he quickly ran through several scenarios as to what this woman could want.

"*Then again, maybe I left something at the Tax Office, or possibly the judge had not been as thorough as he had seemed.*"

His facial expression shifted from a look of anger to that of being stern. The clerk caught a glimpse of his seething from a distance and seemed extremely uneasy when she approached.

"I have this message for you, Sir," the clerk hesitantly spoke. As she held out the piece of paper, she attempted to anticipate Ryan's reaction to her interruption.

"Oh, thank you," he said, as he took the note from her.

She turned to walk away, but Ryan stopped her.

"Wait," he said as he reached into his pocket.

He handed her a $5.00 bill and smiled.

"Thank you, sir," she spoke with a relieved smile. She turned and walked back toward the desk.

Ryan pushed the button of the elevator and the door promptly opened. As he stepped inside, he opened the note. It read,

Ryan,
I've heard that you are in town. I do hope you will stop by to have lunch before going back to Boston.

Love, Aunt Sally

PS: My new address is 960 Willow Creek Drive (take Main Street east out of town, turn left onto Creekwood Village Road, then the first left will be Willow Creek Drive - it will have a sharp bend to the right)."

Ryan placed the note into his right pants pocket as he stepped out of the elevator and into the hallway.

Everyone knows everyone in this town, either the waitress or the man at the Tax Office must have called her.

He placed the hotel key in the door and opened it. Everything was just as he had left it, except that the bed had been readied for the next guest and new towels were placed in the bath. He quickly gathered his belongings, and carefully placed each item neatly in his bag. Satisfied that he had everything, he closed the door behind him and made for the elevator. Once he arrived at the lobby, he walked over to the front desk.

The same woman who had given him the message looked up and cheerfully questioned, "Are you checking out?"

"Yes, I'll be checking out. Can you tell me how to find Main Street?"

"Oh, yeah. Just head this way, and Main Street will be the third street," she said, pointing the direction with her left hand. "Do you want to keep this on your credit card or pay in cash?" she asked.

Ryan looked over the bill and said, "Just keep it on the credit card." He signed the bill and handed it back to her.

She handed customer copy of the bill to him. "I hope you enjoyed your stay in Brandon Springs, and I hope you'll be back," she pleasantly stated.

"It's been interesting," he said, as he reached down for his bag.

He headed out the rear door to the parking lot behind the hotel. Ryan placed his bag in the trunk, opened the driver's door, and slid down into the comforts of the elegant leather seat. He started the engine. As he listened to the quiet purr of the motor, he reminded himself of why he worked the hours he did and why he became so keenly skilled in the game of office politics. He wanted to live well, drive a very nice car, and obtain corporate power. As he placed the car in reverse, a hollow feeling began to rise within his plastic-coated soul. Since his arrival, he found it more difficult to convince himself of the worth of this game. The familiar comforts of his car couldn't mask an uneasiness building within him.

I can't put my finger on it. Something's not right.

Chapter 4

RYAN HEADED IN the direction of Main Street. As he turned onto Main Street, images from the past raced into his mind. He remembered traveling that way as a child to visit Uncle Andrew. As the buildings melted into countryside, the familiarity suddenly ceased. In what had been a pasture, was now a new shopping center. The highway leading to Uncle Andrew's place was peppered with fast food businesses, a couple of gas stations, and a small car lot. At last, he recognized the barbed wire fencing which separated Andrew's front pasture from the highway and the gravel drive that led to the house. He could see the plant down the road on the right. On the left, about 100 yards beyond the drive, was a decorative brick wall with lettering which read "Creekwood Estates." Beneath the wall was an assortment of shrubs, and he could tell that they partially hid the ground lighting which made the wall visible at night. Ryan turned left onto Creekwood Village Road.

The homes near the highway were made of brick, ranging between 1500-2000 square feet in size. They were elegantly designed, and each rested on a 1-acre lot. As he made the turn onto Willow Creek Drive, he noticed the homes became larger. They also were made of brick, but they ranged from 2000 to 3000 square feet. 960 Willow Creek Drive was on the left. Aunt Sally had come a long way from her days in poverty. The place was beautiful.

As he stepped out of his car, he shook his head in bewilderment.

Where had she gotten the money for a home like this?

His pace hastened as he made his way up the walk to the front door. He rang the bell and then turned to inspect the neighboring houses. They were all very nice homes, with well-kept yards. The front door opened, and he turned back to see a small elderly woman smiling.

"Ryan, I am so glad you came to see me," Sally said as she wrapped her arms around his waist and buried her head against his chest. She promptly stepped back, taking his hands in hers. "Oh, you've turned out to be such a handsome young man." Her moist eyes glistened.

"It's good to see you too," Ryan replied softly.

"Oh, please come in."

With her small right hand clasped in his left, she pulled him across the hardwood floored foyer and into the great room. He noticed her hands were still rough from so many years of hard work. Though her posture was deteriorating, her grip on his hand was strong.

She is a wiry little thing.

She positioned him in front of a large chair and looked fully into his face.

"Sit right here," she said. "Would you like a glass of iced tea or a Coke? Lunch is almost ready, but I can give you something to drink."

"Iced tea would be fine, Aunt Sally," he replied.

He remembered she prided herself on making iced tea. She would lecture his mother on making sure the tea steeped the right length of time, and that one should never allow the tea to boil while the tea bags were in the water. Her instructions were etched in his mind.

The water must be brought to a boil, the pan taken off the eye of the stove, the tea bags placed immediately in the water, and the lid must be placed on for steeping.

She released his hand and patted him on the chest.

"Sit down, sit down. I'll bring it over to you."

She turned to make her way toward the eat-in kitchen, which was to the right of the great room. She chatting to her guest as she walked.

"We are just going to have ham and cheese sandwiches with chips, because I wasn't sure you would make it. That's all right, isn't it?" she questioned over her shoulder.

"Oh, yes", he said. "That would be fine."

Within a minute she returned with the iced tea.

"I'll call you when it's ready," she ordered.

She then scurried back into the kitchen. Ryan observed the room. To his right was an end table which separated his chair from a matching sofa. On the wall above the sofa was a large mirror, and directly across from it was a stone fireplace with windows on each side. Above the mantle was a large two door cabinet that matched the paneled walls. The walls were not made of the prefab paneling that one might purchase in eight-foot sheets, but was made of stained wooden tongue and groove planking. Judging by the quality of the home and the furniture, it was obvious to him that Sally was financially much better off than he remembered.

Where did she get this money? Uncle Andrew couldn't have left her much.

"Ok, come on over to the table. It's ready," she called.

Ryan made his way over to the table in the kitchen and found she had set two places. There was a bowl of chips and a small platter of ham and cheese sandwiches cut diagonally.

"Here, you can sit right here," she coached. "I'll take that glass and pour you more tea."

He sat as she refilled his glass and placed the pitcher of tea on the table. Standing beside him, she took his hand again.

"I just want to thank God for bringing you here," she said. She quickly bowed her head, thanked God for the food and for Ryan, and gave his hand a firm quick squeeze as she finished.

It had been some time since Ryan had prayed before eating a meal, but here with Aunt Sally it felt perfectly natural.

"Don't be bashful, grab some chips and sandwiches," she said, as she seated herself. "But save a little room for apple pie, it's still warm in the oven."

Ryan placed a couple of sandwich halves on his plate, then scooped up a hand full of chips from the bowl and placed the chips neatly between the two halves. He picked up one of the halves and almost started to bite down, when he stopped himself.

"Aunt Sally, thanks for the lunch. It really looks good."

"Oh, it isn't much," she said with a sigh. "I'm just glad you are here."

"Aunt Sally, things have changed quite a bit since the last time I was here', he said, hoping to set the stage for her to explain her newly found success.

"Since the plant was built, the entire community has really picked up," she said. "Most of the people in this neighborhood are employed at the plant. Most seem to be more educated than I am, and they are paid well."

Ryan knew the story about Sally dropping out of high school to get married. He had heard she was probably the smartest child in her family, and that she had only made one "B" in her life. She received the "B" while taking a test with a fever of 103 degrees. Each time he had made less than an "A" on a test in elementary school, his father would give him the same story of Sally's one "B." He had a lot of respect for Aunt Sally's gifted intellect, but he hated the comparison. It was the comparison with her that drove him to study and make excellent grades. He didn't want to hear the lecture from his father, and he never made less than an "A" while attending high school.

After one of the sandwich halves and several chips were devoured, he finally couldn't stand the mystery any longer. He attempted once more to prompt Sally to give him the details of her new financial situation.

"This is a beautiful home, you seemed to have done very well for yourself," he said, leaving the conversation wide open for her to explain.

"Life gives out a mixture of blessings and difficulties, and I have learned to trust God's grace in dealing with both," Sally responded.

She looked intently into Ryan's eyes. Her face was worn by time and hardships, but her eyes spoke clearly of intelligence, experience, and compassion.

"I lost your father and mother to a murderer, and now I have lost my dear brother Andrew. Our family is almost gone. I am the last of my generation, and you are the last of yours. We are all that is left of your grandfather's line of Walkers."

Sally's mention of God's grace reminded him of his parents regularly taking him to church during his childhood. During his teen years, he mentally placed the Bible stories about Jesus on the shelf with the Tooth Fairy and the Easter Bunny. He believed in the existence of God, but hadn't been on speaking terms with Him since the death of his parents. He rarely thought of God; and when he did, it was with bitterness for allowing his parents to be taken so tragically.

"I really haven't been as close to family as I probably should have," he admitted.

"Well, I have never visited you in Boston either," she said, sharing part of the blame. "As long as I had Andrew, I felt fine. Now, I realize that I should have paid more attention to you. I should have stayed in touch, at least by mail. I apologize. I intend to correct that situation, if you will let me."

Ryan was shocked by her words.

I am the one who should have checked on my only elderly relative.

"No, it's my fault," he said. "I knew where to find you. It would have been difficult for you to travel and find me in Boston. Since my parents died, I've acted as if I had no family. I should have visited you and Uncle Andrew."

"Andrew very much wanted to see you, but he was really big on not going where he wasn't invited," she replied. "You were probably more special to him than you knew."

"You can say that again," Ryan blurted out. The words bounced out of him before he thought about how it would be taken. "I mean, I was absolutely shocked to find out that he had left me his land. Why did he do that, Aunt Sally?"

She was quiet for a moment, and then she spoke.

"It's a long story. At first, Andrew had difficulties with your arrival into the family. You were much too young to remember any of that."

"I never noticed any bad feelings towards me," he stated. "He always seemed to be happy to see me."

"You did know that your mother was pregnant with you before she married your father; didn't you?" she asked.

"In elementary school, I did the math and bugged my mother until she confessed" he stated. "Yes, she told me that she and my father had not behaved wisely when they were young."

"Andrew thought your mother had seduced his brother in order to trap him into marrying her," Sally explained. "He treated your mother like dirt during the time she was pregnant. Andrew just didn't trust her. After you were born, he saw how much she and his brother loved you and each other. It wasn't long before he apologized to them both. What he didn't count on was how his feelings would grow for you. At first, he was very nervous around you. He was afraid to hold you or play with you. I think he was afraid he would accidentally hurt you. As he became more comfortable, your parents began to leave you with him while they went out. This went on until they moved away when you were about three. He grew to love you.

After moving away, it was close to a year before your parents returned for a visit. Andrew couldn't wait to see you, but it had been so long. You really didn't remember him or the times you had enjoyed together. You were the only child in Andrew's life, and each year he hoped to rekindle the relationship he had with you when you were very little. It just didn't happen.

Andrew never married. I don't think he could ever bring himself to trust a woman enough to commit to a wife. He wanted a son very much, and you were the closest thing he had to one. He was there when you graduated from high school, and he attended your college graduation ceremony. When you got that job up in Boston, he drove all the way up there to see the building where you worked. He was so proud of you."

"Why didn't he let me know he was in Boston?" Ryan asked. "No one told me he came there!"

"You hadn't called, written, or visited in a long while," she explained. "Andrew was not one to force himself on anyone. He didn't tell you because he didn't want you to feel obligated to invite him to stay with you. He wanted to wait until you invited him. He told me that he thought you might be waiting until you had more money, or possibly waiting until you purchased a home."

"I wish that had been the case" Ryan said quietly. "I was caught up in my own world, and I neglected both you and Andrew. I'm really sorry. After my parents died, I acted as if I had no family. I'm not sure why I did that; and I really wish I had not been that way."

"No one can change the past, and to dwell on past mistakes only robs us of the time we currently have," Sally said.

She went on to tell Ryan of several stories about his mother, father, herself and Andrew. He was captivated. The mixture of her ability to tell a good story, and the newfound information contained in them, kept any thought of Boston beyond the borders of his consciousness. At last Ryan's eye caught the time on Sally's kitchen clock.

"Aunt Sally, does that clock have the correct time?" blurted Ryan.

"Why yes, the afternoon is gone," Sally exclaimed. "Please stay for supper. I have so enjoyed talking with you. Please stay. When do you have to be back in Boston?"

"*Boston*," Ryan remembered.

During her stories Ryan had completely forgotten about it. It was Friday afternoon, and Ryan had planned to be back on Sunday in order to rest up for Monday morning.

"Well, I had planned to be back sometime on Sunday" he responded.

"Please stay for dinner; and then stay the night here," Sally pleaded. "I'm sure it would be better for you not to travel at night, and I have two spare bedrooms that are only used when guest of the church come to town. It would be so nice to spend a little more time with you."

"Actually, I was thinking about going out to the property to look it over," Ryan responded. "Are you sure that you want me to spend the night, Aunt Sally? I don't think you planned for me to be here."

"Oh, I've enjoyed talking with you so much," she exclaimed. "You're my only family, and we have so much catching up to do. I would love it if you were able to spend two weeks here, instead of only two days. Let me show you to the room. Please."

Her eyes dancing with excitement, and the tone of her voice filled with anticipation. It became very clear to him that he was indeed welcome.

"OK, I'll stay the night," he said. "But, please let me take you out for breakfast in the morning. You weren't planning on having to feed two."

Sensing that Ryan was concerned with increasing food costs for a person possibly on a fixed income, she answered, "Does it look to you that I can't afford to feed another mouth around here?"

Ryan saw that his question had caused Sally's expression to change to a more serious nature. "Well, no. You seem to be doing quite well," he apologized.

"I'm doing very well, and I would enjoy sharing with you some of the blessings God has granted me," she said.

Ryan nodded his head, letting her know he had gotten the message. She smiled, and said "Now, come with me."

She led him down the hall and pointed out the main bath on the left. She told him that she had converted the first bedroom to a study, and that it had a sleeper couch which folded out into a bed. Ryan was about to take his bag into the study, but she stopped him. She opened the next door on the right to reveal a bedroom which would be suitable for a man. The wallpaper displayed ancient nautical maps and charts; the colors were deep red, tan, gold, and brown. The trim and the crown molding were oak, stained to match the oak furniture. The full-sized bed had massive posts on each corner which were topped with carved oak spheres. Above the headboard was mounted an oak captain's wheel from a sailing ship. She turned down the dark red comforter, revealing gold- colored bedsheets. The curtains were the same deep red and were parted to reveal the Venetian blinds covering the windows. Except the one of a lighthouse, the paintings on the walls were of a variety of ships with sails.

"This will be your room," she said proudly. "Will this be alright?"

"I'll say," Ryan said with amazement. "This room is very elegant; you've done a wonderful job. In fact, it looks like something you might see in a magazine. I'm impressed."

"Why, thank you," Sally replied. "I thought you might like it. I see that your bag is one of those that folds out into a hanging bag. Feel free to use the closet. It's empty except for a small ironing board and iron. You're welcome to use them."

"Do you have guests here often?" Ryan questioned.

"Our church has guest ministers and speakers several times a year, and I enjoy being able to put them up and feed them," she explained. "The other room is a bit different, not as masculine. I put guest women and couples in that room. Most of the couples are missionaries."

"You have wonderful taste, Aunt Sally," Ryan said. "I never knew that. I mean, I just remember you living at Uncle Andrew's place. That old house was nothing like this."

"Yes, that was Andrew's house," she said. "I was a guest in his house, and it wasn't my business to try to change it. I was so grateful to be there and so grateful for his company. I really didn't want to live alone. To be honest, I still don't like it. When I built this home, I insisted that the church allow me to house our guests. It isn't entirely out of charity; I love having the company."

With that, she patted Ryan on the shoulder and turned toward the door. "Do what you like in the meantime; supper will be ready in a couple of hours."

Ryan decided to take advantage of the offered conveniences of the bedroom. He pulled some of his clothes from the bag, ironed them, and hung them in the closet. After setting his toiletry bag on the nightstand, he spent the remainder of the time until supper examining the paintings.

These are not prints of paintings, instead these are actual oil paintings. Interesting. Sally seems to be full of surprises.

He wasn't familiar with any of the artist. Most of the paintings were signed and dated in the 1930-40s. The time flew by before Sally summoned him for supper. During his visits to Brandon Springs as a child, minutes had seemed like hours and hours were like days. Now, time seemed to melt as butter in a hot cast iron skillet.

The supper consisted of fried chicken, mashed potatoes (real, not the instant kind out of a box), peas, and cornbread. He hadn't eaten cornbread since he was a child and had not even thought about the substance in years. He was surprised at the rich hardy taste and had two servings during the meal. As he was about to have a third, Sally interrupted with a warning that she had prepared a dessert. Although she often prepared food that was a little heavy on the fat and sugar content, she was an excellent cook when it came to taste. Her cornbread was never dry, and her apple cobbler was made by a recipe handed down from her mother. When she brought out the apple cobbler, she asked Ryan if he would like to have a cup of coffee with it.

As they talked, Ryan ate two servings of cobbler and sipped his single cup of coffee. They shared stories of his parents and of those of his childhood. He had never felt so much at home in his adult life.

After a while, Sally announced "Well, old people can't stay up as late as when they were young. I'm going to wash these last dishes and I'm off to bed."

When Ryan glanced at the kitchen clock, he was shocked to see that it was almost 11:00 PM.

"I'm sorry!" he exclaimed. "I had no idea it was so late, Aunt Sally. Here, I'll wash the last dishes; you go on to bed."

"I'm not dead, I'm just ready for a night's sleep" Sally stated. "It won't take me five minutes to wash these."

Sally quickly collected the dessert dishes and headed for the sink. It was then that Ryan noticed she had already washed all the pots, pans, dishes, glasses, and silverware from supper. During their conversation he had been so focused on the stories that he had not even noticed what she had been doing. Sally was so accustomed to cleaning up after a meal, that it had become automatic for her. She had pulled the dishes from the table and washed them quickly while having conversation.

As she was busily rinsing the last cup, Ryan approached the kitchen sink. "Sally, I have enjoyed this night so much. I'm sorry that I didn't help you with cleaning up; I didn't even notice that you were washing as we were talking."

"I don't often get to cook and clean after family anymore" she said, as she dried her hands with a kitchen towel. "Don't even think about washing dishes while you are here. I am so glad to have you visiting; and I am enjoying every minute of preparing meals for us. I just become a little tired at my age. You can watch TV, if you like, but I am off to bed."

"No, I am going to go to bed myself," Ryan replied. "Goodnight."

Sally kissed his cheek, gave his hand a squeeze, and headed down the hall toward her bedroom. Just before she closed her bedroom door, she called back to him.

"Don't forget to turn out the lights."

"OK, see you in the morning," he replied.

Ryan turned out the kitchen lights, leaving only the hall light on as he went to his room for his toothbrush. After a thorough brushing, he made sure all the lights were out before he returned to the bedroom. As he slipped between the bedsheets, he felt peaceful sleep begin to slide over him. He turned out the light on the nightstand, and he reviewed the meal of the evening in his mind. He was somewhat regretful of the fact that he had washed the taste of the apple cobbler from his mouth, as it had been so good. Nevertheless, the thoughts of cobbler quickly surrendered to a heavy sleep.

Chapter 5

RYAN WOKE UP to the rich smell of coffee, eggs, biscuits, and bacon. The combination of fragrances was almost as enjoyable as the taste of the previous night's supper.

If I was to stay much longer in this town, I would have to join a gym in order to avoid becoming as fat as a barn. Boston has many fine restaurants, but there is something about the local cooking here. It's out of this world. The food is not exactly refined. It's definitely not healthy by society's standards, but the taste is terrific.

He was like a kid; he couldn't wait to see what Aunt Sally had prepared. He put on the same pants and shirt that he had worn the night before and headed out the bedroom door. As he passed by the bathroom, he was reminded that he had not yet brushed his teeth. He ignored the reminder and continued toward the kitchen. Ryan could hear the sizzle of bacon. He found Sally removing most enticing large golden biscuits from the oven.

"Good morning, Sunshine," Sally greeted him. "Come over here and make yourself useful. Here's the butter and a knife. Are you awake enough to butter these biscuits without burning yourself?"

He smiled and nodded his head in affirmation. As he took the knife from Sally, the same warm feeling that he sensed at the café returned and rested upon him. There was something genuine about what he was doing.

This is how real people live. No power games, no one putting on airs, no walls, just real life. How could buttering biscuits be so enjoyable?

This simple life bathed his soul in comfort. He understood that the biscuits and butter were not the source of this sensation. It wasn't the small town which rested in the rump of these mountains; it was the people and how they lived. These were real people, living their daily lives in acceptance of who they were. Yet, there was something else that Ryan couldn't put his finger on.

Finished with his task, Ryan was surprised that he had successfully completed the buttering without burning himself once.

"OK, let's eat," Sally said, as she placed the last fork on the table.

Ryan pulled a chair out for her to be seated and gave her a hug as she positioned herself. She reached up and gave his arm a quick squeeze. As he pulled out his own chair, he found himself a little surprised at what he had just done. He had given her a hug without even thinking about it. It was just a natural reaction to the moment and the person. He examined Sally's face to see whether his actions had made her uncomfortable. Behind the facial puffiness of the morning, he saw that her eyes still danced with the happiness provided by his visit. For most, a spontaneous hug would not be significant. However, Ryan made it habit to think things out before committing to action. He had practiced checking his emotions and measuring consequences before taking action. He was ever mindful of what would further or hamper his career. So far, this had served him well.

Aunt Sally had a way of causing him to drop his guard. Hers was a simple and genuine life, which seemed to somehow complicate his. He savored these warm feelings, but he was a bit apprehensive to totally give in to them. He didn't trust his emotions. During his ordeal of wearing the braces on his teeth, he had suffered humiliation at the hands of classmates. His reaction to their taunting had caused him even more embarrassment in several situations.

On one occasion, the high school captain of the football team, Brad Dixon, caused him much grief by a suggestion for a science class project. He suggested the class fix a powerful magnet on the classroom wall, and have Ryan stand on roller skates at the class doorway. The class would have him smile, revealing the braces. They would then time how long it took for the magnet to lock onto his braces and pull him across the room. The room erupted in laughter. Encouraged at the reaction of the class, Dixon suggested that the experiment would provide Ryan with his first kiss. After more laughter, he suggested that the class leave the room so that Ryan and magnet could have an uninterrupted intimate moment.

Over the next week, Ryan faced jeers from classmates in the halls of the school. One announced that he was willing to set Ryan up with a wild French magnet. He assured Ryan that the loose morals of the device would make for an easy conquest. Another announced before a large group that Ryan should go into Mechanical Engineering after high school, because he carried the entire Deluxe Model of an Erector Set in his mouth.

Brad Dixon had started something the entire school carried to wild extremes. If Ryan had handled the original classroom scene differently, the student body may have never made an issue of it. If he had laughed with the class and offered to partner with the football player to enter the science fair, then the school would have had a good laugh and let it pass. Instead, Ryan turned a deep shade of red and his eyes watered. He sat, saying nothing. When the bell rang for class to end, he couldn't wait to leave. He jumped out of his desk and quickly made his way down the aisle for the door. His foot caught the leg of a desk and sent him headlong into Alice Taylor (cheerleader, and Brad's girlfriend). The impact knocked her books to the floor. With his balance already off, he stepped on one of the books. This caused him to spin around and land squarely on the floor on his back. The football player made sure Alice was alright, then promptly started in on Ryan again. He asked Alice to check her purse for magnets, and the class cheered. After she assured him she had none, he grabbed Ryan off the floor and tossed him against the wall. He told him to keep his "clumsy tin mouth" away from his girlfriend or he would attach a magnet to the rear of his car and drag Ryan all over town. After that, Ryan was known for his braces. Guys made jokes about him, and girls avoided him.

Ryan realized his emotional reaction to Brad's comments had made things worse. He decided then he would no longer let people get under his skin. Ryan determined he would allow the situations to pass with humor and deal with them later. He learned to simmer his emotions into a calculated action, to be carried out in his own timing. Over the next few days, he ignored the comments about his braces. He simply smiled and walked on. The jeering and jokes stopped by the end of the week, but Ryan continued to be known for his braces.

A couple of months later, Ryan found a stray cat and felt inspired with the perfect idea for revenge. On a Thursday afternoon, knowing that Brad and Alice would go to the movie theater the following night, he set his plan in motion. He bought liquid laxative and three cans of cat food. That evening he dumped all three cans onto a paper plate and mixed in the laxative. Ryan allowed the cat to eat until it was completely full. Then he placed the animal in Brad's car and allowed his "time bomb" to go off. Overnight, the combination of the cat food and laxative caused the cat to widely redecorate the seats of the car with excrement. When Brad opened the car door the next morning, he was greeted by the speedy exit of the cat and was overwhelmed by the ripe odor that now filled the car. No one ever found out who had done it, but word of the deed quickly passed through the school. Ryan enjoyed every thought of his revenge. However, he did feel somewhat sorry for the cat.

Without his braces, Ryan formed a new image while in college and he was very careful to protect it. His new metal-free smile and the perfect college grades proved to be a steady attraction for women. Armed with good looks and a strong intellect, he set his course for success. High school was behind him, and throughout his college years he learned how to master the games played to promote self-advancement.

As he felt the first hot buttered biscuit surrender to his mouth, he compared it to his normal breakfast in Boston of a couple of bagels and a cup of coffee.

The bagels are pretty good, and the coffee in Boston comes in a large variety of flavors. However, Aunt Sally's breakfast is sinfully tasty. I'm definitely being naughty, and I'm enjoying every minute of it. The breakfast may be a bit evil, by society's standards, but my aunt's life is about as wholesome as they come.

His thoughts were interrupted by Aunt Sally.

"Have you ever been to the top of the mountain?"

Her calming voice reminded him of lazy childhood Saturdays, when he would awaken to his mother's soft voice. It gently brought him back down from the heavenly world of those hot buttered biscuits.

"No," he replied. "I've never been up the mountain. I'm not sure that I will, as I really didn't bring clothes fit for that type of exercise."

He didn't want to tell her that as a child he was afraid to go up the mountain. Ryan always felt ashamed about his fear and made excuses each time his father invited him for a hike. Before he was compelled to offer one of the childhood excuses to his aunt, Sally offered more information.

"Oh, there's a nice trail going up the mountain and a walking bridge over the stream. Your uncle and a friend finished the bridge and trail about a year and a half ago. It was Andrew's last project before he became ill."

"In that case, I would very much like to see it" replied Ryan. "How long does it take to make it to the top?"

Aunt Sally's expression became more serious. It was obvious to him that she was in careful thought before she spoke.

"It takes about two hours to go all the way up to the top, but…." she hesitated. "There is a spot about halfway up where the slope flattens a bit before it rises again. That might be a good spot to rest."

She seemed to have more to say, but she waited for his response. It was as if she wanted him to commit to the hike before saying more.

"I would like to leave soon after breakfast," he said, as he studied her worn face. "Would it be OK for me to shower here before going over?"

Although her eyes were soft, the corners of her mouth slightly drooped. Her usual positive spirit masked what aging and hardship had brought to her life. For the first time during his visit, she appeared frail to him. She was serious, and she studied his face and eyes for signs of openness and warmth. Her words came slowly and carefully.

"That will be fine. I... want you to be aware of something. Andrew and this friend became close, and they had an understanding. There was nothing on paper, but Andrew allowed him to set up a homestead at the area where I suggested you stop for a rest."

Ryan was almost speechless. He found it difficult to force the words out in response to her statement. As he opened his mouth to speak, he reconsidered his reaction.

"You are telling me that someone is living on the side of the mountain?" he questioned.

Different scenarios played quickly through his thoughts, and dread began to take hold of him. Ryan's mind raced to thoughts of an old person injuring himself on his recently inherited property, and of the possibility of a lawsuit filed against him.

What am I going to do about this?

It was if his Aunt Sally was able to read the fear in his heart and had the ability to listen to the intentions brewing within him.

"I would ask you to meet this man, before making a decision," she began. "As a favor to me, please meet him and wait twenty-four hours before taking action."

Strangely, her words calmed him. Ryan felt relieved. He could rest in the safety of leaving the decision for another day. This sense of comfort was very unusual for Ryan, for he normally hated to leave a matter hanging. He had become apt at quickly sizing up risks and making a prompt firm decision when confronted with a situation.

This one is different. She's right. I need to process this when I have more information, and when I have more time to consider my options.

He inwardly welcomed the reprieve, and he assured her that he would give it the time requested.

"Who is this fellow?" he asked.

"I would like for you to meet the man without preconceived opinions," she answered.

Chapter 6

AS RYAN TOWELED OFF from the morning shower, his head spun with recent events. To top it all off, there was a squatter to be found on the property he inherited. He decided that this must be the first of many downsides to being a local property owner. It would be difficult to own land, and not live nearby to take care of it. His mind raced.

I can imagine the squatter inviting several of his fellow squatters to come over and homestead the place. Eventually it might become known as "Squatter's Mountain." I'm an outsider, and these squatters would be locals, whom the town's people tolerated. If an incident arose, I'm sure Brandon Springs would stand by the locals over the rights of an outside property owner. What am I going to do? If Andrew had not befriended the guy, I'd be able to run him off the land without any trouble. This is becoming complicated.

Speaking outside the bedroom door Sally interrupted the battle that raged within him, as he tied his left shoe.

"I need to go to town for a little while. Will you be leaving for the property soon?"

Again, her voice caused calm to pass across his troubled mind and heart, and the spinning of scenarios slowed to a quiet ride. He was amazed at how quickly the matter within him seemed to subside in her presence. Ryan opened the door and found her small frame standing in the hall.

"I'm also just about to leave," he responded.

Her bright eyes scanned Ryan for an indication of how the events of the day might go with him. The analysis didn't take long. She placed her hand in his and led him down the hall to the kitchen.

"Here's a lunch and a couple of cold soft drinks," she offered. "I don't expect to see you for a few hours, and I'm sure the climb will cause you to work up an appetite. We'll have a good supper tonight."

She handed him a brown bag which was neatly creased and folded at the top. Sally then pointed to two soft drinks she had placed on the table. She gave his hand a now familiar quick squeeze as he took the bag.

"Don't worry; things will work out exactly as they should," she said. "You'll see."

Sally had a gift for bringing matters into perspective. She wanted her nephew to understand that this situation was not to be a cause for dread, just another interesting curve in a road called "life."

He wrapped his free arm around her shoulders and pulled her graying head lightly against his chest.

"I'll let you know how things go," he assured her.

As he stepped back, he gathered both drinks in his free hand and placed them under his arm. He gave her a sliver of a smile and turned for the front door. As he was about to close the front door behind him, he heard Sally call out.

"Oh, the bridge and the path are on the right side off the back yard."

He gave her a nod of affirmation; then pulled the door shut as he stepped out of the house.

The sun had already burned the night dew from the grass and breathed warm life into the newborn day. Ryan noticed his car had become filthier than he normally allowed. He had no time to wash it, and there was really no point to do so this morning. He knew the coating of dust on this fine machine would become even denser within the hour, as he would soon encounter the gravel drive to Andrew's old house.

A car moving up that old gravel drive during dry weather always results in the vehicle generating a large cloud of gravel dust.

Just days before, the sun's glow accentuated the car's newly waxed voluptuous curves and sleek lines. Today, it took the form of an aging beauty queen. The car's exterior appearance was now dimmed below a coating of gray dust. However, the interior was just as pristine as when it left Boston. The plush leather seat seemed to caress his body, as he settled himself behind the wheel. He left the lowly world of filth and became reacquainted with luxury and sophistication. Ryan placed the brown bag in the passenger seat. Both soft drinks fit perfectly in the console. He started the engine, and as he listened to its purr he was filled with a sense of satisfaction.

He decided he would have one of the soft drinks on the way and save the other for lunch. The salty morning bacon and the warming sunshine caused Ryan to be thirsty. He finished off the drink as he turned up the drive to Andrew's old home. This place seemed to have changed little. The gravel drive, the fences and pastures on both sides of the drive, and the old farmhouse at the end of the drive; they were all as he remembered. It was as if time had escaped these country acres. He pulled in front of the house and left the car door open as he made sure no one was presently inside the place. Ryan was surprised to find the front door unlocked. He opened it and called out. Except for the faint songs of the birds in nearby pastures, no response was offered. The house was quiet. He shut the door of Andrew's old home and returned to the car to gather the lunch and the remaining soft drink.

After locking his car, he moved around the right side of the house and started for the backyard. The place was not overgrown, as the grass had been cut within the last few days. The grass had also been trimmed around the base of the house.

As he rounded the corner of the house, he spotted changes. There was a nice shed in the backyard, and he also saw the wooden bridge that crossed the stream at the base of the mountain. As he approached the bridge, he began to make out a distinct path leading from it on the other side of the stream. The bridge was well made; it consisted of treated planking and had a hand railing on each side. Someone had poured a concrete pad on each side of the stream, and these slabs supported heavy treated timbers which crossed the clear flowing water. The planking was nailed across the timbers to produce a very solid decking for the footbridge. It was wide enough for two people to easily pass, and it had one step on each end. The only interruption of the gurgling small stream below was the sound of his shoes on the planking. It was solid, not a squeak or a creak. On the other side, a short path of steppingstones led to the leaf covered trail ascending the mountain.

As he left the steppingstones and started up the trail, he realized this was totally new ground for him. He had never before passed into these ancient woods. The path was clearly marked, and it appeared to have experienced heavy use. As the slope of the land began to rise with ever increasing degree, the trail angled to the left to provide for a more comfortable stride. The walk became easier, and he noticed the thick bark covering the trunk of a massive oak. The ridges of bark running up the tree reminded him of long flat plateaus of land overlooking shadowed miniature canyons. He stopped to look up into the rich green leaves and observed with admiration twisting limbs which carried them to great heights. This tree was extremely healthy to be so old.

How many lives of men have passed beneath these branches during their slow steady climb skyward?

He took note that this tree had witnessed portions of his own youth from a distance, during times of his visits. The knotted limbs of these old trees had been the source of dread and fear when he was a child. Now they provided welcome shade and enchantment as he made his way up the mountain.

It seems the fears of young boys often become the comforts of men. The dreaded dark night becomes the quiet environment for much needed adult sleep. Boyhood apprehensions in dealing with the opposite gender later become the foundation for adult comforts in love.

He had come to the first of several switchbacks, as the

trail turned sharply back to the right. After about 100 yards, a small rock cliff fell from the right side of the path. As he walked the cliff became higher. Over the tops of trees, he could see the road which led to Andrew's house. He viewed the pastures below and attempted to estimate the acreage. As he moved to the edge of the ledge, he could feel the sun begin to grow in intensity. On a cooler day, this view would be more enticing. Ryan retreated to the comfort of the shady path and continued up. The trail switched back to the left and then again to the right, as it snaked up the side of the mountain. He estimated that it took about twenty-five minutes to hike each leg before reaching the next switchback.

Ahead, the trail seemed to end at the foot of a large limestone boulder. As he drew closer, he observed a separation of about three feet width in the rock. The massive rock had split ages ago, and a jagged trail passed between the two sections. The rocks rose about twenty feet above the path to produce a small narrow canyon between the pieces. He hesitated at the opening. Because of the uneven breakage, Ryan could not see if the passage exited the rock.

For all I know, this is a dead end. Or, perhaps the opening becomes too small for someone to pass through. It reminds me of the type of setting in old movies where the good guy, while passing through, was always ambushed from above by the bad guy.

As he stood in front of the opening, Ryan noticed a second faint path parting to the left and running steeply up the mountain into a thicket. It seemed to be a rabbit trail, but its location caused him a mix of curiosity and concern. He really wasn't dressed for a primitive route, but he convinced himself that it might offer a view of the rock from above. He guessed it might indicate whether the main trail actually passed through the two huge sections of limestone. He left the main passage and began his ascent, pushing aside small branches that overgrew the path.

Because of the overgrowth, he could only see a few feet ahead. There were several sharp turns, but he could tell that the main direction of the path was bending to the right.

At last, he burst into a flat clearing, and beneath his feet was solid rock. He was on top of the rocky passage, and the view took him completely by surprise. He gazed across the relatively smooth flat limestone to the horizon, where it seemed the world dropped off into blue sky. There were three leafy treetops protruding above the edge of the rocky ledge, but he could not yet spot the crack which separated the two sections. Ryan began walking toward the vastness of the sky before him, and his pace quickened. He was almost captivated by the spectacle. As he made his way, he began to see crests of distant rolling hills rise between the treetops. He became mindful again of the trail below, and he scanned the rock for signs of the separation. At last, he spotted the snake like crack that ran across his path. He knew the purpose of his taking the side trail was to inspect the passage through the rock, but upon arrival he immediately jumped across it and continued toward the edge. By now he saw other trees below and could make out a few farmhouses in the distance.

At the edge he felt a sense of dizziness as he peered between the trees and saw the retreating ground some fifty feet below. There was an overwhelming urge to sit down on the rock and dangle his feet, as if to tease the trees beneath him. He did so and allowed fresh air to fill his chest. The warmth of the sun poured over him. Ryan closed his eyes and imagined himself flying above the treetops and gliding through the valley. He opened his eyes to again view the expanse before him. The initial peaceful urge to fly began to evolve into that of jumping out into the sea of trees. The feeling grew. His eyes were fixed upon the ground and rocks below, and they seemed to call to him. There was a dreamy euphoric enticement to allow his body to drop from the ledge, down to the valley before him. It was almost hypnotic. Ryan became lightheaded, as if his mind was beginning to lift up and float out across the treetops. He closed his eyes and held out his arms to each side, as if they were wings.

As the mountain breeze gently pushed against his face, Ryan leaned forward into it. He suddenly felt a streak of adrenaline course through his body, as a sense of fear brought him back to reality. With one swift roll backwards, his body quickly took him back to safety. His muscles tightened, as he realized what could have happened during that brief moment of rapture. Looking down at the massive rock on which he sat, he remembered the purpose of inspecting the crack.

He rose to his feet and moved slowly back to the crevasse. Ryan followed its twisting path to the point where it exited the rock. Indeed, this portion was wide enough to be traveled. He leaped across the crack and followed it all the way back to its mouth.

Satisfied that the passage was true, he decided it was time to be on his way. Ryan had taken more time than he expected in this diversion. As he made his way back to the thicket from where he had earlier emerged, he spotted a second small path directly ahead. At this distance, he could barely make out the opening in the brush. He moved past his intended point and proceeded to this newly discovered second path. At the point where it ascended up the mountain, he observed that it ran between groups of smaller trees then curved to the left behind them. He stood for about five minutes, contemplating the two paths. With a quick turn, he hurried in the direction of the familiar path which had brought him to the top of the rock.

As he traveled back down to the main trail below, he thought of the second path. He was curious as to where it led, but he had been told to take the main trail to the house halfway up the mountain. After all, the main purpose was to arrive at the top and view his land.

This is now my land!"

These were his views, his trails, and his paths. He could explore the other path anytime he chose. The second purpose was to deal with the squatter. This was his land, his mountain, and his situation with which to deal. There was business to take care of, and he needed to be on his way.

He soon came to the next switchback. He hardly remembered passing through the opening in the rock; he had been too preoccupied with thoughts of how to handle the squatter. The trail turned back to the left and the slope began to be steeper. He was breathing harder as he trudged higher. This portion of the trail did not seem to be as well traveled as the lower part. The trees became more consistent in shape. No longer were there large oaks, as those at the beginning of the trail; and no longer did he see the small saplings grouped in thickets. Instead, the trees were smaller in diameter and very tall and straight. There were no lower branches, and the leaves above formed a type of canopy. Every now and then, a ray of sunlight passed through to the thick bed of leaves covering the ground. The trail was becoming harder for him to distinguish. At last, the slope began to flatten, and eventually his gate became almost effortless.

There it was. Ahead, and on the right side of the trail, stood a small unpainted house. It blended so well with the bark of the surrounding trees, that he was almost upon the spot before seeing it. The time was approaching noon, and his body began to remind him of the sack lunch and remaining drink. He pushed aside the beckoning plea of his belly and the beginnings of a thickening thirst. The house spoke clearly of the presence of a stranger on his mountain. He moved to the base of the steps leading up to the front porch and called out.

"Hello!"

He heard no response, only the echo of his own voice as it danced between the trees. Perhaps the man was inside, but was hard of hearing. He had witnessed an indigent person in Boston approach him with a begging and apologetic loud voice, explaining the fact that he was unable to hold down employment due to poor hearing. He dismissed most of these types as drunken bums, or either those who mastered the talent of swindling down to a fine art.

By my estimation, probably one homeless person in twenty has an element of truth in his sad story. The rest are seasoned manipulators of kind and naive individuals. Individuals, whose compassion and open trust made them easy prey for these self-indulgent hollow souls.

On his way to work he would pass by a mission for indigents. To him the mission seemed like a shrine to a god of

58

laziness, and a school to learn predatory practices against the kindhearted. In his eyes, these bums practiced the life of freeloading as one would a religion. One day he parked his car and watched as they entered and exited the mission as in a ritual practice.

There at the mission they were able to fellowship with other believers of like faith. Faith in naïve mankind to be foolish enough to fork over hard-earned money to them in the name of compassion.

He was sure that the foolhardy personnel on staff at the mission had good intentions, but he believed them to be unknowing enablers.

He moved up the steps and onto the porch. The air was still, and the home of this unknown person offered only silence. The porch had a very plain appearance. However, the structure was tightly made. It quietly spoke of the builder's skill. Ryan felt the same strength in the wooden structure beneath his feet, as was given to the footbridge which crossed the stream below.

He gave a quick three raps on the door and stepped back as not to encroach or violate the space owned by the unpainted wooden door. He heard nothing. He heard no shuffling of feet inside the house. As he stood tall waiting for an encounter, he realized that his knocking on the door resulted in no rattling or vibration. It was if the door had been nailed shut. No movement, it was tightly shut. He stepped closer and took the knob in his hand. Behind him, and over his right shoulder, he heard the clear voice of a man.

"May I help you?"

ROB WILLIAMS

Chapter 7

RYAN FELT A CHILL, as if someone had placed a cold hand on his back. He was on someone's porch, and he held this person's doorknob in his hand. He was caught. As the shiver of the event descended back down his back and into his legs, his hand slipped off the knob. He remembered his position on this matter, and he was able to quickly place his emotions in check.

This is the habitat of a mere squatter, and this is my mountain. This is my land.

Courage climbed back into his heart, and he turned to face his adversary. Instantly, he recognized familiarity in the person at the bottom of the porch steps. Ryan was momentarily stunned.

This is the same fellow I bumped into back in town as I rounded the corner. This is the same man who caused the waitress to burst into tears. He was acquainted with my uncle.

"I'm Jerry Prescott, and I would guess that you are Andrew Walker's nephew" the man stated in a calm steady voice.

The man patiently stood, waiting for a reply. Ryan moved slowly away from the door and toward the direction of the man. Standing at the top of the steps, he answered.

"My name is Ryan Walker. Uncle Andrew left me this land, and it appears that someone may be living on my property."

He then reassured himself.

I believe I've laid out the matter plainly, boldly, and in a manner that shouldn't be construed as offensive."

In his dealings with high-ranking executives in Boston, he had learned to state the main point first and then address details if time permitted. If the opening statements generated interest in an executive, then he would have the full attention to proceed with the details. If the party was uninterested, then he had not wasted much time of a busy person. This approach was often appreciated by a high-ranking executive and would often be noted. As a young professional, just out of college, Ryan had been fortunate enough to attend a meeting that included top corporate personnel. In the meeting, he witnessed a bright young man attempting to discuss a matter by first laying the groundwork details. The fellow was cut off by the corporate Chief Financial Officer after only presenting about three sentences. "Get to the point; I don't have time for this. Here, we have a dollar waiting on a dime! Before you come to a meeting like this, have your position well thought out and present it in a clear concise manner." The young man was marked as a babbler, and soon left the company for another job. Ryan never forgot this lesson.

Prescott smiled, and in a somewhat elegant and kind tone responded.

"I would be the person living here; and with your permission, I would like to remain. Your uncle and I had an agreement, but I am aware that he is no longer the property owner. I assure you; I fully intend to abide by your decision on the matter."

"What type of agreement?" Ryan replied. "I understand that you had nothing in writing; nothing legal was drawn up."

"That's true" Prescott stated. "It was based on our word and a simple handshake. I see that you've brought food with you. Please bring your lunch inside. I've become a bit hungry. Please come inside."

Silently, Ryan's mind raced.

This man is no indigent. He's like no street person I've ever come across. Professional bums are sometimes experts at reading the people they approach. When they perceive that the approached person is an educated professional, some of the more accomplished in their craft attempt to pass themselves off as educated and well-mannered individuals who have just fallen on hard times. They try to convince the person that, except by the grace of God, they too would be suffering this same pitiful lot. Some of them are amazing actors. Hollywood talent scouts should spend a lot more time in bus stations and under freeway overpasses. I've seen character roles played by several bums, but this man seems genuine. This home is on MY property! Of course, I can go in and have lunch. In fact, I should go in and inspect this place. If it turns out to be filled with filth, I will have perfect grounds to have it condemned and demolished."

"Sure, I'll come in for a few minutes," he answered as he stepped aside and motioned for the man to open the door.

Prescott moved up the steps and to the door. He placed his hand on the knob, and smoothly turned it until the latch gracefully released. It wasn't locked. Prescott entered the home as if it were his own. Turning to Ryan, he invited him to enter.

"Please, come on in."

The home was simple, but extremely neat and organized. The floors, walls and ceilings were of tongue and grooved wooden planking. He could only see three rooms. They consisted of the main living area, a kitchen area, and a bedroom. The living room floor was covered by an oval braided area rug, and the seating consisted of four wooden rocking chairs. Each had a matching padded seat and back. To the left was a fireplace, with a window on each side. There was a wooden box containing split logs for the fireplace under one window, and under the other was a small table upon which looked like a Bible and a kerosene lamp. There were two matching windows on the opposite wall to the right and across from the fireplace; and he could see one window on a rear wall in the kitchen. Each window had very plain curtains. The kitchen area contained an old wood fueled cooking stove, a sink, a hutch, and a small pantry. In the center was a small wooden table with four chairs. The bedroom was the only room with a door for privacy.

"Here, have a seat at the table," Prescott offered.

Ryan was determined to have this issue settled quickly, as he was beginning to feel a bit uncomfortable in this unfamiliar environment. Ryan suddenly realized that he had just given up some of his advantage in any confrontation, as Prescott had moved the conversation onto his own turf.

Outside the house, the location gave me a more commanding position. It was obvious that the man was standing on my property. Inside this man's living quarters, this seems to put things in another perspective.

Prescott had politely taken control of the situation by bringing Ryan into his personal space. Never mind the fact that the space technically belonged to Ryan, this interior was a very personal area. It is a bit like a landlord entering a tenant's apartment. Ryan immediately became aware of the lost tactical advantage as soon as he entered the home. He was kicking himself on the inside and was becoming more nervous. In one quick move he had shown Prescott his inexperience. He was now inside, and he would have to do his best to recover.

Ryan seated himself as he watched the man lift the lid from a small pot on the stove. The fellow turned to the hutch and opened one of the doors, where he took out a small dish and a bowl. Jerry set them on the hutch work area. He then opened one of the drawers of the hutch. Reaching in, he brought out a ladle, a spoon, and a huge sharp knife.

Something is wrong! The place is too neat and too orderly for a man living on a secluded mountain side.

Ryan sensed his stomach begin to turn at the sight of the knife. A shower of fear flowed from the top of his head and covered his entire body.

How could I have been so stupid as to come inside with this guy?

An overpowering dread rushed into the deeps of his now stiffening body. He was paralyzed with fright. He tried to stand to run out, but he found that he was immobile.

Ryan's head remained still, leaving only his eyes running in every direction. They moved from the man before him, down to his still tightly clinched hands, and back to the man.

This brief moment seemed to go on forever. Frustrated and afraid, he questioned his non-responsive body.

When most needed to serve me, why are my legs locked in a motionless state?

His frame was fixed in position, and his eyes were now fixed on Jerry.

"Now, I will have to see how fresh that zip lock plastic bag kept my cheese" Prescott whispered as he glanced over at Ryan's pale bleak face.

Their eyes met, and at once they both understood the false message the knife had conveyed. They stared at each other for a moment; then both burst into full harmonious laughter. Ryan laughed until tears streamed down his face. Jerry Prescott covered his mouth with one hand, and laughter shook him down to the tip of the quaking knife blade in the other hand. He then wiped his tear-soaked eyes with the backside of the hand which held the knife. Although both men had presented confidence in their demeanor, they each were masking gut wrenching tension within. Once the façade was gone, the stress broke like a dam, flooding them with irrational and uncontrollable laughter.

Between gasps, Ryan blurted "Make sure you don't blind yourself with that knife! I don't have a stomach for that sort of thing, and I'm afraid I would end up making a mess in this place."

Jerry said nothing; for he was still wiping tears and trying not to make eye contact with Ryan.

"Just cut the cheese. No! Second thought, please don't!" Ryan exclaimed, as he held his ribs.

A couple of minutes passed before either could utter another word.

Finally, Jerry squeaked, "You're killing me, Walker."

This statement made it even worse. The building tension of the day was released in this comic flood. Earlier, Ryan had no clue that he had been so uptight about the confrontation with Jerry Prescott. As the laughter subsided into simple abdominal pain, Ryan tossed out another question.

"Do your friends just call you Psycho?" He wiped his eyes with his shirt sleeve, as his vision had become blurred by the tears.

"Don't start it again; I've got a knife" Jerry chuckled.

Shaking with silent laughter again, Prescott pointed the knife blade at him and warned "Stop it. I mean it."

He reached into the other drawer and brought out a healthy block of sharp cheddar cheese encased in a large zip lock bag. He took a deep breath. The tears and shaking subsided as he removed the cheese from the bag. He placed the cheese on the plate, and with surgical dexterity carved off several very thin slices. With the ladle he scooped out a large portion of pinto beans from the small pot and poured them into the bowl. He placed the thin slices of cheese on top of the beans and placed the bowl on the table.

"Would you mind if I asked God's blessings?" Jerry asked.

"I'm not closing my eyes with you in the room; if that is what you're asking" Ryan quipped.

He noticed Jerry's tone had become more serious. Taking a deep breath, he then stated "No, I really don't mind."

Jerry closed his eyes, dropped his head, and asked God to bless both their meals.

It had been so long since Ryan had been under the power of such laughter. This event destroyed any chance of him regaining an authoritative position with Jerry. As a swimmer giving up the fight against a swift running current, he allowed himself to flow. He had lost all control, and he found it difficult to bring himself back in line. It was somewhat refreshing to be out of the game. It was like a basketball team losing by eighty points, with only a minute left in the game. The players have the choice of finishing the game in a frustrated sense of desperation, or they can now relax and have a good time. Ryan chose the latter. Seeing the cheddar cheese begin to melt over the hot pinto bean before Jerry, Ryan began to chide Jerry.

"You're going to eat pinto beans and cheese? I know what that stuff does to the gastric track of some people. So, you do plan to kill me after all! Good grief, open a window. At least, give me a fighting chance."

"Help yourself," Jerry responded through a muffled mouth full of beans.

Ryan moved to the kitchen window and noted that it was not like the rest of the house. It was a modern brown vinyl double hung window, and he opened it effortlessly. Jerry advised him to open a second window if he wished to catch a breeze. Ryan opened one of the windows in the living area and sat back down to his sandwich and remaining drink. After five large bites the sandwich was almost gone.

"Tell be about this agreement," Ryan questioned.

"Your uncle and I became very good friends, and together we cut the trail up the mountain and built his small house," Jerry began. "He had always wanted a small place up here. It's a long story, but the real agreement was simple. Your uncle's health was beginning to fail. In the beginning, Andrew did most of the work on the house. However, by the time it was finished, Andrew could do no more than to bring me material. We hooked a small trailer to a four-wheel ATV, and we strapped the material to the trailer. He was having a lot of trouble making the walk, and eventually he had to rely totally on the ATV. He wanted someone to help him take care of the house below, the bridge, the trail, and this small house. The agreement was that I would live here as long as I maintained everything."

"So, you're the one who has been cutting the grass and trimming around the house?" Ryan asked.

"That's true, but it is a little more involved than that" Jerry explained. "I can't take full credit. I do the work, but Andrew's sister pays for gas and oil for the mower. She pays for materials to repair the house below, and she pays the power bill. The house is on a well, so there's no water bill. Your aunt and I had an understanding also. You're a younger man, and in much better shape than Andrew. You may wish to handle the place without anyone's help; and if that's the case, I'll go elsewhere."

"Do you have time to do all this and work a regular job?" Ryan questioned.

Jerry had just finished the last bite of beans and cheese. He pushed the bowl aside and leaned back in the chair. Placing both hands on the table where the bowl had been, he replied.

"I have a simple life, and I really have few needs. Two days a week I help a couple of elderly widows in town. I earn enough to buy food, kerosene for the lamps, a few clothes, and a book every now and then."

"That's pretty simple, but I would guess that you could become tired of this after a while," Ryan advised. "I'm not really sure how long this arrangement would work."

Jerry nodded his head in a manner to denote that he fully understood Ryan's concerns. He then tried to put his own personal priorities in perspective for his guest.

"I'm sure you have a number of plans for the future, and you probably are a fairly ambitious young man. I'm content to enjoy each day on this earth, and I'm not concerned with future plans. I take each day as God provides and do my best with it. I have no family here, and this place is my only responsibility. Ryan, I want you to understand something. Andrew wasn't sure you would come back here. He thought you might, and he hoped you would. He often said that he didn't know if you would be able to work in Boston and take care of the place, but because of his love for you he decided to leave the land to you. It's up to you. I you want me to leave, I will. I'll accept your decision - whenever and however you chose to make it."

With that, Ryan stood up from the table and gathered his empty drink container and sandwich bag.

"I'll let you know soon. I plan to walk up to the top of the mountain today, and I don't want to have to find my way back down after dark. I need to be going."

"That will be fine," Jerry replied. "The walk gets a bit steeper from here, but I think you will make it in time."

"Thanks for your time," Ryan said.

Ryan put his hand out toward Jerry. The man's large work-hardened hand seemed to wrap around Ryan's. It was the same powerful, but gentle, hold that a young boy senses when his father places a comforting arm around him.

Jerry replied, "I am so glad to finally meet you and I've enjoyed the conversation. No matter which way this goes, there will be no hard feelings."

Jerry took the leftover lunch trash from Ryan's other hand and walked over to a plastic bin that sat on the floor between the hutch and the pantry. He popped the lid open, to reveal a black plastic garbage bag with a pull string. He opened it and deposited the trash.

Ryan thanked him and assured him that he would see him later. Walking out the door and onto the porch, he noticed a small path leading from the trail and down the mountain. He guessed that this might be the other end of the second small path he had seen at the rock, but he decided this was not the time to find out. One of his main goals for the day was accomplished.

He felt relieved as he started up the main trail towards the top. Jerry was right, the slope increased almost immediately. Limestone rock became more prevalent, and it wasn't far beyond the first switchback that he came across a small cave. After this point the clearly marked trail became a smaller path and was somewhat obscure in places. The slope became even steeper. Ryan encouraged himself.

This means that I'm ascending the mountain at a faster rate.

At last, he arrived at the top. The density of the trees made it difficult for him to take in a wide view of what was on the other side. It was obvious that Ryan had hiked the steeper of the two sides. On the side he had traversed, he could catch enough of the landscape to be in awe. It was almost a clear day, and the countryside before him was beautiful. Ryan had always requested a window seat when taking flights. He loved to see the changing scenes below. This was different, in that the land never passed from view. It was open for lengthy inspection. Though the view was still; it was alive with tiny birds in the air, with distant rare vehicles traveling slowly down strings of roadway, and with changing shadows as small puffs of clouds passed overhead.

He looked at his watch and realized that hours had passed

very quickly. Ryan had much less time to return to his car than he had taken to come up the mountain. With one last glance at the land before him, he started back down the small path.

As he made his way down, he began to understand Aunt Sally's request. He had been wise to listen to her. She had not told him the facts and had also provided him the opportunity to gather them for himself. He considered Jerry's point to be a strong argument.

I have little time to properly care for this place while working in Boston. Uncle Andrew entrusted the property to me, and I'll honor his generosity by making sure things were well taken care of. I need to settle the matter regarding Jerry; there's no reason to drag this out any further.

As he approached the small home in the woods, he wondered if Jerry was still inside. Ryan quickly ascended the steps and knocked on the door. This time he heard the footsteps inside and waited patiently as they became more distinct. Jerry greeted Ryan as he opened the door.

"That didn't take long. What did you think of the top?"

Ryan again held out his hand toward the man.

"I can understand why my uncle loved this place. I would like to continue the same agreement that my uncle had with you if you don't mind. Please stay. It's my place now, and I will pay for the gasoline used to mow the grass and power bill. I will work out something with Aunt Sally, so that you receive it through her. I do have one additional request. I would like for you to call me twice a month to let me know how things are."

"Are you sure?" Jerry asked, looking Ryan squarely in the eyes.

Ryan smiled and said, "Yes, I am."

Again, Ryan found the rough large hand of Jerry's in his. Jerry's muscular hand was so thick and solid that he didn't need to provide very much of a grip. It was almost like holding a brick, just the firm squeeze of Ryan's against his made it seem like a clasp. Jerry smiled and patted Ryan on the shoulder.

"I'll call you, if something out of the ordinary comes about," Jerry said.

Ryan took a business card out of his wallet, and on the

back wrote his home address and cell phone number. Jerry informed him that the small path across from the front porch provided a shortcut to the rock below.

With a wave from his hand, Ryan started down the path. About twenty feet along the way, he found that it led to an outhouse. He felt compelled to stop and look inside, for he had never actually seen one before. He was surprised that there was no real apparent smell.

How had Jerry handled that? I'll have to ask him on another occasion because the sun is dropping fast. I still have a fair distance to go.

By the time he crossed the wooden bridge, it was completely dark. The moon was full and strong, and once he was beyond the trees it provided a glow to the ground under him.

For a few moments Ryan stood alone in the backyard and took in the view of the night around him. He was astounded at the display of stars that filled the sky. Ryan observed how the dark form of the mountain hid those shining just below the horizon. He studied the dark small house. He imagined it with warm lights glowing inside, and of pale smoke rising from the still chimney during a cool winter night.

Ryan then walked to the front of the home and stood on the lonely, darkened porch. He imagined a porch swing and how peaceful it would be to quietly rest in it after supper time. This was his, and on occasion it would provide a welcome retreat from the fast-paced life in Boston. He had never imagined that he could feel this way about a simple place in the country. This was going to be an adventure; and he planned to make a few changes in his life. Most of all, he had a family again; and he was going to treat Sally as such. Remembering Sally, he decided that he had best return for that supper she promised.

He easily found his car and slipped into the familiar comfort inside. There was much to tell Sally, and he eagerly anticipated tonight's meal and conversation. Tonight, he would tell her all about the events of the day. Ryan would tell her of his plans, and how he would do things a bit differently.

He wanted to handle the property in a way that would be fair for all. Tonight, he would draw up a document of agreement stating that Jerry had a right to live in the homestead, but that he would retain clear ownership of the land and all that was on it. He started the car, and gingerly crawled down the gravel drive that led to the road back to Sally's home.

Chapter 8

AS HE PULLED INTO SALLY'S DRIVE, Ryan felt complete peace. Entering her front door, advertisements of the meal to come filled the air. He quickly made his way to the kitchen. Delighted to see that the invisible savory promotions in the air had substance behind them, Ryan gave Sally a hug.

"I thought we would informally serve our plates at the stove," she announced.

"It's like being part of a Pavlov experiment," Ryan thought.

His mouth watered instantly, and he couldn't wait to start the feast. The meal was all that his nostrils had promised. Ryan ate until his side hurt.

After the meal, he and Sally discussed his inheritance of Andrew's old home. He decided he would repair the place and asked her opinion regarding almost every idea he had for the refurbishment. Sally suggested they go to the old home and spend the night. Thanks to Sally's continued payment of the utility bills, the home had power.

"That settles it," Ryan said. "We'll drive over in my car and spend the night in my newly acquired home. I can bring you back to your house before leaving for Boston tomorrow morning."

"I'll put you to work washing dishes, while I pack food

and bedding," she eagerly replied. "I'll bring a broom and a dustpan. I'm sure it needs to be swept."

Reaching inside her hall closet, Sally brought out a roll of toilet paper. She called for her nephew's attention and tossed the roll down the hall in his direction.

"We can't forget this item!" she exclaimed.

ONCE AT ANDREW'S OLD PLACE, Ryan brought the packed goods inside. He began placing food in the refrigerator, while Sally made the only bed and prepared the old couch for sleeping.

"You are not sleeping on that couch," Ryan insisted. "As the new homeowner I've determined that you'll have the bed. Tonight, you're the guest!"

The two talked at kitchen table. Sally's devout faith in God seemed to be at the core of who she was.

"Regarding faith, is it easier to have faith during good times than during periods when your life was tough?" Ryan asked.

Sally thought for a moment, then answered.

"It depends on how you want to look at it. Perception plays a significant role in how people deal with aspects of life. When life for me was physically difficult, it was probably easier to have faith. I had little else to count on. I became more prosperous after Andrew's death, but I've had to learn to deal with loneliness. Being alone is a different matter. I know what it is like to be without physical and material comforts, and I know what it is like to have plenty. I have known years of deep constant friendship and know what it's like to be alone. I have found God's hand to be in it all. I believe He meets each individual person where they are. Situations change, and people change. No matter what, He can always be counted on. You just have to look for Him in all the places life carries you. Whether wealthy or poor, a person can choose to live a miserable or a fulfilling life. It is a matter of choice. We all have the choice, and we all make that choice."

She went on to explain how our choice determines how situations and events in life shape us. She used the illustration of how geodes stone must suffer the blows of the hammer and chisel by a stone mason so that the inner beauty of quartz or amethyst may be seen.

"The plain looking geode has that potential beauty all along, but the impact of breaking it apart reveals it," Sally explained. "We have the choice of being thankful for God opening us up or complain about the brokenness. Diamonds in the rough are ground down in to shapes so that the true beauty of the stone be seen in cut diamonds. We can focus on the beautiful gem that God is creating out of us or we can be terrified or angry at the sight of the broken pieces of ourselves that we see on the ground. It is entirely up to us."

She humbly explained that this illustration of cut rock was not original, but one she had heard in a church sermon as a child. It had helped her put life's events in perspective, and it had been a source of strength during trying times.

From the outside, this small unimposing woman looked to be as insignificant as an old chipped and discolored clay pot. God had taken such a small unassuming vessel and poured from it a river of riches into Ryan's thirsty soul. Ryan had asked a thoughtful, but simple question. The answer he received was the wisdom of the ages. Sally and Ryan talked until she could hardly maintain eye contact. It had been a long and eventful day, worthy of a night of hardy sleeping. Ryan made sure she was alright, cut out all the lights, and then dropped into the soft large couch.

Before drifting off to sleep, he thought about the interior of his inherited home. It was just as he had remembered from childhood. The living area in the front ran the entire width of the house, with a single fireplace on the left wall. There were windows on each side of the fireplace, but the opposite wall had only a single window. The couch faced the fireplace and small tables sat under each of the two windows flanking the fireplace. There were a couple of old chairs in the room, and a box containing firewood sat beside the front door. A short center hall ran from the living area and emptied into the kitchen, which occupied the right rear portion of the house. From the hall, there was a door to the left leading into an empty bedroom. Across the hall from the bedroom door was the door leading into a single bathroom. This bathroom had been added much later after the house was built. In fact, the bathroom originally had been a small dining room. The largest bedroom was in the left rear portion of the house, and it was entered directly from the kitchen. The home's only bed was in this room. It was a tall featherbed, and the mattress was hollowed in the center from many years of use. In some respects, it resembled a large rectangular catcher's mitt. The room also contained the home's only matching dresser and nightstand.

His thoughts then shifted to his earlier conversation with Sally, as well as the life behind her words. Ryan evaluated his own reactions to situations he had encountered in life.

I've been bitter over the facts that my parents died so young and so violently while I was away at college, but I could have been thankful for the time I had with them. I didn't lose them while I was a young child. At least their death was quick. They didn't die from a lengthy and painful disease. Life is filled with choices, even about situations which weren't of our own choosing. Sally said that bitterness could be as dangerous as a cancer eating away at a person. I can see that. She also said that self-absorption leads to a confused and meaningless existence. She's right. Sally has really been around and seen life from a number of perspectives. I'm amazed at her wisdom.

As Ryan pulled the comforter around him, he made a decision to look for positive aspects in situations. He also considered how he should change his relationships with other people. As an adult, he had made a point to maintain a certain distance from people. He had viewed people as short-term investments. Ryan based the continuance of a relationship on the degree to which the people contributed to his career. He hadn't limited his relationship to only powerful and successful individuals. When convenient, he also made associates of people he perceived as being below his own status, but he wasn't genuine. He had discovered he could learn from people of all perceived levels of influence, and this knowledge could serve him in his own journey towards success. When he perceived there was little left to be learned from the person, the association would begin to wither. He wasn't a true friend; so, he really didn't have true friends. His relationships would die before coming into maturity.

I see that there are givers in this world, and there are takers. Compared to Sally, I guess I've been a taker. Not a hostile taker, but a subtle one. I don't like what I see. Things are going to change.

He realized his attitudes had helped shape his perspectives about God. It was clear to him that his views on God were similar to those he had regarding people.

I can't see God, hear God, or touch God. It's difficult for me to see how a person's allegiance to an invisible God could do more than tie him down to abstract and fruitless boundaries in life. It's apparent the world was put together so tightly and perfectly that it must have design behind its existence. I guess I have a general belief in some kind of godlike being. I just don't have an active faith like Sally's.

Although he didn't consider himself to be a spiritual person, he had considered joining a church for two reasons. He felt church offered him another opportunity to meet successful people. Secondly, perhaps a preacher's sermon could give him insight into human nature. He could see value in that. However, he decided church was not the place for him. TV evangelists turned him completely off, and the idea of being a religious fake simply to establish successful associates didn't really appeal to him.

Sally was absolutely right about the perception of circumstances, and she seems to have a solid understanding of life. I've always viewed her as a genuine person, and I've had respect for her. She doesn't seem to have any need for people games, and her faith seems real. It's not a showy, in your face, type of religion. Rather it seems to just naturally be a part of her. She doesn't push it on people, but she doesn't hide it either. Sally doesn't make a point of acting a certain way; it's just there. Just as a person's breathing is not usually noticed during conversation, there is an almost transparent natural spirituality beneath the words she speaks.

Ryan had heard people talk about God, but he realized he had no real understanding of Him. He considered the possibility that maybe he really didn't know enough about spiritual matters to have valid opinions concerning God. Because of Sally's faith, Ryan made a decision to look for God's hand in circumstances which arose in his life.

If God really does deal with people on an individual basis, why would He bother to do so in a vindictive manner — especially with people who don't purposely go against Him? A supreme being has to be much bigger than that. Regardless of my understanding of God, I'm going to make an effort to look for aspects in which to be thankful.

Ryan thought about people who were in much worse situations and realized how good he had it. He thought about Sally and the difficulties she had faced. Sally had still found the goodness of God and purpose in her life. Ryan viewed her as a very special person. As he lay there, he listed blessing after blessing in his life and thanked the invisible God for each. For the first time in memory, he thanked God for numerous situations for which he had earlier launched curses. He began to look for ways in which God might have been present in unpleasant situations. Ryan looked for opportunities during his life, in which God may have been attempting to use situations to shape and strengthen him. He looked closely, and he sensed God in the borders of each picture of his life.

The still night was almost deafening. As he listened intently, he could faintly hear crickets sing their perfect lullaby. Lying on the couch, he closed his eyes and replayed in his mind the climb to the top of his mountain. He breathed in the fresh air, and he relived the glorious elements of each scene. He was now free to return home to Boston. The night began to slowly cover him in a blanket of sweet sleep.

Chapter 9

RYAN AWOKE WITH A SHARP

headache, and to the sound of approaching footsteps. A woman's voice sang, "Well, look who has decided to join the world!"

"*Who is this person?*" he thought.

The voice seemed somewhat familiar, but he opened his eyes to a very unfamiliar room.

What in the world is going on? Am I awake, or did my dreams shift to another scene? This doesn't seem real. It's possible I'm dreaming that I'm awake. That would be too weird!

As he lifted his hand to rub his eyes, he felt the cold touch of an IV tube drop across his face. Now he was awake. His eyes popped open to see a young nurse holding out a glass of water and a pill.

"Here, this will help. I bet you feel lousy, but this will make your head feel a little better."

How does she know I have this awful headache?

There was something refreshing about the cheerful tone of her voice. He attempted to sit up, but the throbbing in his head pounded him back down onto the pillow. Ryan closed his eyes. The pain in his head seemed to soften, and he opened his eyes again.

"Am I in a hospital?" he asked.

"Don't try to sit up too quickly," responded the nurse.

"Just take it easy. Yes, you are in the hospital; and you took a pretty heavy blow to the head. In fact, you suffered a concussion. Just take it slow; things should start coming back to you."

I must have had an accident on the way back to Boston. I don't remember driving back there at all.

He couldn't tell by the dialect of the nurse's voice whether he was back in Boston or somewhere along the route from Brandon Springs. He then reminded himself of the fact that Boston is home to a wide variety of persons from all over the world, and not everyone there has a strong New England accent.

"How did I get here?" he asked the nurse.

As the nurse adjusted the curtains around his bed, she smiled.

"Well, I believe an ambulance brought you here."

Seeing he was not in the mood for a smart answer, she again responded in more serious tone.

"You have an injury to your head. I'm sure you feel somewhat disoriented. Try to relax. The doctor will be by any minute now. He wanted to talk to you as soon as you awoke. I buzzed the desk as soon as I saw that you were stirring…and here he is. Doctor Adams, he is all yours now."

She handed the charts to the tall slim doctor with thinning hair. He quickly scanned at the charts and introduced himself.

"Hello, I'm Doctor Thomas Adams. Do you know where you are and what has happened to you?"

"I'm apparently in a hospital," answered Ryan. "According to the nurse, I came here by ambulance. I feel pretty dizzy. It's like being in a fog. This is due to an injury to my head?"

Ryan placed his hand on his thickly bandaged head.

"I don't even remember driving back from Brandon Springs. I just remember…"

He closed his eyes as he tried to make sense of what had happened to him. He was confused; nothing seemed real. His head began to spin, and he had an overwhelming sensation of dizziness. Ryan thought maybe he blacked out for a moment. He calmed himself with the thoughts that he was safely in a hospital and surrounded by a calm confident professional staff. He opened his eyes again.

Ryan continued his conversation. He was about to say that he remembered parking his car at Andrews house, but suddenly remembered parking on a dark street. Ryan remembered the frustration of a flat tire, and the three young men who offered to help him change the tire. He remembered rolling the deformed deflated tire to the trunk after placing the puny spare onto his fine automobile.

"I had a flat tire," he whispered.

"And you came close to having a flattened head" the doctor continued. "Apparently you had a flat tire on the freeway and pulled off onto a side street to change it. Soon after the spare was put on, you were hit hard over the head with a tire tool. Three men stole your car, and you were very lucky you are not much worse off. They could have killed you, but they couldn't wait to get that car. They took the car and sped away quickly. A neighbor heard the screeching tires as they peeled away. She looked outside, saw you lying across the curb, and then phoned 911 for help. You're very fortunate."

"I guess I owe that woman," Ryan stated. "What about my car?"

"Forget the car, son' the doctor advised. "You've been unconscious for a while; just be thankful for your health. I'm sure you have insurance on a vehicle like that, and you can settle up with them later."

"I would rather just get my car back, as soon as the police catch the guys who took it!" Ryan exclaimed.

"The car is gone; you are still here," the doctor reminded his patient. "Listen, the car is completely totaled. Those idiots didn't think about the fact that there aren't many cars like yours. The police spotted them almost immediately on a freeway, and a chase followed. Those punks thought they could outrun the police in your car, but the police called in back up to cut them off. Someone said the car was traveling at about

120 miles per hour when the driver attempted to take an exit ramp onto a side street. He lost control, and car flipped several times and finally hit a barrier. The driver never considered the fact that he was trying to outrun the police on one of those tiny spare tires. Those tires are not meant for high speeds, and they are only to be used temporarily. Like I said, the car is gone. Forget it, and deal with the insurance adjustor."

"I would guess the crash killed the three guys?" Ryan questioned.

"The crash killed the two in the front, but the one in the back seat survived," said the doctor as he glanced back over the charts. "The survivor is in another hospital and should stand trial when he is able."

Ryan was almost dazed by the news of his car, and the fact that two people had been killed driving it. His head was spinning as he attempted to adjust to the situation in which he found himself. Ryan decided to take one step at a time and prioritize the information he had been given. He needed to replace his car, or at least get a rental until he could buy one. His head began to feel better.

"How long do I have to stay here?" Ryan asked. "I have a lot to do."

Glancing up from behind the charts, the doctor replied.

"I would like to keep you, at least, overnight for observation. You did receive a concussion, and you should be careful for several days. You may experience headaches and you may not sleep well. I'll give you a prescription for pain before you check out. You're welcome to call your insurance agent from one of the emergency room phones, if you like."

"I have a cell phone," Ryan responded. "I need my wallet. Where are my clothes? My wallet should be in my pants pocket."

"Your clothes, everything you had on you should be under the cart," the doctor replied, while pointing in the direction of the cart. "Your personal effects should be in a separate bag. Would you like for me to get it?"

"Please…"

Ryan stopped in mid-sentence, as he had become somewhat dizzy again. His head began to throb. He had attempted to sit up quickly again and was paying the price.

"Just sit up slowly," the doctor advised. "Try coming up on one elbow, rest a few seconds and then come on up. Don't make sudden moves for the next day or so."

The doctor reached for the cart, carried the bag to his patient. Ryan began to search the bag. Stopping himself, he spoke to the doctor.

"Thanks for explaining things. I'm feeling a little better now. Thanks for your patience."

Doctor Adams excused himself to attend another patient, and Ryan thanked him again for his help. He retrieved the wallet and found the insurance card. Ryan also found his cell phone in the bag.

Using the cell phone, he explained the situation to the insurance agent. Ryan expressed his frustrations and found him to be very reasonable.

"I can't go without a car, and I want this situation to be very short lived," Ryan explained. "What can you do to take care of this?"

"The salvage yard will be called, and I'll confirm the status of the car using the vehicle identification number," the agent answered. "Since the car is a total loss, I should be able to send a check to pay off the loan. I would advise you to keep the policy active for at least ten days, so that I'll able to transfer the policy to a new vehicle within that time."

The next phone call was to his boss. She advised Ryan to take advantage of the company's health coverage which allowed him a week of recovery after leaving the hospital.

As the minutes wore on, he felt better and began to grow impatient to leave the hospital. He was now fully aware of some of the dangers of owning an expensive car and convinced himself the next one would be a less costly one. Ryan hated the thoughts of being without personal transportation. He decided, once discharged, he would immediately take a cab to a car lot and resolve that situation.

A different dark-haired nurse pulled back the curtains from around his bed and reached for his bag of clothes under the cart. She looked through the clothes for a minute, then smiled and placed the bag back in its original position. She had a kind face, but he could tell she was hiding something. Scenario after scenario played over in his head, and he began to be a bit frightened.

Maybe I've been injured more seriously than I thought. Maybe she knows I'll be in this hospital for longer than the doctor first indicated, and she's about to place my clothes in long term storage. Maybe the doctor didn't give me all the information regarding the mugging. Perhaps the police consider me to be an associate of those thugs. Maybe they're thinking a drug deal went wrong, and the other three decided to do me in and take my car. Maybe the police are looking for something in my clothes. What do they want?

"What in the world do you want with my clothes?" Ryan quizzed the nurse.

"Stop being so nosey," the nurse replied. Still smiling she departed, closing the curtain as she left.

His head was killing him. He closed his eyes again and tried to shut out the pain. During the next two hours, he recalled the events of last couple of days over and over in his mind. Ryan relived each part of the trip to Brandon Springs. The only part missing was the trip back to Boston. He felt confused, and wished he had evidence to indicate something about the missing time. Then it hit him.

There's the document stating that Jerry Prescott has the right to live on the side of the mountain. I just don't remember taking it to the Probate office. Why can't I remember something of so much importance?

The headache was now a constant dull pain. Ryan decided to examine the bag under the cart containing his clothes. He fumbled with the side railing of his bed, until he was able to lower it. Slowly he turned and hung his legs over the side of the bed. The earlier lesson of quickly sitting up had made an impact on him. This time he moved slowly. He slid his feet down to meet the cold hospital tile flooring. Ryan stood for a moment to make sure he was not teasing a return of the sharp headache. He had no plans of allowing one of those to sneak up on him again. After taking only a couple of slow determined steps, he felt a tug at his arm. Looking down, he found the IV still clipped to his hospital bed. He unfastened the clip. Ryan was delighted to see wheels at the base of the IV stand. This was the first real good news since he had awakened. He took hold of the stand and cautiously rolled it across the floor. Like a caravan crossing a desert, he and his traveling partner moved slowly toward the cart.

Still holding onto the IV stand for balance, he reached for the bag of clothes with the other hand. Slowly he opened the bag and examined the contents.

I recognize these pants as being mine, but I don't remember wearing them or bringing them on the trip. Then again, I don't remember the drive back to Boston.

He carefully went through the pockets of his pants and shirt and found nothing. The collar of the shirt was covered with blood. He needed to find out whether he had taken the document regarding Jerry to the Probate Judge, or whether he still had it. He continued his search through the contents of the bag and did not find it.

This would have been the most pressing issue to accomplish before leaving Brandon Springs. If I took it to the courthouse, I would have some notarized copy. I just can't remember it. If I neglected to handle this important matter before leaving, I should still have the document. It's possible that it was left in the crashed car.

Shortly after making the return pilgrimage from the cart to his bed, his head began to pound again. He sat on the bed and slowly laid back. Trying not to make any sudden movements, he gingerly brought his feet up onto the bed. Ryan closed his eyes tightly, attempting to squeeze out the pain. It didn't work. His head was spinning, and he began to feel sick to his stomach.

Ryan felt someone pat him gently on shoulder. When he opened his eyes, he noticed the young nurse had come into the room.

"I'm here to remove your IV. How are you feeling?"

He wasn't sure how to respond. Ryan's head was hurting, and he felt a little confused. He tried to focus his concentration on the nurse.

She's much smaller than the dark-haired nurse. There's something calming in her voice. Her bedside manners are relaxed.

Ryan intently watched her small hands as she carefully removed the needle from the back of his hand, commanded him to hold his arm above his head, and instructed him to apply pressure on the cotton pad she had placed over the slight wound. She updated his charts and turned her attention back to her patient. Removing the cotton, she examined the place where the needle had entered his skin. Confident the bleeding was negligible, she returned the cotton and promptly placed a small bandage over it.

"Are you feeling better?" she asked.

Ryan nodded slowly. Seeing no need for further discussion, she then turned to roll the stand toward the door of the room. As he watched his former traveling companion being taken away, he asked the nurse if the hospital had a method for him to buy clothes. He had begun his explanation of the blood stained shirt, but was interrupted by the sight of his boss at the door.

"You wouldn't be needing clothes, would you?" she asked while holding up a bag from a department store.

"You brought clothes for me?" Ryan asked, as his boss laid the bag in his lap. Her eyes were smiling.

"Socks, shirt, and a pair of jeans; you'll have to get your own underwear', she responded. He opened the bag and began pulling things out.

"You are a Godsend!" he said in amazement.

She's like an angel. I've never seen a human side to her before. Normally, while at work, she's as cold as polished brass.

"If you don't like them, just donate them to a charity," she offered.

"No, these are great!" he said, still a bit overwhelmed. "You really have nice taste. How did you know my size? I mean, you pegged everything perfectly."

"After your phone call, I called the emergency room and asked if you had a need. I was connected to an attending nurse who informed me that your clothes were bloody. I asked the nurse to get your size, and within fifteen minutes she called me back. She said you looked like an Arab nomad in your hospital gown, while sporting the bandage on your head. It would be a poor reflection on the company to leave you in that shape. The office chipped in for the clothes, I just bought them."

His boss was mindful of the persona she usually projected, and she didn't want to appear less human than Ryan's fellow employees. Nevertheless, her smile was real. A living human being existed inside that polished armor, and she seemed relieved to be able to let down her guard for a time. She could hide behind the company image, while relating to him on a personal level.

Ryan noticed she seemed a little awkward, and slightly apprehensive. He had carefully taken steps to promote his own career, and he could only guess about the challenges which would have been his if he had been a woman. He began to see her in a slightly different light. Ryan had now seen personal warmth in her, and it caused him to consider the professional difficulties she might have faced in obtaining the position she held. He found a growing respect for her abilities to overcome obstacles and assume the responsibilities and pressures of management. He began to think of her as a person.

This line of thinking was cut short because the doctor returned to inform him that he would be moved to a room for overnight observation. Still smiling, his boss excused herself.

"I really should be getting back to the office," she stated.

"I sincerely appreciate what you've done for me," Ryan replied. "Please pass my thanks to the others who contributed to the clothing."

The young nurse arrived with a wheelchair. Ryan was eager to be out of the hospital and informed the doctor that he would like to leave as early as possible. The doctor told him he would check on him after breakfast the following day to determine his condition.

"If there are no complications, I would be delighted to discharge you from the hospital," stated the doctor. "However, after leaving our care, it's important that you rest several days before returning to work."

As the physician moved through the door to continue rounds, the young nurse quickly lowered the side railing of the bed.

"You'll be moving up to fourth floor for observation, and I will be your nurse for the remainder of this shift" she explained. "OK, now just carefully slide those feet to the floor and turn around."

He obediently followed her directions. Ryan stood on the cold tile floor with his feet between the raised footrests of the wheelchair. As soon as he made sure his balance was stable, he made the turn so that his back was to the chair. Feeling cool air on his backside he became conscious that the hospital gown was open in the back. He immediately reached back with both hands to pull the gown shut.

The nurse chuckled. The two sides of the gown coming together presented her with a mental picture of curtains closing at the conclusion of a theatrical performance. A performance, where the cast consisted of a lone butt covering the entire stage. She then envisioned a giant butt taking a bow while on stage.

Chuckling again, she whispered, "Everyone hates those gowns. Don't worry. In this job, I've seen butts by the thousands. White butts, black butts, brown butts; butts of every color, size, and shape. Still, I find it a bit funny when patients catch a breeze and realize the thing may be open."

The nurse wouldn't have said this to just any patient, but she felt remarkably at ease around Ryan. Hearing her words, he turned a slight shade of red and began to laugh at both the comment and his situation. Inexplicably, she found the scene of the butt on stage replaying in her mind. It was one of those quirky things, and she was doing all she could do to downplay the entertaining aspects of this theatrical performance. The fatigue from many hours of work and little sleep was beginning to cause her emotions to be overly sensitive to events and situations. She placed a hand over her mouth in an effort to resist giggling.

"Well, this is a first for my butt," Ryan explained. "I'm afraid it's a bit of a recluse. You see, my butt has no public life."

His comments caused her to lessen her grip for a moment. Her building giggle spilled over into a snort of a laugh. Remembering herself, she made a gallant and successful effort to contain things. As she rolled him into the elevator, Ryan said "You see, my butt is somewhat shy. It doesn't get out much."

With that comment, the gallant fight came to an end. As the elevator doors closed, the nurse exploded into laughter that was akin to a scream. She quickly hit the 'Close Door' button and gasped, "Stop it! Don't do that to me. I have to finish this shift, and I'm so tired that I've become punchy."

"Tough day?" he asked her.

"This is the second shift that I've worked, because another nurse called in sick," she answered as she began to regain her composure. "I was supposed to be off six hours ago, but I was asked to stay on."

"I'm sorry" he responded. "My name is Ryan Walker, and my butt goes by the same name."

She exploded again. Still holding the 'Close Door' button, she begged "Please, I have to finish this shift. Just let me make it out of this elevator and take you to your room."

"Not until you tell me your name" he threatened. "Just the name your face goes by, you don't even have to tell me if YOUR butt goes by an alias."

She slapped his shoulder.

"Please! OK, my name is Patsy Smith."

"You made that up!" Ryan accused her.

"No" she responded. "That is really my name. See, look at my name tag."

She stepped around to the front of the wheelchair where

he could see the tag. For the first time, he took thorough note of her face.

She's really cute.

Even though her eyes were still red and a little moist from the laughter, and though she wore no makeup, he found her attractive.

She doesn't have the type of beauty that's striking, but she is really cute. Nurse Patsy doesn't seem to be the type that worries about how she looks. She appears to be very comfortable with herself. I like that.

"OK, I believe you," he said.

She released the 'Close Door' button and stepped back behind the wheelchair. The doors opened and she quietly pushed him down the hall to the room. Once in the room, Ryan quickly realized that he would not be given a private room. His roommate occupied the bed near the window.

Patsy smiled at Ryan as she let down the bed railing and opened the wheelchair foot rests for him to stand. As Ryan sat down on his new bed, he introduced himself to the roommate.

"I'm Ryan Walker, I plan to be here just overnight for observation."

"I'm Nick Pearson; my girlfriend shot me in the leg," other patient responded in a clear low voice.

Ryan looked Patsy squarely in the eyes and quietly whispered, "Please tell me that you are not his girlfriend."

Controlling her amusement, she softly responded.

"No, I'm not. But you had better not cross me. I've been known to administer pain."

"I bet you have," he said.

Still smiling, she pushed the wheelchair from the room.

"This was the first time I've heard that nurse joke with anyone," said Nick. "I tried to flirt with her when I first arrived, but she was all business with me."

"I should remind you that your girlfriend shot you, and that should be reason enough for you to be careful in your relationships with women."

"Point taken," Nick agreed.

They talked and joked for some time before falling asleep.

THE NEXT MORNING, Ryan awoke to the sound of the breakfast being placed on his tray. Sitting up slowly, he was pleased there was no return of the severe headache. As soon as he had eaten breakfast, he readied himself to exit from the hospital. After placing his feet on the cold tile floor, he gathered his new clothes and slowly walked to the bathroom. For the first time since the injury, he looked at himself in the bathroom mirror. Unshaven, he was disgusted to see the bulky turban shaped bandage on his head. The combination made him think that he looked like a Far-Eastern snake charmer. Ryan found a disposable razor on the sink and decided to make use of it.

Now I look like a shaven snake charmer. One step at a time, I guess.

He was careful not to make sudden movements that could result in a headache. Deliberately and gingerly he put on the new clothes. He felt much better to be shaven and dressed.

He had just finished dressing when the doctor arrived. Doctor Adams asked several discharge related questions as he examined Ryan's head wound, and then issued him instructions.

"You're free to go as soon as the nurse redresses the wound."

A middle-aged nurse entered the room while pushing a cart. "Time to give you a bandage lesson!" she sang. "I see you have new clothes. Are you ready for a smaller bandage for your head?"

To some degree, Ryan found her to be a bit irritating. However, he reminded himself that she was just trying to make conversation.

She's attempting to be nice. Some in the medical profession have excellent knowledge and skills in healing, but have awkward bedside manners. She's trying.

He often found that he could easily be irritated when he was on the mend. When sick or hurt, he was usually thankful for the help offered by those on whom he was dependent. When well, he could more easily be in control of his emotions. It was in the state of being between sick and well that he was most grumpy.

OK, I'm out of the gown and I'm shaven. I'll make a conscious effort to make sure any point of irritation won't take hold and ruin the morning. However, it would have been much easier if that younger nurse was seeing me off. She's cute.

"I feel almost normal just to get out of the gown and into clothes," Ryan responded.

"Well, the turban styled bandage will soon be replaced with a new style of head covering this morning" the nurse replied. "Your sheik days are coming to a close. You will need to change this new dressing each morning for the next two days. I'm going to show you how to take care of this wound."

The doctor departed to continue his morning rounds. This left Ryan at the mercy of the nurse; and she showed little. The wound had drained somewhat after being stitched. Now dried, the seepage formed a bond between stitches and bandage. The removal was painful, and he was glad that he could not see what she was doing.

Man! My head is really sore. I'm almost convinced that she enjoyed pulling the dressing from my scalp. Maybe she sensed that I'm a bit irritated with her bad jokes and decided to take it out on me.

Once the bandage had been removed, she promptly presented him with two mirrors. Using both of them he could easily see the ugliness of the wound. His head been shaven around the area of the gash, and his swollen scalp was stained by betadine. Several blood clotted stitches formed a blackened ridge across his orange tainted skin.

That's just disgusting.

"You can take a shower tomorrow, but remember to pat the area dry as not to pull the stitches," the nurse instructed.

"It's pretty sore," Ryan replied. "I'm sure I'll take it easy."

"Now it's time for bandage lessons; and this is a much lighter one than the original," the nurse stated. "You'll have to change this daily, and you should inspect the wound with the mirrors before replacing the bandage. If you observe any sign of swelling or infection, you should either come back or see a doctor."

She placed a gauze pad on the wound and wrapped an ace bandage around his head.

"I look a lot like a wounded fife player from the Revolutionary War," joked Ryan

Yankee Doodle came to his mind. In fact, the tune would pop into his head several times that morning. Before leaving, the nurse gave him a plastic bag containing clean gauze pads, a small tube of antibiotic ointment, and an extra ace bandage.

Just before being discharged, the insurance adjustor called Ryan on his cell phone to confirm the car had been declared a total loss.

"A check has been sent to cover the auto loan," he began. "In fact, I called the bank to let them know the check was on the way. I would advise you to contact the bank in order to know the extent of your current line of credit before shopping for a car. Once you select your new vehicle, just give me a ring and I'll be glad to provide you with immediate coverage."

After the conversation, Ryan took the advice and called the bank to confirm what he had been told. Things were proceeding more smoothly than he had imagined. He only needed to have the bank to FAX a letter to a dealership.

He took the bag of old clothes from the cart and stuffed them in the trash can. Ryan sat down in the visitor's chair to wait for the nurse. He saw the door open, and he was about to deliver a planned oration regarding his readiness to be discharged. However, the face did not belong to the nurse. It was his closest work associate Marc Sutherland.

"Wow, I didn't expect to see you up and dressed," Marc declared.

"I'm out of here!" Ryan replied. "I have things to do, and I am so ready to be out of here."

"Well, I heard you may be released, and I got permission from work to give you a lift home," said Marc.

"Hey, I would love for you to drop me off at a car lot!"

exclaimed Ryan. "Could you do that for me? I need to go to a Ford dealership."

"Ford dealership...?" Marc stammered. "I don't know; … I think you need to go home. Ford dealership? I heard someone bashed you on the head. Now, I know you aren't right. You hate American cars. Ford?"

"If you don't take me, I'll walk," Ryan threatened. "Or, I'll take a cab."

"OK… OK," Marc said.

Marc would have tried harder to talk him out of it, but the conversation was interrupted by the presence of the nurse. She entered the room pushing a wheelchair.

"I'm ready to go as soon as the doctor releases me," Ryan stated emphatically.

"I have your charts right here, and he has signed the discharge," she responded. "Because of the concussion, I will have to escort you out of the hospital with the wheelchair. The doctor left these prescriptions for you."

She could be very compassionate with deathly sick or hurt individuals. However, she had little concern for the irritation of a recovering jerk who was quickly on the mend. She almost shoved the discharge paperwork and prescriptions in Ryan's hand.

"Take one tablet twice a day to ward against infection," she instructed as she motioned for him to sit in the wheelchair.

Ryan was a little taken back, but he wasted little time obeying her command.

The rule regarding the wheelchair is unnecessary and silly, but I'm ready to leave. I have transportation to obtain, and then I have to take care of another matter. I can't forget to verify that I filed that document with the Probate Judge in Brandon Springs. I have to make sure that Jerry Prescott has the right to live on the side of the mountain. I seem to remember everything from that trip, except this one item of legal importance. I never understood the difficulties some people experience when receiving a concussion. I hate this.

Chapter 10

AS RYAN AND MARC pulled into the Ford dealership, Marc continued to try to talk him into going home to rest for the day. He tried to convince Ryan that it would be better to bring him back on Saturday to shop for a car. It was obvious to Ryan that Marc needed to go back to work.

"I assure you that I've thought the matter out, and it should take no longer than an hour before I'll be driving out with a new vehicle," promised Ryan.

Marc was uncomfortable at the thoughts of this bandaged fellow driving alone and told him that after the purchase he would follow along to Ryan's condominium to make sure he was alright. Ryan attempted to relieve him of this duty, but Marc would not back down.

"I'm following you, and that's it."

Marc wasn't sure about his associate's ability to make a costly decision involving the purchase of a vehicle in such a short time. However, in less than an hour Ryan drove a white Ford SUV from the dealership.

"I selected a vehicle that I expect to be common," Ryan explained. "I've endured enough with the ownership of the previous one. Two deaths, two people admitted to the hospital, and an upcoming prison sentence of one is enough tragedy for one car."

The thoughts of two men dying in his luxury car was a

little disheartening, and he would not be reminded of it while driving this new vehicle. Marc dutifully followed him to the condominium; then departed for work.

Ryan entered his living quarters and found everything to be in its place.

Apparently, I came home before having the flat tire. My travel bag is where it belongs. I don't remember any of this. I just assumed I had the flat tire on my way back from Brandon Springs.

He searched the bag for the legal document he had drawn up for Jerry and was satisfied that he must have dropped it off before leaving Brandon Springs. He sat on the couch and tried to watch TV, but his mind was racing on to other things. The doctor had instructed him to rest, and his boss had reminded him of the recovery days allowed by the company. He knew he should take it easy, but he felt he was about to jump out of his skin with boredom. There were too many issues to take care of, and he couldn't stand to leave matters unsettled.

It's not in my nature to procrastinate. I should go by the insurance office and finalize the policy for the new SUV.

He grabbed his keys and left. Ryan only traveled a few blocks before realizing he was hungry. He glanced at his watch and saw it was already 1:00 PM. He didn't want to eat lunch in the new vehicle, so he selected a fast-food restaurant and ordered a hamburger with fries. He was so consumed with his mission, that the food was devoured in short order. He hardly remembered tasting any of it.

When he arrived at the insurance office, he found the paperwork was completed. The only items lacking were the agent inspection and Ryan's signature. The duty was finished in less than thirty minutes. He had earlier thought he would feel relieved by completing this task, but still he was uneasy. He could not stop thinking about Sally, Jerry, and his land. His boss told him to take a week off from work, but he didn't see the need to spend the week in Boston.

It would take two days to return to Brandon Springs and two days to return. If I leave in the morning, I could be there by Sunday evening. I would have a week to rest there, and I could drive back the following weekend.

Ryan found himself at peace with the idea, and his mind began to settle. Once the decision was made, it was as if an itch had been scratched or a splinter removed. He felt relief.

As he traveled in the direction of his condo, thoughts of the mountain filled his mind. He wanted to go back up to the top, but realized that climbing up and down in the same day would be too much for his wounded state.

I could spend a night with Jerry. No, this time I want to be alone on his mountain.

He spotted 'Johns Outdoor Sporting Goods'. At once he had his answer. The idea came to him almost as if it were inspiration.

I'll experience the mountain by camping in a tent on the mountain top! That's it!

Ryan could feel adrenaline surge through his body. He pulled the vehicle in front of the store, got out, made sure his new form of transportation was locked safely, and went inside. As a Boy Scout he had done some camping, but that had been several years ago. He decided he would tell the manager what he had in mind and ask his advice regarding equipment for the adventure. Before leaving the store, he purchased a framed backpack, which included a water bladder. He also bought a small flashlight, a two-man domed backpacking tent, a goose down sleeping bag, a sleeping bag pad, a box of power bars, and a bag of trail mix. The manager of the store demonstrated to him that all of the goods could be fastened to, or placed inside, his new backpack with room to spare. The manager adjusted the frame to personally fit Ryan and was more than pleased to place the charge on Ryan's credit card.

With the backpack readied, and on his shoulders, Ryan hiked through the store to the front door. Before exiting, he spotted a battery-powered lamp. He toyed with the idea of buying it. Remembering his current bill, he decided he had spent enough on camping gear. The march continued out the front door and to the rear of his parked SUV.

I'm amazed at how light it feels on my back. There's a lot of bulk, but the manager balanced the weight and had made the correct adjustments to the backpack frame. It's perfect.

He opened the back of the SUV and placed the backpack inside. All he had to do was to fill the bladder with water, and he would be all set. He sat for a moment behind the wheel of his new vehicle. Ryan sensed the excitement of this new adventure begin grow. He imagined the hike up the mountain to be different from the first trip to the top.

This time I won't be carrying a load of apprehension about dealing with someone I fear to be a freeloading squatter. I can take my time and enjoy the fresh air and beauty of the pristine hillside.

Still excited about the upcoming trek, he drove past a neighborhood mission for indigents. He was stunned as he witnessed a man walk through the front door of the center.

"That guy could be Jerry Prescott's twin!" Ryan shouted aloud.

He immediately stopped the SUV in the street. This caused a concert of disharmonious horn honking from vehicles from the rear. He didn't care to make anyone in this neighborhood angry, so he decided to make the block. The more he thought, the more he was convinced this had to be Jerry. As was common with Ryan, scenarios began to quickly flow though his mind.

Why would he be in Boston? Maybe something happened to Sally, and Jerry came to find me. I gave him my cell phone number, but I neglected to check my messages during the short stop at the condo.

Checking his cell phone for messages, he found none. As he pulled in front of the mission the second time, he found a convenient place to park.

He entered the front hall of the mission and spotted the office just to his left. He couldn't help but notice a huge room through the open doorway directly in front of him. He moved into the large room, which was filled with tables and chairs. It seemed to be much too quiet to be a place which housed indigents. He was a little afraid to call out, so he returned to the office. Seated behind an old metal desk with a laminate top was a man in his fifties. He was busily going through papers in manila folders. A sign on the desk read, 'Staff Supervisor – Walter Bounds.' After about ten seconds of making notes, the man looked up at him and apologized.

"I'm sorry, I needed to document a few things before I forgot the information. My name is Walter Bounds; what can I do for you?"

"I'm looking for a man named Jerry Prescott," Ryan explained. "I'm almost sure I saw him just come in the front door."

"I don't know a Jerry Prescott," Mr. Bounds responded. "Then again, some of our clients fail to give us their real names. Can you give me a description?"

Ryan was not sure how to answer, for he was a little taken by the term 'clients'. This was not a high-class stockbroker catering to wealthy investors. He found the thought of 'indigent clients' somewhat amusing. As a smile grew, he began to describe Jerry in great detail. Mr. Bounds knew no one by that description, but made a couple of phone calls to staff members in various parts of the three story building. No one had seen anyone by Jerry's description. Mr. Bounds explained that the 'clients' were currently on work detail. At length, he explained the rules and arrangements at the mission.

"There are two buildings, and this one strictly houses men. The program is divided into three phases. The men in the first phase live on the second floor, and they endure strict rules. These men are allowed very little personal time, and they work together in large work details. The mission contracts with rental properties to clean, paint, and repair apartment units which have been abused by previous tenants. They have very little privacy in a barrack style large room with bunk beds. During the second phase, men live on the third floor. They have more privacy with only two men to a room, and they all share a single TV in a common room. Each of the third phase men live in their own small apartment in the building next door. They work at a variety of jobs, but they still must report to me weekly. These men live on the second floor of the building, with the few women in the program living on the first. The two groups have separate exterior entrances to their areas of the building."

The went on to explain that the men from all three phases had to attend two worship services at the mission per week, were not allowed to drink liquor, and had to maintain steady employment. The vast majority of the men were in the first phase, and there were only six in phase three. The bulk of the lot returned to the street over time. Mr. Bounds felt the program was worthwhile if only a handful returned to society leading productive lives. Still feeling suspicious about the sighting of Jerry, Ryan thanked him for his time and departed.

By the time he left the mission, dusk was beginning to fall. As he reached his own neighborhood, he had become hungry again. He dropped by a Chinese drive-thru and picked up dinner. He had almost forgotten to have his prescription filled, so he made the pharmacy his last stop before returning home. By the time he arrived the Chinese food was cold and had to be heated in the microwave. He was beginning to feel the strain of the attempted recuperation on his body. He consumed most of the dinner, but was exhausted. His head began to throb.

I need sleep in a bad way. It's been some day, and I hope I haven't overdone it.

The exercise of brushing his teeth was an abbreviated endeavor. His bed beckoned, as a siren. It called to him, and he obeyed with no resistance. He was under its spell, and it never felt so good to slip between the sheets.

Ryan awoke the next morning remembering he must change the bandage daily. He also remembered this was the first day he was allowed to wash his hair. Gingerly removing the bandage, he was surprised to note that the dressing was not stuck to his wound. Examining his head with the two mirrors, he was also pleased to see that his hair was beginning to mask the betadine-stained scalp. He immediately started the shower and treasured the warm flow that fell upon his tender head. After a couple of minutes, he carefully began to work the shampoo into the healthy portions of his head. Cautiously, his fingers worked closer to the stitches. His touch moved so lightly across the shaved scalp that he could barely sense the motion. He moved his head back under the flow as he vigorously scrubbed the rest of his body. Ryan didn't leave this position for several minutes.

Afterwards, he began the toweling by very gently patting the scalp. After a few pats he would examine the faintly stained area using the bathroom mirror and one of the handheld mirrors. He was pleased. He had been so eager to shower that he forgot to shave first. Shaving was usually the second order of his morning bathroom ritual, which followed the opening ceremony of relieving his bladder. He quickly backtracked to handle the shaving; then got dressed for the day. This was the day he would make his way back to Brandon Springs. Visions of mountain top views bubbled through his imagination.

The backpack was still in the rear of his new SUV. He gathered the clothes for the casual trip and placed them in a couple of plastic grocery bags.

I don't need to bring much. However, I remember from my childhood Boy Scouting days, that one should never intend to spend the night in the woods without a roll of toilet paper. I also should pack the garden spade that I use for the potted plants on the back patio. You never know when you may need to dig a cat hole.

He started for the freeway, but thoughts of the lantern redirected him in the direction of 'Johns Outdoor Sporting Goods.' He had to get it and extra batteries. The adrenaline diminishing, he began to feel exhaustion set in. As he neared the shop, he passed by the mission again. Glancing over at the front door of the facility, Ryan caught a familiar glimpse of a man pulling the door shut behind him as he entered. A chill came over him. He slowed the car and began to question himself.

Is my mind playing tricks on me as a result of the concussion, or is it possible that Jerry is actually in town looking for me? Jerry has very distinguishable characteristics. How could I be so mistaken? This man looks too much like Jerry.

This time he was able to pull in front of the mission

without having to make the block. As Ryan exited the SUV, fear suddenly began to rest upon him.

If I'm hallucinating sightings of Jerry, then my head must really be messed up. Perhaps everyone was right; maybe I should spend the week resting at home. But I can't stand the thoughts of sitting alone in my condo for a week. I would be crazy, for sure. I have to find out if this is Jerry.

He entered the door of the mission. Moving straight for the large room, he saw a sea of homeless men playing cards at tables. He heard a man announce that it was time to be off to work. The men stood in murmuring unison and put the cards away.

It should be easy to spot him.

He followed the men out of the large room and out into a parking lot behind the building. There he witnessed as they boarded three old school buses.

Jerry is not among them. Of course, he wouldn't be with them if he had come to find me! He would be questioning the staff.

He raced back into the building to find someone on staff. He stood in the large room and saw no one. Finally, a young woman entered from another door. She tossed an apron into a bin and headed for the front door.

"Hey, stop!" he shouted.

The woman stopped, turned in Ryan's direction, and then began to laugh. It was his nurse, Patsy Smith.

"You're the nurse!" he exclaimed. "What are you doing here?"

"I should ask, what are you doing here?" she responded. "I'd know that bandaged head anywhere!" She began to chuckle again.

"I'm looking for a man" explained Ryan. "Do you know a Jerry Prescott? He would be new here."

"No, I only know a couple of them" she said.

Ryan went on to explain seeing a man resembling Jerry enter the front door as he passed by. She took him to the Director of the mission, and the Director assured him that no one by this name was on the list of those staying at the mission. Ryan gave him a thorough description, but no one had seen anyone fitting it. Ryan and Patsy went back to one of the tables in the large room and continued the conversation.

"I often come to the mission on Saturdays to help serve breakfast," explained Patsy. "Several years ago, I began coming with my father. He was a Viet Nam veteran, and he visited a war buddy at the mission. He came to help serve lunch, but sometimes would find work for his old friend. My father's war acquaintance received a purple heart and had spent a year as a POW. My Dad never talked to me about what the man endured as a POW, but said he was never the same after he returned home. His friend began to drink heavily after coming back to the United States, and his wife left him. Eventually, he was unable to hold down a job, and lived in the streets and under bridges. My father recognized him while passing him on a sidewalk one day and brought him to the mission."

"Your Dad sounds like a good man," Ryan said.

"My father died last year, but I sometimes still come to help at the mission from time to time on Saturdays," she explained. "Not long after my father's death the war buddy drifted on. I never saw him again. Several of the men at the mission are veterans."

"Do you still have your mother," he asked.

"My mother left my father and I for another man while I was a small child," she said. "I lived with my father, and for a few years I had regular visitation with my mother. While I was in high school, my mother and new husband moved to another state. She sometimes called, but I rarely saw her."

"In some ways, we are a little alike," said Ryan. "I lost my parents, while I was away at college. They were murdered while their home was burglarized."

Ryan and Patsy were very different in that she volunteered her time to those who could never advance her career. He had focused his efforts on those who could influence his. She had done the opposite. He felt a degree of shame, because he realized how self-absorbed he had been since his parents died. Nevertheless, they really enjoyed each other's company. It almost seemed they were pieces of a puzzle that fit.

I'm on my way to see my aunt," Ryan explained. "I'd like to tag up when I get back. Here's my cell phone number. If you'll share yours, I'd like to call you the weekend after I return back from Brandon Springs."

With her number, he returned to the SUV and continued down the street to 'Johns Outdoor Sporting Goods'.

I still can't believe that for a second time I've seen a man identical to Jerry enter that mission. This is just weird. This happened two days in a row; and on both days the man vanished. What are the odds of this? Perhaps it really was something to do with the recent blow to my head. Maybe I hallucinated. The thought of that scares the crap out of me! Maybe I should reconsider the wisdom of driving all the way to Brandon Springs in my condition. Maybe this is a common symptom of this type of head injury. The doctor was probably right in his advice for me to rest.

The fear of being mentally unsound was suppressed by the overwhelming urge to return to Brandon Springs. He felt driven to go. Ryan decided it would be wise to be very careful.

I'll make frequent stops, and I'll limit the hours of driving before stopping for the night. I don't have to make the trip in two days. I can take longer if needed.

It was almost noon before he finished his purchase of the lantern and batteries. He had a very long drive ahead of him, and he was already feeling very tired.

Sure enough, he only made it half as far as he had planned. He had to remind himself that he had been recently discharged from the hospital, and that his imagination might be prone to play tricks on him when he was tired. Not long after sunset, he found a very nice motel along the freeway. It also had a nice restaurant. It wasn't long after a hardy supper that he decided to leave a message for his boss on her work phone, informing her he had gone out of town to rest with a relative. He knew she was serious about his taking a week off, and she expected him to be resting at home. He figured the idea of recuperating with a relative should sound acceptable to her. However, he neglected to mention his plan to hike up a mountain and camp in a tent. Ryan made a second call to the front desk for a 6:00 AM wake up call.

It doesn't mean that I have to check out and leave early. I just need to rise up early enough to take the option, if I fell up to it. Besides, I'll take a number of rest stops. An early departure would help me stay on track, to some degree.

He settled himself into bed and began to watch a movie on TV, but this was short lived. With the remote still in his hand, he soon fell into a deep sleep.

Chapter 11

THE 6:00 AM WAKE-UP call didn't do much for Ryan's head. Moving quickly to answer, his head began to throb with a dull pounding. He lay back down and closed his eyes. Within a few minutes the pain subsided. This time he sat up more slowly. Similarly to his practice in the hospital, he slid his feet to carpeted floor and cautiously stood up. After entering the bathroom, he cautiously began to unwind the ace bandage.

This was to be the last day to wear the dressing and ace bandage. If not for the morning headache, he may have decided to end the bandaging practice today.

One more day of this bandage won't hurt. I need to decrease the likelihood of complications. Today, I need to drive as far as possible to make up for lost time. I'm nowhere near a major city, so I anticipate the traffic on the interstate to be light.

HE WAS UNABLE to make it to Brandon Springs. By 8:00 PM, he made a decision.

I'm so sleepy that I'm a little afraid of crashing this new SUV. I really don't need another head bashing event in such a short time. I've got to stop and call it a day.

Afraid of falling asleep at the wheel, he selected the first motel. After pulling up to the building, he had doubts as to the wisdom of this selection.

It's obvious this motel has not made it into the tourism guide; and if it had, it could not rank higher than a half star out of four. I'm exhausted. Left with the choice of killing myself in a highway accident or taking my chances at this fleabag motel, I think I'll chose not to die tonight.

Gathering his backpack, Ryan awkwardly shuffled into the lobby. The lights were dim. After confirming to the foreign clerk at the desk that he would be staying only the one night, the clerk filled out the appropriate paperwork. Ryan made a more thorough review of the place and became more aware of his dingy surroundings. He decided to use cash, as not to provide anyone there with his credit card number.

With the bill paid, he returned to his vehicle and proceeded to drive to the rear of the building. He was glad his room was located on the first of two floors, but he was uncomfortable with the poor lighting in the parking lot. After a couple of tries, he successfully unlocked the door of the unlit room and reached inside to flip the switch for the main light. Upon inspection of the room, he began to feel dirty. As he turned on more lights, he became more disgusted. It had the smell of commercial cleanser, mixed with stale cigarette smoke. There was a neglected cobweb draped from the side of the nightstand to the nearby wall. He placed his backpack on a small table and made his way to the bathroom.

Gross! There are rust stains in the tub and toilet, and there are a couple of broken tiles near the tub. The smell of cleanser indicates that someone recently slid a mop over the stained tiles on the bathroom floor. It's obvious no one bothered to sweep before mopping, because there are small clumps of debris in the corners of the floor. Now for the good news! The towels appear to be clean.

The sink had two different styles of knobs, and the shower curtain was torn so that three of the curtain rings offered no support. Exhausted, he felt he had no choice. He immediately covered the bathroom floor with a towel, leaving only one for the morning shower.

He pulled back the covers to inspect the bed. He found that the very old and worn sheets appeared to be clean.

This is comforting. I dare not inspect the room further. I just don't want to know, at this point. There's no reason for a wake-up call. I should make it to Brandon Springs within two hours of driving.

He undressed and pulled the covers all the way down. Satisfied that no critter had made its home between the sheets, he entered his place of rest for the night. Ryan used the remote to search the TV for something to relax his mind and found fifteen available channels. Three were movie channels; one showing soft porn. He found an old western and turned the last remaining light off. It wasn't long before he drifted into an uneasy sleep.

Ryan was startled by the sound of a crash against the headboard wall. A man and woman in the next room were screaming obscenities at each other. He could tell by the intense conversation, that one of them had thrown something heavy at the other. Over the next hour, the voices lowered to a dull murmur. Then as if there was a totally different couple in the next room, they both broke into laughter. They would howl in unison, and then taper off into mumbling. After a few minutes, one of them would let off a scream of delight and the gut-wrenching laughter would commence again. One would beg for the other to stop, complaining of abdominal pain. This cycle continued for another hour, and then silence.

When the screaming started, Ryan had lowered the volume of the TV to just a whisper. He was afraid someone was being murdered, and he wanted to make sure he was aware of what to report when questioned.

After all, the police would certainly interrogate the occupant of the room closest to the scene of the crime.

Once the tag team in the adjacent room quieted, he realized he was wide awake. Frustrated, he turned the volume back up and found an archeological documentary.

RYAN AWOKE THE next morning wanting breakfast. He glanced at the clock on the nightstand.

Man, it's already 9:30 AM. I need to be going. I'm very hungry, but I really don't want to take chances at the adjacent restaurant. I can think of two solid reasons not to dine there. First, the motel and the diner probably co-exist on the same customer base. I don't want to try to digest a meal while seated near the couple from the next room. I would be directly in the line of fire, if they explode into another fight. The second reason is that I imagine the restaurant is probably as filthy as the motel. I doubt the very existence of a heath score.

He opened the curtains. Daylight offered a more complete evaluation of the room, and it wasn't a pretty picture. There were mysterious stains on the chair and bedspread, and he really didn't want to know the source. He could now see the coating of dust on the dresser and TV, and there were heaps of dead bugs on the inside windowsill. The worst discovery was a pair of lace thong panties peeking out from under the side of the dresser.

This motel was much worse than the hotel in Brandon Springs, so he immediately performed the morning rituals in preparation for the day. He wasted no time. The longer he resided in the room, the stronger the sensation that a variety of deadly diseases were closing in about him. The only occasion to linger was to inspect the wound, after patting it dry after a hurried shower.

After returning the motel key and loading his backpack, he ventured down the highway in search of breakfast. Several minutes later he pulled into an acceptable restaurant. The specialty was breakfast food, and it was served at all hours. Before he allowed himself to be seated, he visited the restroom and diligently scrubbed his hands. He wanted no remnants of the motel room to come in contact with what would enter his mouth. He was exhausted from little sleep after he finished the mean and ordered a cup of coffee to go. It was about 1:00 PM when he final left the freeway for the small tar and gravel road leading to Brandon Springs.

The surroundings seem somewhat different than what I remember from the previous trip. But then again, I arrived as a storm was ending.

Today offered a beautiful afternoon. The sun was shining, and the road was dry. He was surprised at how well the SUV handled it, and marveled that the ride was actually quieter than that of his previous vehicle.

He passed the center of town and took the road to Sally's new home. As he passed by Andrew's old homestead, he came to an abrupt stop. He was almost in a state of shock.

"I trusted Jerry to keep me informed of significant events at the place, and it's apparent he neglected to do so!" Ryan shouted. "I can't believe the front pastures on each side of the long gravel drive are freshly plowed! What is going on?"

Ryan turned up the drive and became angrier as he approached the house. In the front yard sat large pieces of farm equipment. Parking the SUV behind a tractor, he jumped out of it and headed straight for the house. As he started to ascend the steps, a stranger came out of the front door.

"Where is Jerry?" barked Ryan.

"I don't know any Jerry," replied the man. "Who are you?"

"This was my Uncle Andrew's home, and I am in town to see my Aunt Sally," Ryan said as his anger reached its peak. "I can't believe the pastures have been plowed under! I demand an explanation!"

"Your, Aunt Sally?" the man questioned in a more somber tone. "Son, I'm afraid you missed your visit with her. She died three months ago."

"What are you talking about?" Ryan gasped.

"You didn't know?" the man asked. "She didn't last long after Andrew died, and the funeral was small. I'm really sorry, son."

Ryan's head began to spin.

Am I suffering from lingering effects of the blow to my head? What is this man saying?

He took a step back and realized the house was not kept as it had been on his earlier visit. It needed to be painted, and weeds grew around the foundation.

As Ryan took hold of the porch railing, the stranger asked, "Are you OK? Here, sit down on the porch swing for a minute."

Ryan turned, descended the steps, and hastily ran around the house into the backyard.

There's no wooden footbridge! There's no shed in the backyard.

He saw large gaps in the mountain where someone had obviously harvested some of the larger oaks. All at once, he felt dizzy and somewhat sick to his stomach. As he stepped backwards, he felt the presence of the stranger who had followed him. Turning to this man, he could hardly speak.

"What has happened here?" Ryan stammered.

The stranger first expressed genuine sorrow at Ryan's loss of both aunt and uncle. Ryan stood there shaking his head, as the man explained the facts to him.

"Andrew died, owing a large debt to the bank and a substantial amount of back taxes," the man explained. "He had used the land as collateral. I purchased the farm by paying the debts to both the bank and to the state. I'm a farmer. The name is Alvin Gibbs."

Ryan was numb, and his face began to grow pale. He felt as though he was dreaming. At this point he wasn't sure where reality stopped, and imagination started. For the first time in his adult life, he was totally unsure of himself. He heard the words as Alvin attempted to explain, but it was too much to take in. His eyes darted around as Alvin spoke.

The experiences with Sally and Jerry must have been dreamed while unconscious at the hospital. I've lost my only relative; and due to a self-absorbed life, I missed her by three months. God help me.

Seeing that Ryan was visibly shaken, Alvin suggested that he introduce the younger man to Sally's minister who conducted the funeral. Ryan nodded in agreement, but was still very much in a state of shock. It was if someone had cut off both his feet, and blood was quickly vacating his head. He was visibly pale, and he began to shake in small quivers. The farmer took him by the arm, led him around to the front porch, and had him sit on the steps as he went inside the house for pencil and paper. As he sat on the steps, Ryan examined the deteriorating planks on the front porch.

This is a porch which is no longer mine; and behind the house was the mountain which is no longer mine. I have nothing. No land, and no living relative.

It was the thought of losing Sally that finally overwhelmed him. When Alvin returned with paper and pencil, he found Ryan sobbing and physically shaking violently.

Alvin settled on the front steps beside him and explained what he was putting on paper. He had written the name and phone number of Sally's pastor and was beginning to draw a map to the church. The grave site was in a small cemetery behind the church. Whether it was out of respect for Sally or compassion for Ryan, the farmer was exceptionally kind and patient. He rested a large hand on Ryan's shoulder and asked if he was going to be alright. After Ryan nodded, the farmer told him he was proud to meet any relative of Andrew and Sally. He then scribbled his own name and phone number on the sheet of paper and handed it to Ryan.

"Call me anytime, if you need me," he whispered.

The placement of the rough hand on his shoulder, and the comforting kind words made Ryan feel as if he was speaking with Jerry. Without thinking, Ryan grabbed the farmer and buried his face into his muscular shoulder. Realizing what he had just done, Ryan quickly released his grip and apologized.

"That's OK, son" the farmer stated. "You've had some pretty hard words to hear, and I'm sure it took you by surprise."

Ryan stood and thanked him for his kindness. In a somewhat dreamy mental state, he walked back to his SUV. As he sat in the vehicle, he wondered if he was alright to drive. He questioned his ability to separate reality from fantasy.

Maybe I'm insane. Am I a danger to myself and to others? I must have suffered brain damage. Why didn't they notice this at the hospital?

He looked up and saw the farmer still looking at him. Ryan had to go; he couldn't stay there any longer. He started the vehicle and headed down the road. He was traveling toward what he had envisioned as Sally's new home, and in the direction of the new plant.

This was an imaginary home and an imaginary plant, for neither

*exists. This means the skateboard park and children were imaginary. I
have to concentrate. I have to separate the important from the non-
important things. I've got to get a grip on reality.*

He pulled over onto a dirt shoulder and stopped the
vehicle. Ryan pulled out the sheet of paper and his cell phone.
He was relieved to see that he could get a signal. This was the
first positive thing that had occurred since coming to Brandon
Springs, and he found himself surprised to be so grateful for
such a small thing. Composing himself, he called the minister.
The farmer had given him the minister's home number,
knowing he would probably be at home resting during the
afternoon.   When the preacher answered the call, Ryan
explained that he was Sally's nephew. He explained that he had
only recently found out about her death and was on his way to
the church to see her grave. The minister expressed sympathy
and told him he would meet him there. The name of the pastor
was Percy Ivans. He assured Ryan that he would meet him at
the gravesite a second time.

After the call Ryan re-examined the map and was relieved
that he was headed in the direction of the church. Ryan was
afraid. He needed help and felt totally vulnerable. He was
beginning to have real doubts as to his sanity. Ryan grasped
for any positive moment, in an otherwise chaotic and tragic
day. As he entered back onto the paved road, he audibly
thanked God for the simple fact that he was now headed in the
right direction. He thanked God for a kind farmer, and for the
fact that he was able to contact the minister. He begged God
to help him handle the events which were happening to him.
He still felt almost sick to his stomach, but the dizziness began
to pass. As he prayed, he felt calmness come over him.

He pulled into the church gravel parking lot. Ryan was
alone, as the minister had not yet arrived. He departed the
vehicle and made his way to the cemetery behind the old wood
frame church. As he scanned the small cemetery, he spotted a
grave which still wore some of the baldness of a fresh burial.
The tombstone was small. He moved toward it and strained to
read the inscription. It was hers. Just to the right of it was a

plot that was sparsely covered with grass.

This must be where Andrew's body was buried.

He felt strangely comforted that they were buried side by side, rather than resting alone. Overcome by exhaustion and grief, he dropped to his knees and wept. He was crushed by a wave of guilt which pummeled his mind.

Why didn't I make time to see them? Why was my career more important than the lives of these two last relatives? What if I had begun to visit Sally after Andrew's death? Would she have been stronger. Is it possible she would have had a greater will to live? I left her to a lonely death.

Ryan felt the kind hand of the pastor upon his shoulder. He was an old man. At the sight of this wounded individual, he joined Ryan on the ground. On his knees, he held Ryan's sobbing body against his frail chest. The younger man asked him the questions that continually bruised him. The pastor told him the Biblical story of the adulterous woman who had been rescued by Jesus.

"She was to be stoned to death for her offense," he began. "Jesus pronounced that only a sinless member of the crowd would be qualified to throw the first stone at her. Without a stone thrown, the crowd dispersed. Jesus asked her where her accusers were, and she responded that none were present. He told her that he didn't condemn her either. He then told her to go, and to discontinue her sinful activity. There's no one present to condemn you either; stop condemning yourself. The Bible speaks of Satan being the one who enjoys accusing and condemning people. Jesus came to save the world, not to condemn it."

Feeling the dampness of the soil on his knees, Ryan suggested they continue their conversation inside the church. The pastor was all too pleased to agree. Ryan helped him up. Not mentioning the intense pain he was experiencing in his legs, the old man simply stated that he could no longer walk as fast as when he was younger. Though his arthritic knees felt as if nails had been driven in them, the loving expression on the pastor's face never changed. Arm in arm, they slowly entered the small church.

Sitting on a pew, they talked for a long time. The old man told him that Sally had spoken of him and was very proud of him. The pastor explained that she and Andrew had moved on to a wonderful realm in the hereafter, and that they were very happy there.

"Don't let mistakes of the past haunt you," he stated. "It's more important to serve the living than to hurt for the dead. Everyone should learn from mistakes, and you should take this opportunity to look for ways to be helpful to the living."

Ryan was beginning to calm down, but was intensely weakened by exhaustion. Still, he felt the need to talk to someone about what had happened to him. He began by showing the pastor the stitches in his scalp; then he explained how he received the blow to his head and the concussion. He was initially reluctant to share the experiences of seeing the Jerry-like figure on two occasions. Though he was presently grief stricken for Sally, he was troubled deeply and doubted his mental state. The fact the minister was a stranger enabled him to let down his guard, and he eventually went into detail regarding what he thought he had seen. He thought it was fairly safe to confess his fears because he doubted he would ever see the preacher again. The minister didn't appear alarmed by the conversation. Instead, he told Ryan of a man who had once been kicked in the head by a mule.

"The man was unconscious for several hours," the old man said. "After regaining consciousness, the fellow behaved rather oddly for over a week. However, it wasn't long before he was back to normal."

Prompted by Ryan's doubts regarding his mental state, the pastor quoted a scripture which stated, "For God hath not given us a spirit of fear; but of power, and of love, and of a sound mind."

He suggested Ryan spend the week resting in Brandon Springs, as he had originally planned.

"I assure you that the pace here is extremely slow, and it would be the perfect place to recover," he said. "I've lived alone since the death of my wife. I understand what it's like to have no living relative. Why don't you stay at my place? I've got plenty of room."

Ryan normally wouldn't have accepted the invitation of a stranger, but he was exhausted and felt in need of the pastor's advice and companionship. He accepted, but insisted that once a day he treat the pastor to a meal in a local restaurant in payment. They struck a deal. It was when they stood from sitting in the pew that Ryan began to notice the extent of the old man's physical pain. The pastor never complained, and his facial expression never gave any indication. Ryan noted how gingerly the pastor rose from his position, and he witnessed the way the man's body quaked as he straightened his legs. It was if he was able to sense everything the minister felt. During the entire process of meeting at the gravesite, moving inside, and the conversations; Ryan had been focused on himself and his own needs. Seeing nothing but his own pain, he hadn't a clue as to the physical torture the old man was experiencing. Ryan thanked the pastor for the conversation, and for the invitation. He was mindful to walk very slowly, as to allow the old man to set the pace in leaving the sanctuary. They both left the church grounds in their own vehicles, with Ryan following the minister to the house.

IT WAS NEARING DUSK as they passed Andrew's old place in route to the pastor's home. Ryan was almost sure he saw Jerry walking down the gravel drive toward the house. He sensed a sudden cold shiver pass down his back. It was if he had gotten out of an outdoor swimming pool after an evening swim, and felt a cold breeze catch him from behind. He didn't slow down, and he didn't look back. He was petrified. Ryan's hands gripped the steering wheel, and his eyes were fixed on the pastor's car ahead. He was not about to let this old man out of his sight. Emotionally, he clung to the thoughts of the minister as if the old fellow was the lone rock jutting out of a raging sea.

God help me. I think I've totally lost it. Am I insane? Is this what it feels like to be crazy? I'm seeing people who aren't there, and I remember events that never happened.

He thought of the minister's words, and of what he had stated about God saving those in the world. He prayed earnestly and left himself at the mercy of God. Ryan repeatedly thanked God for how the events of the day had unfolded. He attempted to focus on the positive aspects.

What if I had found out the truth of Sally and land on my own, without the kindness of the farmer and strength of the minister? I can imagine myself a babbling lunatic, sitting alone before Sally's grave. Would this have been too much for my brain damaged condition? What would I have done?

When they arrived at the minister's simple small home, Ryan felt somewhat numbed by what he thought of telling Reverend Ivans that he imagined seeing Jerry again. He was afraid the old man would become apprehensive, and not allow him to stay. Ryan desperately did not want to be alone. He was afraid he was losing his mind, and he needed someone to help him stay in touch with reality.

He helped the minister make supper and felt comforted as the night wore on. Ryan was like a small child standing close to his father in a strange and perilous place. He drew strength from this stranger. Before this day, he would have never considered opening his deepest personal thoughts to someone he just met.

The supper was delicious, and the conversation was golden. After the kitchen had been restored to its earlier immaculate state, the pastor showed Ryan the spare bathroom for his use and the bedroom where he would be sleeping. The old man explained to him that his bedtime had become earlier as he approached his late years, and he excused himself for the night. Ryan was emotionally and physically drained, and he retired to his appointed bedroom. He closed the curtains on the windows. This was not because of modesty, but due the fact that he was afraid to look outside. He wanted to give himself no opportunity for any apparition of Jerry to display itself in the dark outside his window. Ryan was thankful for the lamp on the nightstand beside the bed. He didn't want to see anything before dawn. Yet he left the lamp light on, because he found he was too afraid to be in the dark. It was if he was a child again. He undressed, but made sure not to approach the mirror over the dresser.

I can't risk looking in the mirror. If I caught a reflection of Jerry standing in the room behind me, I would totally freak out. I need sleep.

He was consumed with fear. After making sure the bedroom door was locked, he slipped in between the sheets. Whether due to any coolness of the fresh sheets or the chill of fear, he felt cold. He began to shake, but within a few minutes it subsided. Ryan closed his eyes and remembered again the words of the old pastor. He began to pray, and sensed a peace come over his tired soul. With the covers pulled up around his neck, he fell asleep.

Chapter 12

RYAN HEARD THE old man cough, while clearing his throat. He felt comforted by the presence of Reverend Ivans. The minister had given him sound advice and provided him with a safe place to recover from his injuries. Ryan prepared to take on the new day.

This is a new day, and I plan to take the old man's advice. I will not allow past mistakes to rob me of future successes. I'll look for opportunities to serve the living, and I'll ask God's help.

Entering the kitchen, he was greeted by Reverend Ivans. The pastor had begun to fix the morning meal. The old fellow began to make comparisons between breakfast cooked in years past by his wife to his present feeble attempts to prepare her recipes. It was obvious the pastor missed his deceased wife greatly, and the old man spoke honestly about the loneliness of spending the last years of his life without her. During the conversation, Ryan mentally compared the current treatment of senior citizens to what was practiced by societies in the past.

In the past, the elderly lived out their last days in the homes of their children. Out of love, appreciation, and a sense of duty the children would take care of those who had cared for them in their youth. In today's busy society, the old were usually sent off to die under the care of strangers in impersonal homes for the elderly. It's common for today's adults to visit their parents only when it doesn't cut into career time or fun time. I have to question, which culture is the more enlightened and more civilized?

Breakfast was great. As he adjusted to the new facts in his life, Ryan was beginning to feel more normal. Still, he was bothered by the repeated sightings of Jerry. He thought he had seen him twice at the mission, and again the night before in Andrew's driveway. It was Monday, and Ryan felt like he had only a few days in Brandon Springs to figure things out and settle his mind. It had become fairly apparent that things in this small village were not as he thought. It appeared that an actual visit by Ryan to Brandon Springs had never actually occurred. He desperately tried to make his memories fit with what he now knew to be fact.

I'm not comfortable with the idea that the earlier trip was totally imagined. I'm learning that Andrew and Sally are dead, and the land is not mine. It appears the pastures have become plowed fields, several of the old oaks are no longer there, and there is no footbridge. How do I know the farmer told me the truth? I guess it's possible for someone to take over the farm as his own and plow the fields. Someone could even sandblast the house to remove some of the paint, as to make it appear to have been left neglected. The bridge could have been removed, and the shed could have been taken. Someone would have to go to a great deal of trouble.

Ryan stopped midstream in this line of reasoning.

What am I thinking? Sally is dead. I visited her grave with the minister who buried her. The grave was at least a couple of months old. The minister is a kind man. I'm grateful that he provided calm and sanity in this crazy new world of mine.

Is Jerry imagined? The images in my mind seem to be incredibly real, as real as what I'm currently experiencing. I'm almost sure I've seen him three times. Honestly, I only caught a glimpse of this person at the mission. In a city the size of Boston there could have been another person who strongly resembled someone from Brandon Springs.

Ryan quickly realized his mind was rambling along a very shaky path. The more he considered the issue, the more he was convinced that the possibility of spotting Jerry in Boston was very unlikely. To some degree, it made perfect sense for Jerry to be walking up a driveway of a homestead which contained a cabin on the side of the mountain. However, if he had never actually visited Sally on an earlier trip, his meeting Jerry was seriously in doubt.

His hope of holding on to memories of a recent visit Brandon Springs was quickly fading. Still, he desperately felt the need to confirm the fact he had made the trip. Ryan had to see if there was really a cabin on the side of the mountain. He wanted to fully establish that reality for himself. After breakfast, he told the pastor that he would be going out to check on things. Ryan informed him of the possibility that he planned to be gone overnight and would back by the following evening. The old man was concerned with the condition of his visitor and reminded him about the needed rest. After assuring the pastor that he would be alright, he grabbed his backpack and headed in his SUV for Andrew's old place.

He found the farmer making repairs to one of his tractors. The fellow pleasantly greeted Ryan, but his voice was filled with apprehension. Ryan told the man that he was staying with the pastor, but that he had a request of him. He asked the man's permission to hike the mountain and camp overnight, as a wish to pay a last visit to his Uncle Andrew's land. Ryan explained this had been an intended plan for this trip to Brandon Springs. The farmer kindly consented. The only condition he required of Ryan was that he was not allowed to have a fire at his campsite. This was due to a concern that a fire might spread if the wind increased. Ryan agreed and thanked him. He parked his SUV behind the old house, adjusted the backpack, and started in the direction of where he had imagined the footbridge. As soon as he got to the stream, he saw no signs that a bridge ever existed.

There are no concrete slabs for the support, and no path on the other side of the water. This evidence seems to immediately settle the matter. I'm convinced that I did not make that earlier trip. Everything that I thought I remembered looks to have been only a dream. I'm sure the cabin never existed.

He now doubted his reasoning for making the hike. Nevertheless, this was his opportunity to see the mountain as it really was. It would seem foolish for him to tell the farmer that he had changed his mind about camping. Though he questioned his own mental stability, he was not about to advertise this fact. He didn't want to risk the appearance of not having his wits about him.

He carefully crossed the stream on a series of stones and climbed the bank on the other side. There was no path, so he forced his way through a thicket. After several feet, he broke through into a forest of large trees. There was little underbrush, as the leaves of the huge trees blocked the sunlight from reaching the ground below. Without the series of zig-zagging paths and switchbacks, he began the ascent straight up the mountain. Before long the slope began to increase.

At last, he came across a newly formed logging road used to remove some of the huge hardwoods. The absence of the grand and sinister oaks was the cause for the gaps in the trees he had noticed the day before. As he viewed the massive stumps, he allowed his imagination to fill the void where the trees once reached high with twisting limbs. Though the space allowed sunlight to break through to the ground, his heart was darkened by the sight. Ryan missed them. As a child he could not have imagined he would have found fond feelings about something that had caused him such dread. In their stead, sunlight fell across a muddy floor of disturbed soil and rock.

He had no idea as to where the logging road began, but it would provide an easier hike up the mountain. After a couple of switchbacks, he spotted a bright yellow bulldozer at the end of the road. It appeared to have been abandoned for the day. He began to become hungry, but he didn't want to stop until he confirmed in his mind that no cabin existed. He wanted to visually inspect the spot on the mountain.

So much of this is different from my memories. I never saw the large split rock, or the trail that led through it. But then, I took a different course up the mountain. Still, I have doubts that massive rock exists.

Ryan came to an area in the forest that had little slope. This was much like the place where he had envisioned the cabin. He decided that this would be a good place to eat a late lunch. He ate a couple of his power bars and drank from his pouch of water. After eating, he felt refreshed. However, reality had begun to finally settle in.

There was no cabin. I'm pretty sure Jerry never existed. While unconscious in the hospital, Jerry must have been a very strong character in a dream. Somehow that memory became fixed in my awakened mind. It was probably due to the blow to the head. Maybe I should see a shrink. My parents are dead. It's possible that I subconsciously sensed a need for a strong stabilizing character in my life. Maybe I was looking for a parental figure.

As he tackled the incline straight on, he continued to work things out in his mind. He put his emotions aside and rationally reviewed the situation.

I received a blow to the head. Subconsciously I must be missing my parents to the point of making up an imaginary person. It's common for small children do this, and they aren't considered to be insane. I'm sure I'm not insane.

After a short distance, he became winded from the combination of the pace and slope. He stopped to rest, and he turned to view the land he had traveled. Through the trees, Ryan could see part of the flattened area illuminated by a single beam of sunlight. It reminded him of scenes he had seen in paintings. He felt that maybe this was some type of sign.

I'll take this as a confirmation that I'm becoming enlightened to my condition. I plan to reach out and take hold of reality. In order to make it to the top before the sun goes down, I need to press on. I expect the hike down to take less time. Yet, there's no real way to compare this to an imaginary hike taken in a dream.

Just as dusk began to fall, he arrived at the top. It was incredibly similar to his view in the dream hike. Because of the density of the forest, he had no real view on the backside of the mountain. Looking back through some of the trees he had passed, he saw the patches of fields and a string of roadway in the distance. He set up the tent and spread out the pad and sleeping bag inside. Ryan turned on his lamp and inspected the area around the tent. Satisfied the spot was good, he then consumed two bars from the backpack and drank water from the bladder. He topped it off with some of the trail mix.

Lying on his back in front of the tent, he could make out

a few stars through the large opening in the leaves above him. He entered the tent and turned off the lamp. Returning to the spot in front of the tent, he laid back down to face up into the night. It seemed as though the sky exploded. He imagined he was on the edge of space in some sort of craft. Ryan thought about the fact that he actually was riding a type of craft through space, and the craft was planet Earth. He wasn't sure if he had ever seen stars like this before, and he realized the lights of Boston dulled the view of this spectacular display of the heavens. He was fascinated. He thanked God for the view, and for His creation.

The hike had taken a toll. Ryan's head began to throb, so he took one of the pain pills the doctor prescribed for him. It wasn't long before the combination of the tiring hike and the prescription drug caused him to become drowsy. He retreated into the tent, zipped up the tent screen, but left the tent door open as to enjoy the fresh air. He slipped into the warm sleeping bag. Within no time, he drifted into a heavy sleep.

RYAN FELT THE COOL morning mountain air on his face, as he awoke the next day. He rolled out of the sleeping bag and unzipped the tent netting. The trees and grasses around him were alive with morning doves and quails. He slipped through the tent opening and observed the sun sliding up from its hiding place. Its rays broke across the dew-covered grass in a display of glittering hue he had never witnessed. Ample puffs of flaming clouds hung above him Ryan couldn't speak; he could only watch and listen in stillness.

He was amazed as the sun rose above the neighboring hill, and its glory began to warm every living creature by its silent and gentle touch. This sense of awe and worship was finally interrupted by a sensation in his empty stomach. Ryan reached back into his tent for his backpack and snatched a couple of power bars. As he consumed them, he scoured the terrain for details. The view and woods around him seemed to be very familiar. Things weren't identical to what he had envisioned in the dreamed hike, but it was all very familiar. Although this mountain was not his, he felt at home. It was one of those moments in time where one senses that the life is truly good; being at a place where one is meant to be, and all is well. He breathed in the clean morning mountain air, and peace bathed his soul.

Ryan sensed the presence of God, like never before. He was totally at peace, with himself and the world around him.

This is how things should be, no care for enhancement of career. There are no feelings of failure or guilt regarding my lack of care for Sally and Andrew. I feel no bitterness for the loss of my parents.

It was as if God, Himself, had His arm around Ryan. He thanked God for blessings of life, and he expressed his love to God. This was something beyond words.

Soon this warm feeling began to dissipate, because in the distance he saw angry clouds forming and moving in his direction. Ryan realized that he needed to make a hasty retreat down the mountain. He quickly finished dressing and packed his belongings tightly in the backpack. Ryan descended at a rapid pace, only slowing to maintain his balance. There was no time for a leisurely lunch along the way. Introducing the coming storm, gusts of air swayed massive branches in the trees. Empowered by the winds, the shaking leaves sung a song of warning. In unison they sang, at times in a low soft melody, and at other times a crescendo.

As he moved down to the flattened area, the foliage began to lose its harmonious tune. By now the music had lost its rhythm, and the sounds were becoming more chaotic. Some lifeless branches were discarded by the ancient trees, and Ryan was careful to glance up from time to time in efforts to avoid them. He was growing tired by the time he reached the stream, but there was still no time to lose. As he began to step across the stones positioned in the clear water, sheets of cold rain suddenly pelted his body. The wind blew hard, and the speeding drops made his skin sting as they landed. He was regretful that he had neglected to purchase a poncho while back in the sporting goods shop. Ryan quickly and painfully raced across the backyard towards his parked SUV. Once there, he tossed the backpack in the rear, opened the front door, and dropped into the driver's seat.

It was there that he realized that he was completely soaked all the way down to his underwear. He felt violently chilled and began to shake so badly that it was difficult to place the key into the ignition. Ryan started the engine, turned the air to defrost, and turned the heat up to the highest setting. The wet clothes caused him to become aware of every inch of his body. As the air warmed and the glass portals of the vehicle cleared, physical exhaustion became a factor. His quick dissension was enabled by the awareness of the growing storm, but now his body ached. At this point, the heavenly experience on the mountain top seemed to be very distant.

He dropped the vehicle into gear and moved toward the gravel drive. Cascades of rain fell so strongly that he could hardly see through the windshield. The wipers sloshed back and forth at the highest speed, and they tossed massive quantities of water from each side of the vehicle. The saturated ground started giving under the weight of SUV, and the tires occasionally lost their grip. With mud shooting from the rear of the vehicle, the tires made vain attempts to take hold of the gravel drive. Instead, pebbles were launched angrily from the back of the vehicle. He decreased the pressure on the accelerator, and the SUV began to take a firm hold on the drive. Torrents of rain pounded the windshield as he crept down the gravel drive toward the road.

Once he reached the road, the wind dropped to a sporadic series of smaller gusts and the rain lessoned to a steady shower. This was fine by Ryan. He couldn't wait to get back to the minister's home, take a hot shower, get dressed into something dry, and relax on the large couch.

As he pulled in front of the pastor's home, he felt somewhat relieved. He exited the SUV and squished around to the rear to retrieve his backpack. Reverend Ivans was home and heard him pull up. He met Ryan at the door, and the sight immediately caused him to chuckle. The minister asked him to remove his boots at the front door. Ryan was surprised to see that even his socks were soaked. He had neglected to purchase a good set of hiking boots for his adventure. As he waddled down the hall to the bathroom, the old man's slight amusement turned into a knee slapping burst of laughter. At first Ryan was irritated at the minister's cheer, but his mood reversed when he was able to view his state in a mirror.

He looked like a drowned rat; and standing in socks, he looked like a silly drowned rat. He couldn't help but laugh at himself. Hearing the laughter inside the bathroom, the old man asked, "Are you OK in there?"

Ryan responded in the affirmative and continued to snicker. The pastor suggested an early supper. Ryan glanced at his raindrop speckled watch and saw that it was 4:00 PM. Time had passed quickly as he had galloped down the mountain in the effort to outrun the storm, and it was obvious why his body ached. He had been moving at a quick pace for hours. He was hungry, and he quickly agreed to the early supper.

Once the wet clothes were removed, Ryan passed up the shower in favor of a hot bath in the tub. As he relaxed in the soothing water, he almost fell asleep twice. Eventually, the water began to cool. This was a signal that supper might be nearing. The thoughts of a hot meal strengthened his weary body to rise from the liquid bed. He toweled his tired frame and opened his backpack. Ryan had spent money wisely on this item, for his clothes inside were dry. He pushed the wet discarded clothes into a pile in the corner of the bathroom and slipped on dry ones.

In dry socks, he lumbered down the hall toward the kitchen. The smell was wonderful.

"Have a seat," the minister called out. "You look much better."

"Thank you," Ryan replied.

"I won't ask any questions; just enjoy the meal, young man," the minister stated in an assuring voice.

Ryan sat, and they thanked God for the food and the day. After the first bite was swallowed, Ryan began to tell him of the hike. He went into the details of the night in the tent, and of the morning experience. Still very tired, he helped the pastor clear the table when the meal was finished. Ryan was at peace in his heart, but he was becoming even more aware of his aching body. The events of the day had been too much. He slowly moved to the couch, settled into the soft cushions, and closed his eyes.

Chapter 13

RYAN AWOKE with a dull headache and the sound of soft chatter. It reminded him of voices from the front porch he had heard as a child while visiting Uncle Andrew. He felt comforted, as if the combination of sounds was a gentle massage working away tension and stress. He distinctly recognized one of the voices, but this caused a wave of confusion to sweep over his mind. Ryan opened his eyes to a somewhat familiar room, but the lighting caused him to close them. He allowed his ears to absorb clues to his situation.

Am I awake or dreaming? The voice I heard sounds like my Aunt Sally's, but that's impossible.

Confused, he listened for the second voice in the gentle conversation. It, too, sounded familiar. However, in his dizzied mind he was unable to match the voice with a face or name. As he attempted to rub his eyes with his hand, he felt the cold touch of an IV tube drop across his face.

"Oh man, this experience is much too familiar," he mumbled.

With his eyes still closed, a thought swept across Ryan that unsettled him to the core.

Maybe I have indeed lost my mind.

He was afraid to open his eyes. The peace he found on the top of the mountain was a world away, and he struggled to bring reason to what was happening around him. As he lay listening to the conversation around him, he realized that this was no dream. He now became very much awake, and much more aware of his surroundings. He opened his eyes.

The voices stopped. Though the lighting still bothered him, he clearly recognized the caring face that moved over him.

It's Sally. If I've lost my mind, would I really be able to distinguish between being awake and being asleep? Am I in heaven? I seem to still be the hospital. What is real?

Totally confused, he again closed his eyes. His aunt placed a warm hand on his cheek and asked, "Ryan, is the light bothering you?"

"Some," he responded.

"Can we lower the lights in here?" she asked the other person.

"Oh, sure," the other voice answered. "Let's try this. Ask him if this makes it better."

The lighting softened, and his surroundings were easier to observe. The second person's face moved in view beside Sally's.

This is the cute short nurse from the hospital and the mission. I must be in heaven.

Still not raising his head, he reached with his left arm to feel the presence of the IV in back of his right hand.

This is not heaven. I'm back in the hospital.

"How are you feeling?" Sally asked.

"I'm not sure," Ryan said. "I'm a little confused. Are you OK, Aunt Sally?"

"I'm fine," she responded. "You're the one we've been worried about, but today you seem to be more alert."

"Am I in a hospital?" he asked.

"You are starting your second day with us," the nurse said sweetly. "It's normal to be confused after a concussion; and it's normal for you to be sensitive to light. You should be fine soon, but you have to take care of yourself."

"I think I dreamed of having a concussion; or maybe not," Ryan mumbled. "I don't really know".

"This was no dream, honey," the nurse explained. "You

may not remember several things. That's common. You just have to make sure you don't bump that head of yours again any time soon. Do you remember the accident, at all?"

"Accident?" he asked. "I thought maybe someone hit me on the head, or something."

With his left hand, he felt the thick bandage that covered the top of his head. The larger portion of it was on the left side.

"The important thing is that you are going to be alright," Sally interrupted. "The car is totaled, but I am sure you have insurance."

"Seems like I've had this conversation before, but with a doctor," Ryan said.

"That's good; so, you remember talking to Doctor Adams?" the nurse asked. "I'm really surprised, because you were drifting in and out of that conversation."

"I thought someone had hit me on the head," Ryan explained. "I don't remember an accident. I thought the car had been totaled by a car thief. Wow! I just can't seem to piece things together."

Ryan attempted to sit up, and it felt as though something was pressing his brain against his skull. His head was killing him. He slowly settled back down onto the pillow.

"Take it easy; you can't just sit up the way you normally would," the nurse explained. "Let me raise the head of your bed a little. Just let me know when you want me to stop."

He heard the electric motor under the bed hum, and he felt the bed begin to slowly elevate his head. About halfway up, Ryan began to feel nausea set in.

"OK, stop now," he pleaded. "I'm feeling a little sick."

"That's normal," the nurse answered. "Here, I'll back it off a little. We'll take it a little at a time."

Her voice was so sweet, so understanding and kind.

"You had us worried a little. Twice yesterday, your blood pressure dropped for a short while. Each time, we were afraid you had bleeding in your brain. We took you down for a scan, and everything seemed to be OK."

"I am so glad you're doing so well, today," Sally said.

She hadn't spoken much because she wanted the nurse to explain the situation to Ryan. She began to gingerly stroke his left arm; then suddenly stopped.

"I'm not hurting you, am I? You have several large bruises, especially across your chest and left shoulder. I think maybe the seat belt caused that during the impact of the accident."

"No, that didn't hurt," he replied. "But I am really sore all over."

"You look more alert today, young man!" Doctor Adams cheerfully exclaimed as he entered the room. He leaned over the bed and shined a light in each of Ryan's eyes.

"I know the light may bother you, but I'm glad to say that you're looking much better. Do you have a headache, or have you experienced nausea?"

"Yes, a lot of the first and only some of the other," Ryan said.

"You may not remember the conversations we've had, but don't worry about that," stated the doctor. "You've survived a tremendous auto accident. After being discharged, you need to rest for two more weeks before returning to work. Take more time if you need it. Don't rush things."

"I remember talking with you before, but I am confused as to what was said," Ryan replied.

"You may have trouble remembering certain things," the doctor explained. "There are no broken bones, but you do have a concussion. Because of that, you may feel confused at times. It might not be a bad idea for you to write things down, as you begin to remember. This exercise may trigger other memories. I'll have the IV removed sometime this afternoon if you continue to respond well. That should make it easier for you to write. I had Sally place a pen and pad on the nightstand beside the bed. As for the catheter, I will have someone take that out immediately."

"Catheter?" Ryan blurted. He looked down to see a yellowed tube escaping from under the left side of his hospital gown and passing over the left side of the bed. He looked over at the nurse to see if she was grossed out by it.

"Don't look at me!" she exclaimed. "I'm not taking that out. That is what orderlies are for!"

"Come now, I bet you would do a fine job," the orderly chided, as he slipped into the room. "Doctor Adams, I understand this is ready to come out."

"Yes, he won't need it any longer," the doctor replied. Doctor Adams moved toward the door, and then turned back to instruct Ryan. "You'll need help standing and walking to the bathroom. If you need to go, just buzz the station and instruct the attendant that you're in need of help. Joe, or another orderly, will help you. You're in great hands."

Doctor Adams smiled at the nurse, then excused himself to continue his rounds. Joe reached and took the catheter in his hand.

"Come on over here, Patsy," Joe teased. "Let me show you how this is done."

"I'm out of here," she responded. "You probably would get a kick out of that, wouldn't you?" she said as she left the room.

Ryan heard the orderly call the nurse by name. He felt relieved that her name was consistent with what he thought to have remembered. However, this positive feeling was quickly diminished by the immediate situation he faced. He had a tube running from the back side of his hand, and another more sinister tube protruding from a much more sensitive and personal area of his body. This was not going to be an enjoyable experience, and a sense of dread filled him.

Why couldn't they have done the removal of the catheter while I was asleep? Of course they couldn't, that would defeat the purpose for having it. The deed had to be done after a patient was capable of having conscious control of urination.

Joe then glanced at Sally. Without him having to say a word, she understood.

"I'll just step out in the hall for a few minutes," Sally spoke.

As she left the room, Joe pulled the curtains around the

bed. At the thought of what was about to occur, a sense of humiliation flooded Ryan. He had never been in a situation quite like this. In his mind he knew that the catheter had been placed for his welfare, but he still felt as if a very personal part of his body had been somewhat violated.

Joe pulled back the sheets to lay bare the subject of the next action. Upon seeing his physical condition for the first time, Ryan felt a strong mixture of fear and sickened abasement. He normally wasn't intensely afraid of pain, but this was an incredibly sensitive and private area. There is a strong natural drive in man to protect this part of the body from trauma or injury.

"Oh, God help me," he thought to himself.

"I really don't like the idea of another man handling this part of my body," Ryan explained. "Can I do this myself? Can you just talk me though the steps so that can do it?"

Joe realized the desperation in Ryan's voice and attempted to settle him.

"I don't care for this anymore than you do," Joe said, reading the expression on Ryan's face. "It won't take long. I've done this a million times."

"Well, I haven't!" Ryan exclaimed.

"You are right; you haven't done this before, "Joe quietly and firmly explained. "If you were to attempt to take it out, you would probably damage yourself. I don't think that is what you would want."

The desire to avoid self-mutilation quickly replaced thoughts of humiliation. Ryan relented.

"OK," he said. "Go ahead, get it over with."

"I just have to release the balloon, and slide it out," Joe calmly stated. "Now, you may feel a slight burning sensation."

Joe was right; the catheter was out quickly. Ryan felt discomfort, but he was really glad to be done with that event. It was over, and the experience was now behind him. Joe pulled the curtains to the original position, placed the catheter in a plastic bag for disposal, pulled off his latex gloves and placed them also in the bag.

"Don't hesitate to buzz me, if you need to go," Joe offered. "Make sure that you don't try to make it to the bathroom on your own. The last thing you need to do is to fall and bang your head. I'm serious; don't try to make it on your own."

Joe left the room, and Sally reappeared.

"Sally, can you hand me that pad and pen?" Ryan requested.

As Sally attempted to place the pen in his hand, she noticed his difficulty in gripping it with the needle in the back of his hand. She suggested that he allow her to write down what he wanted to record.

"That would probably work out better," he said. Thanks. I seem to have difficulty sorting reality from things I apparently dreamed while asleep. If you would, just take notes and maybe later we can discuss things. Some of it may not make sense. I'd like to record everything as I think I remember them, before attempting to connect the pieces of events together. I just want to get it all down on paper for now. We can sort through it and try to make sense of things later."

He could remember driving in the rain, but could not remember having an accident. Sally suggested that he tell her everything that he thought he remembered or dreamed.

"Whenever you're ready, I'll be glad to review the details with you to confirm the real events and rule out those that are untrue," she said. "Perhaps detailing even some imagined experiences, could trigger remembrances of real occurrences."

Ryan told her of each of the two visits he thought he made to Brandon Springs. He started with the most recent. He told about the three days in Brandon Springs, where he had visited with the minister and stayed overnight on the mountain. Then he detailed the first visit he thought he had made. This was the one in which he had stayed with her in the new house. He realized that this version of the visit also lasted three days, and that one night was spent in the old hotel. Each time he had spent three days in Brandon Springs. He went on to explain how he had thought his condition in the hospital was the result of a mugging during a car theft. Ryan told her the details of seeing a fellow named Jerry, and of how disturbed he had been to see him in various locations.

She didn't say a word while he talked. She quietly wrote everything onto the pad.

At last, he said, "Well, I think that's all I remember. Or maybe that was all that I remember dreaming; I'm not sure at this point."

"That is quite a lot," she replied, trying not to show her concern.

"I know that it doesn't make sense," Ryan said. "I realize that now. I just wanted to tell you everything, because I am not sure if any of it really happened. Tell me; did any of that happen?"

She was not sure how to answer his question, but thought that it best to be direct.

"Portions of the conversations with Doctor Adams and the nurse were real," she began. "You never made it to Brandon Springs, because you lost control of your car about twenty miles from there."

"From there?" he asked. "Where am I?"

"The ambulance took you to this hospital, which is about thirty-five miles from where I live." she explained. "We don't have a hospital in Brandon Springs."

"So, that's all?" he asked. "What about Jerry Prescott; does he exist?"

"Maybe you met someone by that name while driving to Brandon Springs," she answered, trying to console him. "No, I don't know a Jerry Prescott. Maybe there really is such a person, and you just can't remember where you've met him."

"I can't remember the actual drive from Boston; only the imagined trip," he said with concern in his voice. "I can't even remember why I was coming to Brandon Springs."

"I think you probably received a letter from the Probate Judge," Sally explained. "His name is Walter Owens, not Peacock. Andrew died, and he certainly did have a will. You didn't come for the funeral, so the judge determined that he should send you a letter. No, you didn't inherit the property. I'm surprised that you even dreamed about that, since you never showed any interest or affection regarding the land. In fact, you would never cross the stream and play in the woods on the other side. Now, that part was true. You never went there. Were you really afraid of the woods on the mountain?"

Feeling a little embarrassed at revealing his childhood fears, he avoided the question.

"So why did the judge send me a letter?" he asked.

"Judge Owens said that he would pay you a visit this morning, and I will let him handle that explanation," Sally replied. "Andrew left you a package, and the judge feels personally responsible for seeing that you receive it."

"What's in it?" Ryan asked in a bewildered tone.

"The will stated that a package was designated for you," she explained. "Andrew had left it exactly where the document detailed. It was in his top dresser drawer in his bedroom. I have no idea as what it contains, and I don't know how long it's been there. He never mentioned it during all the years I lived in that house."

Within a few minutes, the judge arrived. He was not at all the distinguished man of Ryan's dreams. He was no Ira Peacock. This fellow was short, fat, and had a head full of brown hair. His introduction of himself took Ryan by surprise, as his voice was high in pitch and reminded him more of a used car salesman than that of someone of such legal statue.

"So, this is the Ryan Walker you said so much about?" the judge asked Sally.

"In the flesh," she responded.

"I'll let you perform the presentation to him," the judge said, as he handed the package to Sally.

Once in her hands, her fingers gingerly moved over the gift. It was wrapped in plain brown paper and was tied securely with twine. A label on it read, *"To Ryan Walker – personally."*

She held it out to Ryan as if it were a lost mysterious treasure. Sensing her personal reverence for it, he slowly took it from her. She had loved her brother deeply, and she gave

Ryan a glance of devout earnestness as she released it into his hands. It was as if she were passing an urn of ashes of a departed loved one to a family member.

"Should I open this here, or should I wait?" he asked.

"It's yours to do as you please," she replied.

"I will need something to cut the string, and I don't have anything," he stated, looking about the room for a sharp object that might suffice.

Sally reached into her purse, and with a slight smile brought out a pair of sewing scissors.

"I thought you would be interested in seeing what is inside," she answered as she passed them to him. "Do you want me to step outside?"

"No," he said. "I very much want you to be present when I open it."

"I'm also somewhat interested in seeing what's inside," the judge said in almost a whisper. "Mind if I stick around for a minute or two?"

"Sure, that would be fine," Ryan answered. "I appreciate your bringing it to me. The least I could do is to let you see what's inside."

As if to grant the twine the least bit of damage, he carefully cut only two members of the binding. He had quickly assessed that these two cords would free the twine to be slipped off two ends of the package. He delicately placed them on his hospital bed spread and handed the scissors back to Sally, handles first. He waited until she had returned the tool back to her purse, then carefully pulled the taped portions of the wrapping apart. He made sure not to make a tear near the label. Under the paper was a box. Placing the paper near the discarded twine, he removed the lid from the box.

"Well, we still don't know what you have," Sally said, breaking the silence.

Inside were several large envelopes, neatly stacked one upon the other. There was also a small box.

"I think I should open the envelopes first," Ryan stated.

Just as carefully, he opened the first sealed envelope.

There were several old photos of family members. Some of them were of Andrew holding Ryan when he was a baby. Others were of his parents and Sally, taken many years before. They were so young, so different. There were pictures of people Ryan did not know. Sally explained that they were ancient pictures of his grandparents and their families. Sally identified each person and mentioned memorable stories relating to some of them. Ryan asked her to writes the names on the back of the photographs and also on a sheet of paper. He asked her to place a distinguishable title for some of the stories with the names and place the sheet with the photos back in the envelope. He wanted to make sure he had the names and stories straight. Ryan naturally had a strong talent for organization.

Realizing the personal nature of the items contained in the box, the judge politely dismissed himself. He gave Sally a gentle pat on the shoulder, wished Ryan a speedy recovery, and left the room.

The second envelope contained a book. Ryan was surprised to know that it was Andrew's journal. He had never even considered Andrew to be the type of man who kept a journal.

"I'm not sure that I have the right to read the personal writings of Uncle Andrew," Ryan stated.

"If Andrew had not wanted you to read it he would not have included it in the package," she assured.

He opened the first page and read out loud the first entry. Previous to that moment, he had viewed his uncle as uneducated. But the prose was well written, and the penmanship was exact. He closed the book and set it aside with the photos.

At once, he realized that it was he who was unlearned about his uncle. Andrew had left him a treasure. This was treasure in the imagery of pictures, of insight into Andrew's personal feelings and thoughts, and rich in information regarding family members and events. As he browsed the photographs and read excerpts from the journal, it was becoming more apparent to him that his perception of Andrew before this day had been formed from a very limited perspective. He was being reintroduced to his uncle.

Next was a thin envelope, and Ryan proceeded to gingerly open it. He slid the contents out of the envelope onto the bedspread. Ryan was left in disbelief. As his eyes meet Sally's he could tell that she was very much surprised, and he watched as she placed her hand over her mouth. As he opened each folded document, he found shares of stock in Coca Cola and Chevron Oil. There was also a savings bond for $250 purchased in 1971. The shares of Coca Cola and Chevron Oil stock dated back to the 1960s. At first glance, he estimated the total worth of the stocks and bond to be between $3,000 and $5,000. It wasn't the amount of money that the documents represented that caused Ryan to become so overwhelmed, but rather it was the fact that Andrew had been so mindful of him. Ryan had never considered his uncle to be financially astute, even in the slightest way. He looked at Sally in amazement, not knowing what to say.

Sally broke the silence, "Don't ask me. I had no clue that Andrew had ever made investments in stocks or bonds. These were purchased back in better times, but even during hard financial times he never mentioned these."

At last, the box contained only one thick envelope and a little box. He reached for the large envelope and opened it. Inside were a short letter, were the title and owner's manual to Andrew's truck. The signed and dated letter gave Ryan ownership of the truck, and title bore Andrew's signature on the back.

"Did he want me to do something with this truck, or do you think he was just passing it on to me as a gift?" Ryan asked his aunt.

"I'm really not sure what his intentions were, but it is yours to do whatever you wish," she replied.

Placing the title and letter back into their original envelope and returning the stocks and bond documentation back inside their proper envelope, he carefully stacked the items on the bed. In doing so, he noticed the last remaining small box within the larger one.

"What do you think this is?" he asked as he removed it.

"I don't have a clue," she replied. "Open it."

He opened one end of the box and emptied a man's gold ring into his hand. Looking into Sally's eyes, he realized at once that the ring was very familiar to her. Sally's eyes began to water, and then she cupped both hands over her mouth as tears spilled over her eyelids and down her cheeks.

"Where did this come from?" he asked.

Her hands left her mouth. Without saying a word, one hand wiped the wet lines from her face and the other reached out to take the ring from his hand. She gently fingered the ring lovingly and quietly shook her head. Ryan waited for her to speak. At last, she cleared her throat, and with watery eyes glanced up at him.

"This was my father's ring," she explained. "I haven't seen it since I was a teenager."

Ryan immediately tried to imagine her in her teens, but was unsuccessful.

"Your father must have given it to Uncle Andrew," he said.

"He must have given it to him in secret," she replied. "My father was like that. He never put on a performance or made fanfare regarding things. Each of us knew that we held a special place in his heart, and he made sure to spend personal time with each of his children. He died when I was in my twenties, and I still think about him and miss him. After all these years, you would think that I would forget. When I was about nineteen, I noticed the ring was not on his hand and I asked about it. He simply said that he didn't have it anymore, and he offered no explanation. He brought it back from France after serving during World War I, and the ring was very special to him. I don't know any more about it, except the fact that he had it before he met my mother. I haven't a clue as to why it was so special, and my mother never discussed it. There must have been a special reason for him to give it to Andrew, but I wouldn't know what it might be."

Ryan was deeply touched by the personal value of each gift. He was overwhelmed. Ryan's sorrow ran deep, and his eyes began to tear. His emotions were quite volatile. They bounced from one extreme to another, based on the situation at hand. He found it difficult to speak. Some of the smallest thoughts could trigger huge feelings of guilt, sorrow, or thankfulness. However, he no longer felt cold or uncaring. Ryan wasn't sure whether it was because of the concussion or the honest conversations with Sally, but his emotions and concern for others were more alive than ever.

"Sally, I am so sorry that I didn't attend Andrew's funeral," whispered Ryan. "I'm sorry I left you to deal with that situation by yourself. You and Uncle Andrew were the only family I had left. I don't know what I was thinking. You've always been so good to me, and I have been so self-centered. I'm really sorry."

"It doesn't matter; you really shouldn't concern yourself with that," she consoled.

"Do you still live in Andrew's house, and did he leave you the land?" he asked. "Do you owe taxes on the property? Tell me about what has happened with all that."

"You really don't need to be concerned about any of that," she advised. "You need to rest."

"Sally," Ryan said as he looked intently into her eyes. "Please, I really want to know how you're doing. I also want to know what has become of Andrew's property since his death. Are you doing alright financially, and are you able to handle the property taxes?"

Sally was torn. She didn't want to tell him of things that would cause him to worry, but she could see from the tone in his voice that he was beginning to be seriously concerned. She quickly decided that it would be easier for him to handle the truth, than to worry about every imaginary scenario.

"I don't have a new house," Sally began. "I still live in Andrew's old house. In his will, Andrew left me the house and property. Taxes are owed on the property, and there was a small loan that Andrew owes to the local bank. The roof of the old house began to leak before his death. So, Andrew replaced the roof and made several repairs. But he used the property as collateral for the loan."

Ryan pressed her until she finally revealed to him the total amount of what was owed came to just over $20,000. Each year Andrew had sold a piece of farm equipment to help pay the taxes, and now all of it was gone. Ryan placed his left hand on Sally's small right wrist and told her that they would handle the problem together.

"We're family, and we are all that is left of this family." Ryan assured her.

Ryan offered her the $15,000 that he had in his savings, but she strongly refused. He then told her to sell Andrew's truck and use the money. She hesitated, but Ryan persisted until he made her agree. He had her take the pad and write a statement that gave her permission to sell the truck on his behalf, and he then managed to slowly sign and date it with his right hand. Reaching for the stack of envelopes on his hospital bed, he retrieved the one containing the truck title and letter. He carefully and slowly signed his name below Andrew's on the back of the title, placed the items back into the envelope and handed it to Sally. She didn't want to take it, but he insisted that they agree to handling matters together.

"Everything is going to be alright," Sally said. "Just relax and get some rest. I need to go to Brandon Springs to take care of a few things, and I'll be back this afternoon. Just relax and rest."

She stood with purpose, as though she were on a mission. Sally reminded Ryan of the call station buzzer clipped to the bed and made sure he was able to reach it. She told him that she would inform the nurse's station of her leaving, and that she would return during the afternoon.

Ryan's emotions had been pulled in various directions during the eventful morning. Now his soul was at peace, and he could finally relax. Exhausted, he felt his eyes become heavy. It wasn't long after Sally's leaving that he drifted into a sound and restful sleep.

He awoke to the sound of the squeaking wheels, as the nurse had returned with a food cart.

"Are you awake?" she asked in a pleasant cheery voice.

"I think so" Ryan replied.

"I'm going to try to raise your head so that you can eat," she explained. "Just tell me if you feel bad."

He heard the sound of the motor and felt the head of the bed begin to lift him toward a sitting position. He was relieved that he suffered no headache or nausea. However, he did feel disoriented and a little dizzy. The nurse was very patient with her patient.

"I'm sorry, just give me a minute please," he asked.

"Just take your time," she coaxed.

"Is your name, Patsy?" he asked as he began to feel better.

"That's pretty good," she said. "You are remembering things."

"I think I dreamed about you," Ryan whispered.

"I'm not sure I want to hear about this," she cautioned.

"No, it's nothing like that!" he explained. "I dreamed that you pushed me around in a wheelchair, and that we laughed a lot. It was all good. You were a lot of fun."

"Well, that sounds pretty safe," she replied. "I want you to try to eat lunch."

The nurse moved the hospital tray table over his lap, placed the lunch onto the tray table and removed the lid from the food.

It doesn't look bad. But it doesn't compare to any of the imaginary meals prepared by Sally in my dreams.

It contained Salisbury steak in gravy, mashed potatoes, and green beans. He soon realized that he was hungry. The IV still in his right hand, he attempted to fed himself with his left hand. She advised him to eat slowly. He spied the chocolate pudding and gave her a grin. Once the meal was gone, he raised both hands like a cowboy after roping a calf at a rodeo to signify that he was finished. He felt very tired.

"Thanks for the food and for your patience," Ryan told

his nurse.

"Patience?" she asked.

"You didn't give me a hard time regarding my dream about you," he replied. "You could have shut me down immediately, but you allowed me to explain."

"I see."

"I'm also grateful that you didn't hang around for the catheter removal."

She chuckled with the same laugh that he remembered from his dream. As she began to push the cart from the room, he asked her if there was a Gideon Bible in the nightstand.

"I've seen them in almost every hotel in which I've had stayed," he explained.

She confirmed that there was, and he asked her to hand it to him. The nurse placed it on the tray table before him. She smiled as she left with the cart.

I don't know why I asked for the Bible. It was sort of a sudden urge. I'm not even sure what I want to read. It couldn't hurt to look it over.

Using mainly his left hand, he flipped it open. He saw a mixture of red and black lettering in the passages. He had read the Bible enough in his life to know that some texts print the words of Jesus in red. He flipped a few more pages until he came across the book of Acts, Chapter 2.

"And it shall come to pass in the last days, saith God, I will pour out of my Spirit upon all flesh: and your daughters shall prophesy, and your young men shall see visions, and your old men shall dream dreams."

It was the word "dream" that caught his eye. He had dreamed twice of spending three days in Brandon Springs. In reality, he had not yet even arrived. He couldn't remember the drive from Boston, but he remembered every detail of those dreams as if they had actually occurred.

I'm not my normal self. The doctor told me that I could experience confusion, loss of memory, nausea, headaches, and dizziness. But there are other things that are different. I've all but ignored my Aunt Sally during my adult life, but now I feel exceptionally close to her.

He found himself thankful for small things, and for acts of kindness from others. Ryan felt volatile, but at other times he felt remarkably at peace.

I should call my boss at work. I'm unsure of the number of days I've had taken off from work for the trip. In fact, I can't remember even telling her that I was going out of town.

He reached for the buzzer and called the station. A voice on the intercom answered, and Ryan explained that he needed his cell phone. Within a couple of minutes, Patsy entered the room.

"Already calling girlfriends?" she poked.

"Not exactly," he replied. "She's not my girl. She's my boss. I need to tell her what has happened. I can't remember the number, but I'm sure it's stored in my cell phone. Where is it?"

Opening the drawer of the nightstand, the nurse pulled out a plastic bag containing Ryan's personal items. She reached in and handed him the cell phone. He turned it on and was thankful that it was charged and had a strong signal. Scanning the list of stored numbers, he was relieved to find the number. He placed the call and his boss immediately answered. His boss told him to take all the time he needed as he had plenty of sick leave and plenty of vacation hours. She asked where the hospital was located. At that point Ryan asked her to speak with the nurse and handed the phone to Patsy.

"Please tell her where the hospital is located and how to get in touch with the place," he asked.

Patsy gave the boss the address and phone number of the hospital.

"She sounds really nice," Patsy said as she handed the phone back to Ryan. "Are you sure she was not your girlfriend? I think she sounded a bit jealous. She's not the violent type, is she?"

Ryan smiled, and almost laughed at the thoughts of his boss being his girlfriend.

"I'm not entirely stupid," he responded. "That's all I need, a girlfriend who could fire me."

"I've known nurses that dated doctors," Patsy said with a smile. "Not me, mind you. I'm not entirely stupid, either. That kind of thing works only once in a while."

"So, is Joe your guy?" Ryan poked.

"Please!" she responded. "Joe...that's funny."

She smiled at the thoughts of what he had suggested, and then she clasped her hand over her mouth as the smile quickly evolved into a chuckle. She was not about to tell Ryan that Joe was gay.

"Aha!" he exclaimed. "It's true! The laughter gives it away. I knew it."

The look in his eyes, peering from under the head bandage, made the accusation seem even funnier to the nurse. The bandage was wound around his head like a turban. He looked like some type of eastern swami want-to-be, sitting in a lotus position, spouting insightful philosophical nuggets of wisdom. However, these were ridiculous words, thought to be wise only by him. She kept her hand over her mouth in an attempt to capture any brewing humor. What happened next caused that effort to be in vain.

Ryan was very tired. Whether it was his mental state from the concussion, or just the shear physical fatigue; God only knows. Just as he pointed his left index finger into the air, as to make an enlightened point, a loud burst of gas escaped from his rear and into the bed where he sat. The muffled explosion was all it took. She bent over, and with a hand still cupped over her mouth she let out a partially quieted squeal. She shook from the effects of the laughter. It would not be contained. Her eyes began to water and a tear slid down her cheek. She attempted to regain her composure, but not for long. Like a volcano, the seismic activity lying under the surface of her doomed effort to retain composure was at risk of eruption. One desperate statement from him brought it to the surface.

"Oh, dear God!" he exclaimed. "Was that what I thought it was? I hope I'm dreaming all this, and I hope someone will wake me up quickly. It's a bad dream, right? I'm not dreaming, am I? I just hope I didn't crap myself."

First came the silent shaking, as she stood with both hands clasped over her mouth. Then her strained bulging eyes began to weep around the edges. It was no use. There was no brave finger that would be able to hold this leak in the dike. The muffled squeals began again. She shook her head, as if to beg him to stop. Her first recourse was to turn her back on him and pray that he would be silent. The prayers fell on deaf ears. Ryan began a mumbling rant of ridiculous excuses.

"What did you put in this IV?" he questioned. "Oh no, you've poisoned me with a laxative drip! I know that it looks clear, but it has to be a concoction of concentrated juice from some exotic prunes out of the jungles of Costa Rica. I hear it killed millions of monkeys there. What a horrible way to go. I understand that death by fart is one of the worst ways to go. One giant blast of monkey flatus, caused by this substance, would be enough to wreck the entire eco system. Imagine the horrific force of toxic air whipping through the jungle trees and into our atmosphere. This had to be the cause of all those greenhouse gases, eating away at the atmosphere. Indeed, we are all doomed!"

Another muffled squeal, and then she fled the room.

Chapter 14

RYAN WAS EXHAUSTED from his fun with the nurse. Minutes after Patsy left, he fell into a deep sleep. A couple of hours later, he was awakened by an immediate call from nature. He hadn't realized it, but the earlier incident had prophesied of things to come. He grabbed the buzzer and instructed the voice at the station concerning his need. He then detailed the possibilities of what might result if help didn't arrive quickly.

He gingerly braced himself on his right elbow, and slowly raised himself to a more erect posture. For the first few seconds, he felt somewhat dizzied. This soon passed. Using his left hand, he unfastened the IV line that was attached to the bed and released the side railing. Ever so easy he slid one leg over the right side of the bed.

Time is critical! I need Joe on the double, but I can't afford to wait for Joe to do everything. There's no time to lose.

Just as he moved the remaining leg over the side, Joe broke into the room.

"Hold on, hold on!" Joe shouted. "I'm here. Just be careful and don't push it."

With Joe's hand under his arm, Ryan slid both feet down to meet the tiled floor. Joe stepped in front of him and placed a hand under each of Ryan's armpits. Without saying a word, Ryan stood up slowly. He then turned toward the bathroom.

151

As though it was some form of waltz, Joe gracefully moved behind him. He held Ryan's arm with his left hand and took hold of the IV stand with the other. Ryan wasn't waiting to be told, he was awkwardly moving toward the bathroom.

"Hey, are you OK?" Joe asked. "You're walking kind of funny."

"Well, I've got a tight flex on my anal sphincter at the moment," Ryan retaliated.

"Carry on, my good man" Joe replied. "I have a healthy appreciation for that, seeing that I am directly in the line of fire."

"Oh, man" Ryan replied. "Don't make me laugh. It would carry serious consequences for both of us. You're pretty good at this; I bet you've done this a thousand times."

"Yes, lad" Joe said. "I'm a veteran, and I've been in harm's way many a time. I have war stories that you wouldn't believe."

"Don't start them yet; I'm almost there," Ryan begged. "This thing could go at any moment."

He turned his back to the toilet and struggled to gather his hospital gown before easing down onto the seat. He took a deep breath, and then an explosion rocked the bathroom. He could feel the repercussions splash onto the skin of his rear end. A secondary explosion followed the first.

"Oh, gross!" Ryan gasped. "This is nasty! Man, do you have to keep that bathroom door open?" he asked.

Joe replied, "Yes, I have to. Believe me; I would like to let you have it all to yourself. Procedures. I have to keep an eye on you until the doctor says that you can make it on your own. What did you eat? This can't be hospital food! What did you get into?"

By this time, Ryan had started laughing. Once done, he cleaned himself with paper best he could. He then begged Joe to let him take a bath. "Just let me sit in some water for a few minutes," he pleaded.

Joe agreed. He started the water in the tub; and then reached behind the toilet to pull out a large can of air freshener. He sprayed the bathroom until Ryan's eyes began to burn.

Then he blasted the hospital room. He kept spraying until Ryan finally objected.

"This stuff is pretty strong, and it kind of stinks," Ryan said to him. "Can you stop with the spraying?"

"You're an expert when it comes to stink, man," Joe replied quickly. "In fact, I believe you have a corner on the market for stink. When you get home, you can just stink to your hearts content. But this is a hospital, full of sick people. Some of them are dying, and I know their dying wish would not include smelling your stink!"

Ryan was laughing so hard, that it was difficult for him to stand.

"Hold on!" Joe insisted. "I have to help you."

He took Ryan by the arm, helped him remove the gown, and assisted him into the tub. A bath never felt so good. His hand having the IV rested on the side of the tub. Joe made sure Ryan was alright, and then he walked over to the nightstand to retrieve a new gown. He kept an eye on Ryan the entire time. Afterwards, he helped him out of the tub and dried him off. Ryan had never been this dependent on anyone since he was a small child. It was humiliating, but Joe's humor offered relief. It felt good to be clean. By the time Ryan reached the bed again, he was tired.

Over the next few minutes, the spray did its work and the smell dissipated. Things were somewhat back to normal. He was amazed at how so little effort could leave him exhausted. He closed his eyes and slipped into a sweet slumber.

He was brought back to reality by a familiar voice.

"Mr. Walker, I need to remove that IV now," the nurse announced in a professional manner.

Ryan slowly transcended from the land of dreams into the real world.

"Hey, after all of this, are you telling me that we aren't on a first name basis?" he stammered, still a bit groggy.

She smiled and said, "I am your nurse, and you are my patient. I need to remove the IV. I'll be off my shift in a couple of hours, and you will have a new nurse."

153

She continued her work as she spoke. The nurse clamped the line from the IV and removed the tape that had secured the needle to his hand. She took his hand in hers, placed a swab of cotton over the entry point, and then she quickly removed the needle from his hand. For just a few seconds she pressed the cotton swab against the area where the needle once penetrated and lifted his hand directly above him. Although the contact of her soft hand against his was only brief, Ryan couldn't help noticing how gingerly her warm delicate fingers caressed his skin. Once satisfied that bleeding would be minimal, she lowered his hand and placed a bandage strip over the cotton to hold it in place.

"There. Isn't that better?" she asked.

"I liked that part where you held my hand," he said teasing. "Can you do that again? I mean, without the needle part."

Normally, Ryan wasn't a flirt. Whether it was because of the dream he had about her, or the fact that he was behaving oddly due to the concussion, Ryan found himself very much at ease when around Patsy. He was completely comfortable when he was with her. Ryan never felt awkward with her; even during the incident when he inadvertently passed gas in her presence. He genuinely liked her, and he felt at home around her.

"I wasn't holding your hand; I just didn't want you to wiggle around while I took the IV out" she explained.

"Well, I'm just glad that Joe wasn't sent in here to do that," he replied. "I don't think I would have enjoyed holding hands with him."

Collecting the IV stand in her right hand, she smiled as she silently rolled the stand from the room. With the IV removed, Ryan could more freely use his right hand. He picked up the pen and pad and began to make a few additions to what Sally had written down earlier. As he looked over the details of what he had dreamed over the past two days he realized an oddity.

Before Patsy returned to remove the IV, I napped for almost two hours. Yet, I am unable to remember anything I dreamed during that time. That is so weird! My dreams recorded by Sally are still very fresh in my mind. Maybe those dreams were special, or maybe the concussion caused me to remember some things and not others. Whatever the case, I'm not the same person I was before the accident.

In his dreams, he had twice spent three days in Brandon Springs. There were commonalities in each. Jerry Prescott was a key figure in each; the land and mountain were special in each; and by the time each dream ended he learned to look for things in which he could be thankful. Ryan learned to be thankful for small things, and he gained a different perspective regarding what was important in life. In each he developed an appreciation for God. There were different situations in both occurrences, but through them he transitioned into a changed person.

He glanced over at the Gideon Bible and thought of the scripture he had earlier read in the book of Acts.

Young men see visions, and old men dream dreams.

These words were fixed in his mind. He really wasn't sure what they meant, but these actions seemed to be different from the natural order.

I've always thought about young people dreaming dreams, and the old having the perspective of vision. Maybe that was the point of the scripture. Perhaps the scripture was describing something out of the ordinary. Some dreams are caused by inner conflicts in our conscious or subconscious. Other dreams may be caused by eating spicy pizza late at night. The meaning of this has to be different.

He had taken a philosophy course in college that dealt with dreams. It talked about key words contained in dreams, and what they possibly could mean. Ryan wasn't concerned with meanings or interpretations of key word. He believed something deeper had occurred that changed his perspective on life.

I've spent little time in conversation with my Aunt Sally, but I seem to be adopting some of the same perspectives held by her. Perhaps her life had a greater impact on me than I realized, or perhaps God spoke to my heart through the dreams.

His contemplation was pleasantly interrupted by Sally's return and genuine smile. She told him that the debt to the bank and the tax payment was in the process of being handled. Ryan was relieved, but he didn't ask her for details. His thoughts were still captured by the words in the Bible and of his recent experiences.

"Aunt Sally, do you think God talks to us in dreams?" he asked.

She took Ryan's left hand in both of hers, and her eyes danced as she spoke.

"I think He talked to me through one of your dreams," she responded. "I should share something with you, but first I want you to agree to stay with me while you recover. I heard the doctor tell you that he wanted you to rest for two weeks before going back to work. Would you please stay with me during those two weeks?"

"Apparently, I don't have transportation to go anywhere else," he said with a wink. "I hear that my car is totaled."

He paused for a few seconds, and then continued.

"I am so sorry that I haven't come to visit since my parents died. I've been so wrapped up in my career that I neglected you and Andrew. It wasn't right, and I intend to change a few things. Sally, I would love to spend time with you."

"Stop apologizing!" she ordered. "We'll start things afresh today. You need to focus on the positive things in your life. Let's enjoy the time that we have during your recuperation. Let's focus on what we are doing from this moment on. Is it a deal?"

"OK, fair enough," he said. "Now, you wanted to share something with me. Tell me what's happening."

Sally closed her eyes, and a large smile spread across her face. When she opened her eyes, he could see that they had begun to tear. She released his hand, in order to wipe the tears away. She began.

"Your dream gave me an idea. I left here and went directly to Pete Johnston's. He's the largest farmer in the area. I asked him if he would be interested in leasing the front pastureland for farming. He was very familiar with that land. Without hesitation, he said that he would love to farm it. I honestly told him about my situation, and we discussed several options before coming to an agreement. We struck a written agreement regarding his leasing the pastureland for farming. The lease arrangement will enable me to pay off the bank loan and pay the annual taxes on the property. We then went to the tax office together and managed to get an extension on the taxes. In a matter of only a few short hours, my entire situation has changed. Over the years I have seen God step into handle situations, but I have never seen something like this work out so quickly. I truly believe God gave you that dream for me."

Ryan believed he sensed the presence of God that very moment. The feeling was so remarkable that he considered the possibility that he had slipped into one of his dreams again, but he knew this was real.

"Sally, do you think your pastor would come here to visit me?" he asked.

Sally's demeanor changed to that of being quite concerned. "What's wrong?" she asked. "Has the doctor changed his prognosis?"

Seeing that she was beginning to worry, Ryan immediately put her at ease.

"Oh, nothing is wrong," he said. "I'm fine. I just wanted to see what he thought about all of this. I also wanted to ask him to explain something that I read in the Bible. I know that you attend church regularly, and I would guess that you know him pretty well. I mean, he would have to drive over thirty miles one way. Do you think he would want to do that?"

"Sure.' she replied. "I'm sure he wouldn't mind. What scripture did you read?"

He had torn a piece of paper from the pad to mark the passage, so he had little trouble finding it again. He showed it to her. After a few seconds of reading, she answered.

"This is the first sermon Peter ever preached. I'm not a Bible scholar, and I don't really understand all of it. I just know that this was the first sermon that anyone preached after Jesus went up into Heaven."

"It was the part about dreams that caught my eye," Ryan explained. "It's so strange; I don't seem to be able to remember dreams other than those of trips to Brandon Springs that I never made. I remember everything that I asked you to write down this morning. I can remember those things I dreamed very clearly. I've taken a couple of naps, but I can't remember dreaming during those times. What do you think?"

"The doctor said that you might have trouble remembering things, that's why he told you to write things down," she replied. "Have you written down anything else?"

"I just filled in a few gaps regarding those dreams," he said. "I want to ask him about that part in the Bible and am wondering about something else. Why do you suppose I dreamed so much about homeless people? I'm not generally very fond of them. I don't trust them."

"To be frank, some of them are bad people," she replied. "Not all of them. Some of them have temporarily hit difficult times, and some of them are to a point of giving up for various reasons. I remember when you were about five years old, your mother read you the children's story of 'Billy Goat Gruff'. You must have become frightened by the old troll in the story. Your mother told me of a situation in which she was stuck in traffic. She had just begun to cross a bridge when the traffic came to a halt. You were in the back seat of the car, and you looked out the window just in time to see a ragged man come out from under the bridge. You were petrified. You keep screaming at her that a troll was outside the car. She assured you that the doors were locked, and eventually she was able to calm you down."

"I've seen a lot of them in Boston who are just bums," Ryan stated. "I had one spit on me for not giving him some money. He smelled like a mix of booze and rank body odor. He was disgusting."

About that time, he saw Patsy walk down the hall past his hospital door. She glanced into the room, as she went by, and gave him a smile and a slight wave of her hand.

"Patsy!" Ryan called to her.

Not hearing his call, the nurse continued to walk. He then called out more loudly, "Patsy! Nurse Patsy! Hey, Patsy!"

She quickly came back to the door. "What do you want?" she asked. "You can't yell like that; you will have to lower your voice."

He had quickly deduced that she was off the clock and on her way home. She had a bag and her purse on one arm, and her keys in the hand of the other.

"So, I see that you're off your shift now," he smugly stated.

"I was on my way home," she replied. "You have another nurse for this shift. What do you want?"

"Nurse Patsy, I just wanted to see what you are like when you're not on the clock." he answered.

"My name is not Nurse Patsy," she said as she rolled her eyes. "You can call me nurse, or Nurse Smith; but I'm not Nurse Patsy. In fact, I'm not nurse anything right now because I'm off duty."

"So, when you are off the clock you are just Patsy?" he asked.

"That's right," she answered.

"Well, I think it's great that we can be on first name basis now," he said with a smile. "It's OK to call you Patsy when you're off duty, right? Patsy, this is my Aunt Sally. When I get out of here, I'll be staying with her for a while. I wanted you to meet her."

"We've met," the nurse replied.

Smiling, she turned to Sally. "It's nice to see you again, Sally. Is he always like this?"

"Well, I'm not sure," Sally replied. "You see, he recently smashed his head."

"I think I'm beginning to get an idea as how it was smashed," she said while giving Ryan a stern look. However, Ryan's smiling face made it impossible for her to continue the glare.

"Your aunt and I spoke several times while you were unconscious," the nurse said to Ryan.

Turning back to Sally, she continued, "I really have to be going. I feel for you. I think you're going to have your hands full with him. Do you think you can stand two weeks?"

"I've handled worse," Sally responded. "No, I'm going to enjoy every minute of it. It's so good to talk to you again."

Patsy turned and exited the room. Ryan caught her glance back over her shoulder at him as she left.

"I didn't realize that you were so smooth, Ryan," Sally said with a wink.

"I'm not," he replied. "It's just easy to talk to her. I'm relaxed around her. Maybe it has something to do with her being my nurse. Maybe I really was knocked silly. I don't know."

"We'll see," Sally said with a grin.

Their conversation was interrupted by a rather large nurse pushing the supper cart into the room. "Time for supper, Mr. Walker" she called out. "This is the first time I've seen you sitting up. You must be feeling a lot better. My name is Nurse Atkins, and I have you for the second shift."

"My nephew was just telling me that he feels relaxed around nurses," Sally said, glancing over at Ryan.

"As long as he does what I tell him to do, we'll get along just fine," the nurse replied. As she pushed the tray of food over his lap, Ryan glanced at her name tag that read, *"Bernice Atkins, RN."* He could tell by her demeanor that she was a no-nonsense person. Nurse Atkins had an overpowering personality. She was the type of woman that caused males, both boys and grown men, to snap to attention in her presence. He was almost frightened.

"I'll do my best," he said with a shy smile.

"Yes, you will," she responded. "We'll have you up and out of here in no time. As soon as you're finished with supper, I'll change that dressing on your head."

She quickly turned and departed the room. Ryan gave Sally a sheepish look. "OK, it's not the fact that Patsy has been my nurse," he confessed.

"I need to let you rest," she said, bearing a broad grin. "I feel comforted leaving you in the hands of your capable nurse. I'm sure you will find her just as relaxing as Patsy."

"Lord, help me," he whispered. "I hope I don't do anything to make her mad."

Sally chuckled. She gathered her things and gave him a kiss on the cheek. "See you tomorrow," she said as she walked out the door.

Within minutes after finishing the supper, the nurse returned with dressing and bandage material. "All right, Mr. Walker, let's see that head," she said.

He would never have anticipated her skill. She was like an artist creating a work of art. Her touch was perfect; she seemed to be aware of each tender area. Her speed spoke of a fine combination of experience and gifted coordination. The bandage was removed in a flash, and the dressing was taken off with the gentle care that a new mother displays for her first-born baby. He rested in her care. She replaced the large bandage with a much smaller one.

As she finished, she said, "I understand you were in a nasty auto accident. One of the paramedics said that the car rolled several times before flipping off into a ditch. I would guess you hit your head on the side of the car as it rolled. You are very fortunate, and you were smart to have that seat belt on."

Her words were filled with care and kindness. Ryan imagined that she had seen many horrors in her line of work. It was probably encouraging for her to see someone who had come through things well. He had guessed correctly, for her next words confirmed his thoughts.

"You need to be very careful not to hit that head again any time soon," the nurse coached. "I've seen many young men who once felt invincible seriously hurt in accidents. Some of these young men suffered serious brain damage that left them a lifetime of paralysis; or loss of speech; or loss of hearing; or left them in the mental state of a two-year old. You are blessed. You've been given a life that each of those wish for desperately. Don't take it for granted. Use this life well."

"I plan to do exactly that," he quietly said.

She left the room, and he thought about the life he could have lost. He thought about the fact that none of us are guaranteed length of life, or ease of life, or a job, or a home, or a spouse, or anything.

We're placed here on earth for a very short time. Whether we are given two months or 100 years, our life is very short in comparison with the history of man. Viewed against the perspective of eternity, the length of each life on earth is a mere solitary faint blimp on the radar of time. We've been given a life of choices. Some people have a greater range of choices, than others. I think it's fair that those people are charged with a greater responsibility. We hear this charge over and over throughout our lives, and the truth of the statement is inescapable. With great power comes great responsibility. The power of choice is great; and it should not be taken for granted or handled irresponsibly.

Ryan had always thought that a person should be measured by his loves, dislikes, ethics, morals, values, and thoughts. However, he had done nothing in his relationship with his Uncle Andrew. Now, it was too late. After rethinking the matter, it now seemed obvious to him that actions were a more meaningful measurement than feelings.

What a person puts forth in effort, means a great deal more than what someone happens to think or feel. The things that we choose to do in life are mirrors into our souls. They don't reflect the person we think ourselves to be, but rather the person we really are.

He considered the saying 'Talk is cheap,' and he decided that thoughts and feelings were also just about as cheap.

They take so little effort; they take so little commitment on our part. Feelings can be so strong, and some have the ability to consume us if we let them. Because of this, we have a tendency to over value them. Feelings come and go; but our actions become part of the history of mankind and our words are spoken out into eternity. It is the good that we do that remains, whether anyone consciously remembers it or not. We don't have to take credit for good for it to remain after we die. What we do can consciously or subconsciously change the lives of those around us, and their lives impact others. Our deeds become a real part of who we are. Thoughts and feelings are like conception, but it is out of our actions that the good in us is given birth.

His philosophical discussion with himself was interrupted by a urinary urge to visit the bathroom. This time, his need was not as immediate as the last. He pushed the buzzer and notified the station. He again prepared for the event by dropping the side rail and placing both legs over the right side of the bed. Ryan was feeling much better than he had during the morning and considered placing his feet onto the floor. He decided that he shouldn't do anything that might place the orderly's job in jeopardy, so he waited. He sat there with his feet dangling for a couple of minutes before the second shift orderly entered the room.

"I hear you're ready to go," the orderly called out. Ryan dropped to the floor as the orderly took his arm.

"My name is Michael," the orderly stated. "You seem to be doing pretty well on your own. I'm not really sure that you need me."

"How long do I have to wear this stupid gown?" Ryan asked. "Can't I wear underwear, pajamas, or clothes? I mean, I'm done with the catheter and IV."

As Ryan began the process of relieving himself, Michael answered.

"Not my call, but it makes sense to me. I'll ask the nurse at the station to place your request on your chart."

"That's fair," Ryan replied. "Thanks. That would be nice."

As Ryan flushed and started back toward the bed, Michael asked, "Do you feel weak or dizzy? You seem to be walking on your own just fine."

"I'm tired, but I'm not dizzy," he replied.

"Good," Michael responded. "I'm going to tell them to put that information on your chart, as well."

Ryan climbed back into the bed under his own strength and thanked the orderly again. He thought about the patience that everyone at the hospital had shown him, especially Joe. He thought about how Sally had been spending so much time supporting his stay there, and how she jumped at the chance to take care of him at Andrew's old house. She was a doer. She didn't just talk-the-talk, she walked-the-walk. She had taken care of Andrew in his last days on earth. She was a small unassuming woman, but she was a giant in her acts of kindness and care. He remembered the Biblical story of the Good Samaritan. It was the person who acted, who was considered the neighbor. Not the person who embodied higher learning, or philosophical understanding, or spiritual enlightenment. The Good Samaritan invested his life in meeting a need of someone other than himself. It was too late to do anything regarding his relationship with Uncle Andrew, but he was now going to be the nephew he should have been to Sally.

It was still early into the evening, but Ryan was very tired. He closed his eyes and drifted into a peaceful and dreamless sleep.

Chapter 15

SALLY WAS ALREADY SITTING IN HIS ROOM when Ryan awoke. She waited quietly and patiently, as to allow him his needed rest. Sally received a call from Ryan's doctor in the early morning hours, but it had been by her request.

"What time is it?" he asked her.

"I need to tell you something," she replied. Her soft voice was sad and somewhat hesitant.

"What do you want to tell me?" Ryan requested.

"I received news this morning, and I guess I should make you aware of something," she answered. "I had asked the doctor to allow me to talk to you about this, but I'm having some difficulty."

"Are you alright?" he asked.

"Oh, sure," she replied. "I'm fine; I'm just having a hard time finding the words. OK, here it is. You don't seem to remember the details of the accident, and no one has said much to you about it. Ryan, there were two vehicles involved. It was raining extremely hard, and you were slowing down to take the exit ramp. The car behind you was traveling much too close in that kind of weather. The other person didn't realize that you were slowing until she saw your brake lights. She must have panicked and hit her brakes much too hard. Her car hydroplaned and she caught the rear end of your car on the driver's side. Both cars lost control. Yours flipped several times and was left in a ditch. Her car spun around and slammed sideways into a concrete divider. The impact on the other car was directly on the driver's door. She was wearing a seat belt, but there were no air bags in the door."

"She died, didn't she?" he whispered.

"I had requested that the doctor inform me, if she passed away," Sally replied. I wanted to be the one to talk to you about it. He called me about 6:00 AM to tell me that she passed away around 4:00 AM. I hoped that she would pull through. I wanted to have better news for you. It wasn't your fault. She was traveling too fast for that kind of weather, and she was too close to you. The police said that she may not have even seen you until you hit your brakes."

"Did she have kids?" he asked.

"Two children," Sally answered. "She had a boy in middle school and a daughter in elementary school. She was in her late thirties and was a schoolteacher. She was on her way back from a teacher's workshop held in another town. I'm so sorry, Ryan."

By the time she finished the explanation, Ryan was sitting with his eyes closed and both fists were clinched. He took a deep breath; then began to shake as if he were sitting on a block of ice. Though his fists were held tight, the shaking was uncontrollable. He couldn't speak. Ryan could only think of the pain he experienced as a college student, when he heard that his parent's had been killed.

These two kids are much younger; they were at such tender ages. Maybe there's something I could do. Of course, there's nothing I can do to change the situation. Their mother has been taken, and I've been party to her demise. I may be the last person they would want to talk to, but I have to do something. I want to find them, hug them, and offer anything. I want them to know that I understand what they're going through, and that I will be there if they need someone. However, it's possible that I would never be allowed to get near them.

"Ryan, she never gained consciousness," Sally consoled.

"She never woke up."

"Why couldn't this be a stinking dream?" he shouted silently in his mind. *"I've dreamed so many things while in the hospital. Why couldn't I swap this for one of those dreams? Why can't I swap realities?"* His emotions shifted suddenly. Ryan quickly went from deep sorrow to fierce anger. He felt anger at himself for being part of it. If he had not been involved in the accident, he would be able to console the two kids. Then he became angry at the situation.

She died, and there was no reason for it. It was just a fluke. Who knows the mind of God? Maybe it was her time to go. If that was the case, what the heck is God doing? He allowed this. God could have stopped it easily, but He didn't. There are a number of scenarios in which she would have been safe. She could have noticed me earlier; the rain could have slackened; or she could have left her place of origin just a few seconds later and avoided the situation entirely. Any of these things would have taken her to safety. How could God possibly leave those kids in that situation?

He became angry at God.

"Why did God let that happen?" he finally burst out.

The shaking slowed as his eyes filled with tears. The slight tremors were replaced by heavy sobbing.

"What was God doing?" he asked. "Why didn't He take me instead? I have no children. I don't even have a wife who would have to deal with my death."

"Don't blame God," Sally advised. "You don't have to blame anyone. I don't know why she decided to not take things more slowly. She really should have slowed down. Don't blame God, and don't blame yourself."

"You told me to find the good in things, and try to focus on the good," he blurted. "I don't see any good in this; I don't see any purpose or any logical reason for it. I certainly can't find any good in it."

He would have continued down that path, but the conversation was interrupted by the squeaking of the approaching breakfast cart. Soon, Patsy came through the door. She took one look at his desperate and angry eyes and realized what was going on. The nurse had gotten word of the woman's death during her morning briefing.

"I'm not hungry," he whispered, as he wiped his face with his hands.

He felt coldness come over him. His shield was being raised, and he recognized it. He had known it when his parents died. This shield from the world around him kept him a comfortable distance from pain. It also resulted in his neglecting those who loved him. Before the shield could fully be in place, a small sliver of understanding slid through an opening in the armor. This time, it would be a conscious decision on his part. He could either allow a shield to lock the world away from him, or he could leave himself open to the ravages of life. Sally and Patsy both remained quiet, and Patsy continued with the breakfast tray just as if he had said nothing to her.

He glanced at Patsy, and then he looked fully into Sally's eyes. The image became blurred by his tears. He didn't want to shut her out again. She didn't deserve that. He broke into sobs even more violently than before. Every feeling of anger and grief poured from him like rivers. Every corner of his soul was swept clean of all traces of bitterness and self-loathing. He became conscious of the fact that Patsy was witnessing his lack of control. He knew that she could see his weakness, but he was past caring.

Sally wrapped her arms around him and wept with him. He glanced up to see Patsy leaving the room. It didn't matter. After a few minutes he calmed. He realized that he urgently needed to visit the bathroom, and he told Sally of the need. Sally stepped out and informed a nurse at the station. After just a couple of minutes Joe was there. Without thinking, Ryan dropped the railing and dropped down to the floor before Joe arrived at that side of the bed.

"I'm sorry," Ryan stated. "I didn't think."

"You're OK," Joe replied. "You didn't get far. In fact, I wouldn't be surprised if this was my last escort with you."

"Really?" Ryan asked, as he quickly moved toward the bathroom.

"Sure," Joe answered. "I think the doctor will be around soon. On your chart I saw that both Michael and I recommended that you be allowed to go by yourself. I can't speak for the doctor though. I just wouldn't be surprised. Don't tell the doctor that I said so."

"No problem," Ryan replied, as he flushed away the contents of the toilet.

As Ryan passed the door on route back to the bed, he could see that Sally and Patsy were talking in the hallway outside the room. He figured that he must have really freaked out the nurse, by his behavior. Ryan didn't really care about damaging any impression he had earlier made on Patsy; he was still consumed with thoughts of the woman who had passed away.

As Joe left the room, Sally entered. It was as if they were passing guards. Sally sat in the chair near Ryan's bed.

"Are you feeling any better?" she asked.

"Why did she have to die, Sally?" he pressed. "I prayed, and I've asked God to help those kids. I can't see any way that good could come out of this. I just don't see why she had to die."

Sally paused a few seconds, and then replied.

"Try not to be so quick to judge God. We're so very limited in our perception of reality. At best, we may have ninety years of learning and experience. Our understanding is so small. Sometimes we come to understand certain things that occur in our lives, and there are some things that we will never understand in this lifetime. Wait for it. You may see a purpose one day, or you may not. Just don't be so quick to judge God. I want you to be assured that you were not at fault. Based on what was contained in the police report, I would guess that her husband will come to the same conclusion."

"What was her name," he asked.

"Her name was Emily Knox, and her husband is an attorney named Russell Knox," Sally replied.

"She was married to an attorney?" he asked. "Well, if there is any chance at all that I could be at fault, I'm bound to hear about it."

"Don't be so quick to judge him either," she stated rather firmly.

"I'm not judging anyone personally, I've just known several attorneys," he answered. "You're right. He is probably too busy grieving for his wife, to think about me."

"I need to go to town for a while," she said. "Will you be alright?"

"I'll be fine," he answered. "Could you leave me your address? I know how to get there; I just can't remember the address."

"Are you planning on taking a long walk?" she chided, still concerned.

"No," Ryan replied. "I need to have some papers sent from the bank, and I would like to have them mailed to your house. Would that be alright?"

Sally took the pad from the nightstand and wrote down her phone number and address.

"I'm sorry I became so upset," he said.

He then took the pad and pen and wrote down his own name and cell phone number. He told Sally to keep it with her in case she ran into Mr. Knox.

"If you see Mr. Knox, please give this to him," he told her. "Tell him that he or his children can call me at any time. Tell him that I am so sorry for his loss. Let him know about my parents. I know it's not the same as losing a spouse, but I do understand loss."

She leaned over him, gave him a firm hug, and told him that she loved him. A few minutes after she left, Patsy entered the room.

"Are you going to eat this breakfast?" she asked.

Ryan gave her a smile and uncovered the dish. It was a bit lukewarm, but he ate most of it. Patsy waited for him to eat. She said very few words, for she was studying him in an attempt to evaluate his emotional state of mind. She had been told by Sally that the news of the death had touched a personal nerve, and the nurse was considering whether he might do something rash. Just as he was almost finished, she asked him if he was going to be alright.

"I'm fine, but I absolutely hate the fact that I was involved in an accident that took a mother away from two children," he explained. "I suddenly lost both parents when their home was being burglarized. It's hard to explain how I feel."

She told him that she was sorry to hear about his loss. He began to sense the weight of grief beginning to subtly settle back upon him, so he quickly changed the subject. He told her that he needed to make a few calls on his cell phone. He asked her if she personally recommended a local car dealer.

"Car dealer?" Patsy asked. "I don't trust any of them. I'm afraid you'll have to be on your own in that matter."

She left to finish her rounds. Using his cell phone, he selected three dealers that advertised the availability of FAX numbers. Ryan called his insurance agent and told him of the situation. He gave the insurance agent the phone number of the local police, so the agent could obtain the police reports regarding the accident. Ryan instructed him to quickly notify the bank regarding pay-off of the auto loan. He also asked if the agent would retain the insurance policy, so that it would be automatically transfer upon purchasing a new vehicle. The letter of coverage was to be mailed to him at Sally's address.

He then called his bank and explained the situation. He explained to them that he planned to purchase a vehicle soon and asked the bank to FAX a copy of his credit report to each of the three auto dealers. The letter also confirmed the maximum amount for an auto loan that the bank would give him. His previous car was very expensive, and Ryan knew that this type of letter would get the attention of the auto dealers. He then called each dealer and told them to expect the FAX. Ryan informed each of them that letters were being sent to several dealers. He planned to promote competition among the businesses. He told them each to contact him on his cell phone as soon as they received the FAX.

Having successfully pulled his mind away from the death of Emily Knox, he laid his head back on the pillow to catch a quick nap. However, he was interrupted shortly after closing his eyes. A large man walked into the room.

"Is this the room of Ryan Walker?" the man asked.

Ryan's first thought was that this was a car salesman, but he realized that it would be impossible for a car dealer to find him so soon. Then, as if someone had dumped a pail of ice water over his head, a terrible fear ran down to the tips of his toes.

This guy looks far too dignified to be a car salesman. He may be the husband of the woman who died in the accident. I gave Sally my cell phone number to pass on to the husband, but I'm not ready for a face-to-face conversation.

"Yes, I'm Ryan Walker," he answered with much anxiety.

"I'm Pastor John Rawlings," he replied. "Sally told me that you wanted to see me".

"Oh, yes," Ryan said with relief. "I read a passage from the Bible, and I wanted someone to explain it to me. I hope you didn't make a special trip to come here."

"No, I am here visiting a member of my congregation, and thought this might be a good time to stop by to see you." he replied. "What was the scripture? I'm not sure if I can help, but I would be glad to try."

Ryan picked up the Bible and opened it to Chapter 2 of the book of Acts. He held it out to the pastor and pointed to it. He told the minister that he really didn't understand what it meant.

John Rawlings looked over the verses for a moment, and then answered.

"Well, it is obvious that the people of the time understood those words. This passage of scripture describes the first sermon Peter preached. As a result of what occurred that day, three thousand people were converted. Peter was a simple fisherman and was not known to be an orator. The power of the Holy Spirit was the real source of the conversions of the people in the New Testament. Jesus had warned the disciples to not begin preaching until they were empowered by the Holy Spirit. Jesus also told them that He would send a Comforter to them from God the Father, once He reached Heaven. This unseen Comforter, the Holy Spirit, would comfort them and spiritually strengthen them. The Holy Spirit would spiritually give them understanding of the scriptures and all that they had heard Jesus tell them. This Comforter would essentially minister to them as Jesus had, but would also grant them understanding. The disciples did as Jesus instructed. This was the day the Holy Spirit was sent from God to empower, instruct and comfort mankind. Peter was no longer the frightened fisherman who had earlier publicly disowned any association with Jesus out of fear of being crucified with him. He was now strengthened spiritually by the Holy Spirit and was granted enlightenment of spiritual matters."

"I'm not very knowledgeable about the Holy Spirit, and I really don't understand," said Ryan. "I don't have a problem recognizing Jesus as being the Son of God, and I understand the concept of God being our spiritual Father. Matters regarding the Holy Spirit seem to be a little mystical to me, and I'm not entirely comfortable with the idea."

Pastor Rawlings was a member of faith that believed God to be made up of a Trinity. The pastor tried to explain the concept of three spiritual Entities as being a single Deity, by relating the idea to people.

"The Bible indicates that people are created in the image of God," Rawlings began. "To gain a better understanding of God, we need to better understand mankind. I would like for you to explain your concept of your own existence."

"I see myself as being made of body and a mind," replied Ryan.

I commend you on your understanding," said Rawlings. "I'm sure that you are college educated, but I'm personally disappointed in scholars who make man out to be only a physical batch of matter and chemicals. I would like to offer the concept of you consisting of a body, mind, and spirit. Each of these are different, but that they essentially make up this person we know as Ryan Walker. Your physical body is Ryan, your mind is Ryan, and your inner soul or heart is Ryan. They are different aspects of you, but they make up this one person we know to be Ryan. The Father, Jesus, and the Holy Spirit are different; but they are essential God. They are three, but they are one. It's sort of a mystery."

They both agreed that it was a little difficult for a finite mind to understand an infinite God. The pastor went on to explain that the Holy Spirit is the unseen spirit of God who gives us spiritual insight and understanding and strengthens us spiritually. He reminded Ryan that the Bible states that just before Jesus left the earth, He promised to send this Spirit from God the Father to comfort and guide us in His absence.

Ryan thanked him for the explanation and for taking the time to visit him. He told the pastor that the discussion helped, and that he had a better understanding of what he had read.

"However, I don't understand what the scripture meant regarding dreams," Ryan stated.

"To be honest, I'm not sure that I thoroughly understand the issue either, but there were occasions where God speaks to people through dreams," the minister replied. "Both in the Old and New Testaments, two different men named Joseph were given understanding through dreams. I believe this particular scripture in the book of Acts indicates something special regarding prophecy, dreams, and visions. I'm not entirely sure what was meant, but the people in the crowd understood what was being said to them. I apologize for not having a better answer to the question."

Ryan appreciated the pastor's honesty and thanked him again. However, he was still deeply troubled.

"I wanted to ask you about something else," Ryan stated. "Why would God allow a mother of two children to die in an accident?"

"I can't say that I have a corner on the Mind of God," the older man responded. "The Bible says that we see life as though we were looking through a stained glass. We can see that there may be something on the other side of the glass, but we often aren't able to distinguish the details very well. I am sixty-eight years old, and I've witnessed several things in my lifetime. Every so often, I am allowed to catch a glimpse of understanding. I can't tell you why people die when they do, and I certainly wouldn't try to tell those children that I understand why. I will tell you of another situation. I knew a woman who was very distraught because her husband had been suddenly killed in an auto accident. It was suspected that he suffered a heart attack while driving. An autopsy was performed to try to gain an understanding of the condition of the body, and it revealed that a major portion of the man's body was consumed by cancer. The wife decided that it was better for him to have died quickly than to die a long and painful death from the cancer. We just don't always see everything. Sometimes, we never find an answer in this life."

"This mother was less than forty years old," Ryan said.

"We are all going to die," the pastor replied. "We are given the gift of life, and we are not guaranteed how long we will have it. That's part of what makes the gift so precious. If we knew the hour of our death, we might spend our lives in misery waiting for it and dreading the moment. Whether we live one hundred years or two hours, our life is precious; and it is a very short speck of time in comparison to eternity. God deals with us personally; and there are different durations for each of us to stay here in this realm. This isn't Heaven; in this place we often find ourselves in difficult situations."

The pastor and Ryan talked for a while, and eventually the conversation moved to lighter subjects. At one point, Ryan asked him if he was originally from the area. John Rawlings had served as pastor to many large congregations; some were in major cities. He retired at age sixty-five and had intended to spend a portion of his last years traveling with his wife. This was short-lived. Within two months after his retirement, doctors discovered that his wife suffered from a fast-growing inoperable brain tumor. She was dead within the year. It didn't take long for him to realize that he needed to be busy. Sitting around the empty house was no answer to his grief. That was when he answered the call to pastor this small church in this small quiet community. It was perfect for him. The church could not afford to pay a large salary, and he was able to live on his retirement. The church was small, and so was the workload.

The pastor told Ryan to place the grieving husband and children of this woman in God's hands. He advised him to spend some time in prayer for the family. Ryan thanked him for his visit and for the responses to his questions. The pastor excused himself to visit the the member of his congregation who was in the hospital.

It wasn't long before Patsy brought his lunch, and he was now hungry. Ryan didn't have a clear answer as to why the woman died, but he felt a great relief from the intense grief he had been suffering. Thinking about one of his dreams, he asked Patsy if she ever worked with homeless people after hours.

"Homeless people are sort of creepy to me," she answered. "I visit a couple of elderly women in a retirement home after work on Wednesdays. I read to them and explain some of the current world events to them. They basically just want to have conversation with someone young. Their husbands passed away several years ago, and they're lonely. They have a craving for someone to just place a hand on their shoulder or take them by the hand. They're starved for a human touch. Sometimes, I brush the hair of one lady. Both women have family living great distances away, and they rarely receive a visit from anyone. They still very much want to be part of life and be in contact with the living. There is another woman at the retirement home who exists in a lone world of her own creation. She is surrounded only by ancient photos of years gone by and of loved ones no longer living. This woman chose to live the rest of her life in a self-made shrine, awaiting death. It's sad."

Ryan felt a sense of shame. Patsy visited and cared for elderly women who were not part of her family. In a sense, she adopted them. Patsy had one surviving grandmother, living on her own in another state. She called her grandmother weekly and wrote to her every other week. Ryan had not taken the time to visit or call his only remaining relatives. He had been consumed with his career and had basically shut them out of his mind.

This is going to change; in fact, it already has.

He made a commitment within himself to care for Sally. It wouldn't end with her. He decided that he would attempt to be more aware of the needs of others around him. He would adopt these motherless children and their father into his daily prayers.

Patsy left to care for other patients, but her statements remained in his mind and heart. She made him aware that it's impossible to care for everyone in need, but that we are capable of picking out just a few on which to focus our attention.

Our focus should begin with our family members, if those members will receive our attention. If not, there are plenty of other people who are willing to receive it. We aren't to ignore everyone else, but we should focus our attention on the few that we are able to care for.

It had become apparent to Ryan that the world would dramatically be a different place, if everyone did this.

Doctor Adams entered the room. Looking over Ryan's charts he began, "Good news, young man. I'm going to discharge you to the care of your aunt tomorrow morning following one more night of observation. You no longer need the assistance of the orderlies, but I'm sure you were aware of that already."

The doctor looked up from the charts to catch the broad grin those words had caused to spread across his patient's face.

"Does this mean that I can take a shower?" Ryan asked.

"Absolutely," the doctor replied.

Doctor Adams instructed Ryan about the proper care of patting the stitches dry and told him that the stitches would be removed in another week. The doctor removed the bandage, inspected the stitches, and informed Ryan that there would no longer be a need to wear a bandage over the healing wound. Ryan thanked him for the news. Before the doctor left to continue the rounds, Ryan told him about the dreams. He told him that it had been difficult for him to distinguish the dreams from reality. They seemed to be more like memories than dreams. The doctor reminded him that one way for him to divide reality from those events dreamed was to have others confirm real events for him. Ryan also told him that since becoming fully conscious, he rarely remembered dreams resulting from recent sleep.

You shouldn't be concerned," Doctor Adams stated. "Concussions result in a variety of short-term memory oddities. It's apparent that your reasoning abilities are very sharp, and your recovery is making very fast improvements."

Ryan called his aunt using his cell phone. She was delighted to hear that he would be discharged the following morning. Sally was busy with housework, but she promised she would visit him after supper. Ryan laid his head back on the pillow and recalled the various events and discussions of the day. Nothing excited him more than the fact that he was now allowed to take a private shower. He decided to get cleaned up before Sally arrived, so he buzzed the nurse's station and told them of his intentions. Within a few minutes Patsy arrived with a towel, bath rag, soap, a new hospital gown, and a small bottle of shampoo.

"What happened to my clothes?" Ryan asked her. For the first time, he remembered the small travel bag he had packed for the trip to Brandon Springs.

"I think your aunt took your things to her home to wash them," she replied. "I think something happened to them during accident, and they needed to be washed. I don't know the details."

They talked for some time. In fact, Ryan had forgotten about the shower until Patsy reminded him that she had other patients to attend. After she left, he made his independent pilgrimage to the bathroom. The ritual was on. He relieved himself of both forms of common bodily waste, shaved, and then started the shower. Ryan stepped into the tiny streams of water, allowing them to rain upon his head. He stood motionless for about a minute. A shower never felt so good. He began to gingerly apply the shampoo to his head, making sure not to pull any of the stitches. He then lathered up the rag with soap and vigorously scrubbed every inch of the remaining portions of his frame. Afterwards, he followed a similar process during the toweling of his body. He was careful to pat dry the area of the wound, and then firmly buffed the water from the rest of his body.

"Clean at last!" Ryan shouted.

The process was somewhat invigorating. Once the ritual was completed, he rolled the towel up in the form of a makeshift whip and snapped it at the shower curtain.

I'm finally back to my healthy self. Well, almost.

As he tossed the towel into the corner of the bathroom, he was reminded that he was not yet completely back to a normal state of being. Standing naked, he viewed his only available form of attire hanging on the back of the bathroom door. He could shower, but without his own clothes he was restricted to hospital attire. Ryan reminded himself that this would be his last time to robe himself in such a fashion. Tomorrow, he would be free of it. Once he could be clean and wear normal clothing, he was sure that he would be back to his normal self. Donning the gown, he happily climbed back into his bed.

Within an hour, Patsy returned to congratulate Ryan of his impending dismissal from her care. She was off duty now, but she seemed to be a little less comfortable during this conversation. Before she left for the day, they exchanged cell phone numbers. Ryan couldn't help but notice how nervous she seemed, and he wondered if he had said or done something to cause it. Even though she had been gone only minutes, he was tempted to call her and ask. After more thought, he decided to let the matter rest for a day.

As he finished eating, Sally arrived with his travel bag. There was a familiar smell of cologne as she entered the room.

"Wow… are you wearing a new perfume?" he asked.

"Don't blame this on me!" she exclaimed. "A bottle of cologne in your travel bag broke during the impact of your accident. This is your stuff that you smell, not mine. I washed your clothes, and I hung your bag on the clothesline in the sun for an entire day. I can't get this smell entirely out."

"I'm sorry," he said, with a sheepish grin. "Thank you, so much, for going to all that trouble."

She told him to open the bag. He looked inside and found that she had purchased a pair of shorts for him to wear during his last night in the hospital. He was so grateful. He got out of his bed and hugged her. Grabbing a pair of underwear, a tee shirt, and his new pair of shorts, he promptly went into the bathroom to change. He came out of the bathroom, tossed the hospital gown onto the floor, and threw his arms into the air like a gladiator celebrating a victory over an opponent. His life was filled with wonderful small blessings, and he was learning to appreciate each one.

Sally told Ryan that she would not be staying, because she had a lot of housework to finish before he came to stay with her. He tried to convince her not to bother doing anything special on his behalf; for he was just looking forward to spending time with her. He knew that Sally had always been a hard worker, and he suspected his request would be ignored. Sally gave him a quick hug and reminded him that she would return the following morning.

The RN, Bernice, brought him his supper. It was then that he first noticed the few strands of gray that invaded her dark hair. Age caused the skin to loosen under her eyes and chin. However, her eyes were strong with confidence. He imagined that she had seen more suffering than he could ever imagine, and that she had probably dealt with a wide variety of humanity while in her line of work. He guessed her to be in her late forties.

"I see you no longer require our standard gown," she said as she spotted her patient proudly sporting his shorts.

"Yep," he replied. "No more breezy attire for my rear end. I'm back to normal clothes. I'm to be released tomorrow morning."

"You have really recovered quickly," she stated. "Don't take this personally, but I will be glad to see you go. I'm always glad to see people get well enough to leave. In the beginning, I wasn't sure how things would turn out for you. You had trouble gaining consciousness, and sometimes that can be a bad sign."

"I want to thank you for your care," Ryan said. "I was very impressed with your skill and speed in changing the bandage on my head. It's obvious that you're a true professional in your line of work. Thank you."

A smile on the nurse's face revealed a personality that was equally as strong as the commanding air that filled the room at her presence. There was certainly something behind that no-nonsense persona she carried into the workplace.

"You are very welcome," she responded.

With that, she exited the room to continue caring for those less fortunate than Ryan. He listened as her steps faded into the mixture of faint sounds that spilled into the hallway from other rooms. Most of those muffled sounds came from television sets, mixed with quieted conversations.

He lifted the lids from the containers of food and began to quickly consume the contents. The meal was not the best, but he felt hungry. As he ate, mental pictures of Bernice's smile frequently popped into his head. He suspected that she was a much more interesting person than he had first imaged, and he almost regretted not having more time to get to know her.

He had taken a shower and now had access to normal clothes. Ryan thought about how much better he felt. Lying in bed, he lifted the sheet and proudly glanced down at the new shorts he happily wore. He closed his eyes and tried to imagine his Uncle Andrew's home.

I wonder if it is well painted and cared for, as in one of my dreams; or if it has been neglected and fallen into disrepair, as in the other. Understanding the current financial state of Aunt Sally, I guess it probably is in need.

His imagination then moved to the mountain and ancient oaks behind the old home. Childhood fear of them was replaced by the anticipation of returning.

Chapter 16

ANTICIPATION FILLED RYAN'S mind as he awoke. The first order of the day was to perform the morning bathroom ritual. After dressing, he packed up all his belongings and sat in the chair.

I've spent enough time in that hospital bed, and now I'm ready to start behaving as a normal healthy individual.

Patsy brought in the last meal he was to consume before leaving for his stay at Sally's. She said very little, and Ryan was puzzled by the fact that she seemed somewhat cold toward him.

"What's going on with you?" he finally asked. "Is something bothering you?"

"I shouldn't have given you my cell phone number yesterday," she stated. The words seemed to be painfully spoken. "It wasn't your fault; you didn't do anything wrong. It was me."

"What's the problem?" Ryan asked.

"I've been seeing this guy for some time now, and it wasn't fair to exchange numbers like that. You're a great guy, I just shouldn't have led you ..." she stopped in mid-sentence as Ryan interrupted her.

"I would expect someone as cute as you to be seeing someone," Ryan replied.

It was both an effort to make her feel more comfortable,

and an attempt to cover his own feelings. The truth was, he hadn't even considered the fact that she could be involved with another guy. Hiding his real disappointment in hearing the facts of her relationship, he continued.

"I've enjoyed the conversations we've had, and I just thought we might talk again sometime."

Feeling a little relieved, but still uncomfortable, she replied.

"OK, I just wanted you to know before you left this morning. I can't tell you how hard it was to tell you. I really like you."

"I like you too," Ryan said, as he began to uncover the breakfast plate. "My aunt should be here in just a little while, and I can't wait for the doctor to make his official decree."

He was attempting to change the subject to that of simply being her patient.

"He is on the floor; I've seen him already," she said. "That was what prompted me to go ahead and talk with you. I was afraid that he would discharge you before I had a chance."

Doctor Adams entered the room and Patsy excused herself to attend other patients. The doctor proceeded to make a thorough check of Ryan's condition.

"Well, all I have to say is that you are healing at a remarkable rate," he told his patient. "You are free to leave. Just make sure you go by the administrative office before leaving to settle any insurance matters. I wish you the best of luck."

Waiting for his aunt, Ryan thought that it would help take his mind off Patsy if he had something to read. He remembered the Bible in the nightstand. He pulled it out and tried to read it. Ryan's eyes scanned the words, but he wasn't making the connection. His mind wasn't absorbing the words. He couldn't shake thoughts of Patsy. Finally, he decided to turn to a familiar passage. As he read the 23rd Psalm, the words began to become real to him. The passage read, *'Though I walk through the valley of the shadow of death, Thou art with me'.*

He had walked through the valley of the shadow of death,

and that shadow had fallen on the woman in the other car.

It's obvious that God was with me, but was He with her also? I've always considered that verse to mean that God will save us from death when we are in harm's way. I'm not sure that's really what this passage means. The pastor was right; we are all going to die. It would be unimaginable for God to leave us at the point of our death. As we breathe our last in this realm, it's obvious we would be in need of God's presence more than ever. No. It has to mean that God will be with us both when the shadow of death passes over us and when it falls squarely upon our lives here on earth. Whether death comes to us or if we were allowed to live on for a time, I think it is saying that God will be with us.

Sally finally arrived and found Ryan sitting in the chair with the Bible on his lap.

"Am I interrupting a Bible study?" she asked.

"No, I was bored and decided to take a look at this Bible," he replied. "I'm ready to go."

She had expected him to be enthusiastic at his release, and she was puzzled at his quiet and down cast demeanor. Nevertheless, she decided not to pry. She helped him with his belongings and went with him as Bernice wheeled him to the administrative office. His insurance handled the entire account, and nothing was owed.

"Well, you are entirely in my hands now," Sally said. "The hospital has gathered all they can from your insurance company, and I believe your nurse is through with you."

Her comment drew smiles from him and Bernice. The nurse wheeled him out the entrance of the hospital. She gave Ryan a quick wave of the hand as he plopped himself into the seat of Salley's vehicle.

Aware of the fact that Ryan had recently been in a tragic auto accident, Sally was much more cautious in her driving than usual. The drive home was filled with small talk, and Ryan's attention was focused on the beauty of the day. The sun was shining, and temperature seemed perfect. It was a wonderful spring day, and he soaked it in as she drove.

Remembrance of past visits filled Ryan's mind, as they made their way up the long gravel drive to Andrew's old house.

Upon first inspection of the home, Ryan realized that both dreams he had regarding the place were incorrect when it came to the condition of the house. It wasn't well taken care of, for paint peeled and flaked on several areas. However, it wasn't to the point of decay. The wood appeared to still be very solid.

The interior was pretty much like he remembered from childhood. The furnishings were plain and simple, yet they were clean and solid. There weren't many pieces of furniture. Even the interior paint appeared to be many years old. Sally escorted him to the largest bedroom, which had lacey curtains and a matching lacey bed spread. Andrew had been an unselfish person, and he had given her the nicest room with the best bed. She had passed the favor on to Ryan, in providing him her room.

"Where are you sleeping?" he asked her.

"Oh, I sleep in the other bedroom," she replied.

Still carrying his travel bag, he made his way to the other bedroom. It was very plain. There was no curtain on the window. It contained a small twin bed, a single nightstand with a lamp, and lone dresser across the room. He suspected that she was trying to give him the most comfortable bed.

"I'm staying in here!" Ryan exclaimed. "I'm not staying in that girly room with all that lace, and stuff."

"It's not that girly," she responded. "Won't you just stay there anyway?"

"No, Sally," he replied. "I'm not taking your bed. I want to sleep in Andrew's room."

"Well, alright," she replied. "If you insist, I guess you can stay there."

He placed his belongings in Andrew's old room and tried out the bed. At once, he understood the sacrifice she was willing to make. The bed was terrible. There were several springs that poked his back, and it took him a few minutes to settle into a position that avoided them. He sat up and listened to the faint noises coming from outside. He heard morning-doves and other birds singing, and he could hear a dog barking in the distance.

The peaceful soft sounds were soon drowned by the sound of heavy farm equipment. He rose and made his way to the front porch. He had forgotten that Sally had made a deal to allow a local farmer to plant crops in the pasture. The equipment had arrived, and the ground would be turned today. Sally soon joined him on the porch, and they watched as the first machine ripped the soil and prepared it for planting.

Sally gave Ryan's hand a quick firm squeeze.

"It's about time someone made good use of that land," she said.

She turned and went back into the house, but Ryan sat on the porch swing and watched. It fascinated him. He found the smell of newly turned earth to be pleasant; and he was surprised at how easily the machines accomplished the task. As a child, he had once attempted to plant a tree for his father. It took him about an hour to dig the hole properly, and he was extremely tired when the job was completed. He watched the activity until Sally came out to tell him that lunch was ready. During the lunch, Ryan asked Sally if she was willing to sell him a few acres.

"I told you that I have about $15,000 in savings, and I would like to buy some of the property", he explained.

"I have no desire to sell you any of it, but I'd be glad to give you a few acres," she replied.

Ryan protested, but it was to no avail.

"When I die, who do you think is going to inherit this?" she asked. "You and I are the last members of this family; don't you think it to be a waste of money to buy something that you are going to inherit?"

Ryan admitted that her statements made a lot of sense. He talked to her about the house, and whether she planned to paint it. She said that she would, but that it could wait awhile. He suggested several colors for it, but she was adamant on it remaining white. She told him that there was something that seemed clean to her about white paint on the outside of a house. Their discussion was interrupted by a phone call from the hospital. Ryan had left his watch in the hospital bathroom when he earlier washed his hands. Ryan apologized and offered to drive her car back to the hospital to get it.

"I won't have any part of you driving on your first day out of the hospital," she insisted.

She promptly left for the thirty-mile trip to the hospital, and Ryan went back out on the front porch to watch the farm equipment. His eyes shifted to the peeling ancient paint. It was at that moment that an idea came to him as if it were an inspiration. He decided that she was probably right about him not giving her money for property, but it was very apparent that she ought to have the house painted before the wood suffered serious damage.

I'll have someone paint the house! After all, this home will be mine once I inherit it. It would be perfectly logical for me to have it painted. I'll tell Sally that I'm only protecting my future investment.

Nevertheless, he didn't want to hear Sally refuse his paying for it. He realized that he had to act quickly. If he were to wait for her return, he knew she would strongly object to his spending money on the old home.

He reviewed local businesses on his cell phone and called a painting contractor. Ryan told him that he was planning to surprise his aunt and that he had about an hour before she would return from a trip to a neighboring town. An agreement was struck for them to send an estimator immediately to give him a price before Sally returned.

During the discussion on the phone, the contractor told him that they could replace the shutters also. Ryan asked them to bring information about the shutters and paint samples when the person came for the estimation. He then excitedly returned to sit on the front porch. In his mind he pictured the freshly painted house with the addition of shutters. This new project completely replaced the earlier despondency regarding Patsy, and he felt consumed by anticipation.

Within twenty minutes the estimator arrived. He gave Ryan an estimation that included preparation for priming, painting, and replacing the shutters on the house. The house would be painted white, with the foundation and porch painted gray. Green shutters would be placed on the small house, and the front door would be painted the same shade of green. The total came to $2,500. Ryan considered the proposal to be very reasonable; he signed the contract and gave them a check for the required $500 down payment. Sally arrived within ten minutes of the estimator's departure.

They are to start early tomorrow morning, and I can't wait to see Sally's face when the crew arrives!

Sally could tell that he was hiding something; for he wore a silly grin during the remainder of the next hour. She imagined that it must have resulted from a phone call with Patsy. She had seen something stir within them both during her visits to the hospital. She decided not to press him on it.

Ryan thanked her for picking up the watch, slipped it on his wrist, and returned to Andrew's bedroom. He found Andrew's old Bible on the dresser and flipped through the pages. As he did, he came across Andrew's military discharge papers. Ryan had not considered the fact that personal documents might be kept there. He felt a slight sense of guilt as he unfolded the papers. Nevertheless, he told himself that Andrew would not have left the documents in such an obvious place had he not wanted others to see them. He noted that it was a medical discharge. At once he considered whether Andrew had become wounded while in service, and he wondered why he had never been told. Ryan brought the discharge papers to Sally, who was on the porch swing watching the machinery.

"Was Andrew wounded while in military service?" he asked.

She looked at him for a moment without saying a word, as she glanced down at the discharge document. She carefully spoke as if she was measuring ingredients for the first time to make a cake from scratch.

"I'm sorry; I didn't mean for you to see that," she replied. "I planned on you staying in the other bedroom."

Ryan could tell that she was deep in thought.

"There was a time when your uncle was very troubled,"

she began. "I'm not sure he wanted you to see that."

She paused. Ryan felt the earlier sense of guilt begin to creep back into his heart and he could tell that she wanted to say more. He quietly waited for it. He didn't want to say anything that would deter her from continuing.

"You have always been very special to him," she stated.

"Why was I special?" Ryan plainly asked.

"He introduced your mother to your father," Sally explained, gazing out across the freshly turned soil. She paused again.

"There was a little more to it than that."

She looked him full in the eyes and made sure that she had Ryan's complete attention.

"Before marrying your father, your mother had gone with Andrew for two years."

Seeing the shock on his face, she continued.

"Oh, Andrew was a looker back then. He was the older brother, and your mother and father were about the same age. He owned land and had the confidence of an established man. Everyone thought that your mother would marry Andrew. She was completely infatuated with him. They probably would have gotten married if it hadn't been for Tommy Long's death."

Ryan had never heard any of this. His parents had never mentioned it. Ryan sat down on the porch swing beside Sally.

"Who was Tommy Long?" Ryan asked.

"Oh, he was a local kid who enjoyed fishing at the reservoir," she explained. "He was there almost all the time when he wasn't in school. A lot of people in the community fished there, including Andrew. They happened to both be fishing there one day, along with several others. Andrew had parked his car on the hill that overlooked the reservoir. The parking brake failed. Andrew had unintentionally left it out of gear, and the car rolled down the hill into the water. Tommy was fishing directly in the path of the car and never heard it coming. He was pinned under the car and drowned. Andrew glanced up from his fishing just as the car hit the boy and ran to help him. Your uncle frantically tried to get him out from under it. It was no use; they weren't able to recover the body until the wrecker pulled the car out."

"It was an accident," Ryan said. He could picture the horror of the situation.

"It was an accident," she responded. "But Andrew was never the same. He pulled away from your mother. I believe he loved her very much, too much to ask her to share in his shame. He had neglected to put that car in gear, and it cost a boy his life. Tommy's parents were wonderful people. They visited Andrew after the funeral and told him that they knew it was an accident. They told him that he was forgiven, and that they wished him well. However, Andrew couldn't forgive himself. Your mother tried to talk with him, but he completely broke things off with her. He stayed to himself for about six months, just until his crops were in. Then he sold all his livestock, stored his tractor and truck in the barn, boarded up the house, and joined the military. After a few years in the army, he returned.

Now, about your question regarding the discharge, I guess I need to tell you about that. Whether it stemmed from the death of Tommy or from thinking about your mother, he began to drink heavily while he was in the army. Eventually, the army decided that he was an alcoholic and unfit. They released him on a medical discharge. When he returned home, he pulled himself away from the bottle. He dedicated himself to making this farm succeed. Andrew worked hard from sunrise to sunset. He purposely left little time or energy for drinking. He purchased new livestock and brought the farm back to life. Andrew eventually enjoyed being with family and friends again, but he never married.

It was while Andrew was in the army that your mother and father drew close, fell in love, and married. They weren't sure how things would be when Andrew came back, but it turned out that they had a fine relationship. My husband and I joined Andrew, your mother, and your father enjoyed wonderful times every Saturday here in this house. All of us spent most of our free time together, and it didn't change when you were born. After a couple of years, your father accepted a job in sales, and your family moved away.

Andrew loved you. He viewed you as the son he never had. If it hadn't been for the accident with Tommy, it is very possible that Andrew could have been your father. He was fearful for you. Andrew was somewhat afraid to become too close to you. He was afraid that God would punish him for the accident. He was afraid that something bad would happen to you if you were closely associated with him. I don't believe God would never do that. I remember an occasion in which Andrew told me that he was afraid that something like that would happen. He wrestled with the guilt of Tommy's death for many years. It was only within the last few years that he began to sense forgiveness from God, and he made peace with himself."

"I never knew that he cared about me at all," Ryan exclaimed. "My mother and father never told me about the accident, and they certainly never told me that my mother and Uncle Andrew had ever been serious."

"Your parents didn't talk about it because they didn't want you to judge Andrew," Sally explained. "They didn't want you to treat him differently, and they were afraid that he might become upset if you ever brought the subject up with him. They didn't want to place a greater burden on you or Andrew."

"But why didn't they tell me about Andrew and my mother?" Ryan asked.

"I'm not sure," said Sally. "They apparently felt it should remain in the past, and they probably thought it might bring up more questions for you concerning Andrew."

From the front porch, Ryan heard his cell phone ringing from inside the bedroom. He rushed to answer it. It was a call from the bank confirming that the paperwork for a new auto loan had been settled, and that a FAX had been sent to all three requested car dealerships. Within thirty minutes all three car dealers called Ryan. After the discussions with each, he narrowed the selection to the Ford and GM dealers. He was to meet with them both the following day and take a look at the vehicles on the lots.

Sally prepared supper, and she hoped the long-awaited meal would compare to that in his dreams. Her cooking had a prominent role in all that he had dreamed, and she hoped that he had not overestimated her talents in the kitchen. He had not. The hearty aroma that filled the small home was incredible. His senses were filled with anticipation and expectation. To him, the first bite of her fried chicken was fabulous! He wasn't sure what spices had been included in the flour coating, but they seemed perfect. The rest of the meal consisted of field peas, corn on the cob, and hot buttered home-made cornbread.

After they finished the meal, Ryan helped Sally clear the table. Unlike his dream, she allowed him to help wash and dry dishes. They talked and laughed, as she told him childhood stories of his father. His father had been the baby of the family, and he often didn't care to be bossed around by two parents and two older siblings. He had learned to be quite creative in his getting around them all. As the remaining cornbread was being put away, Ryan unsuccessfully reached for one more piece.

Sally warned, "If you don't stop with the cornbread, you won't have room for dessert."

Ryan retracted his hand, and questioned, "Dessert?"

Sally presented apple cobbler, topped with vanilla ice cream. This was to be consumed with a fresh cup of coffee, on the side. As the combination of home-made cobbler and ice cream slipped into his mouth, Ryan thought to himself that life had nothing better to offer than to be able to enjoy conversation with loving family over food this good. However, tomorrow would hold new expectations, decisions, and discovery.

Ryan was excited at the prospects of buying a new vehicle. He and Sally discussed the pros and cons of all types. Ryan found that his requirements for selection were based on more practical needs than his earlier interest of simply projecting affluence and prestige. Silently, the painting of the house held his greatest anticipation.

Once the work was done, she neatly folded the kitchen cleaning rags and drying towels. She hung them over the edge of the sink. Sally explained to him that she preferred taking a bath at night, and she excused herself to do so.

The farm machinery had stopped at sunset, so Ryan looked for something to occupy his time while Sally took her bath. He sat on the couch in the living area and noticed an ad from a department store on the coffee table. The store was in the same town as the hospital and car dealerships. In the bedding section, he was surprised to see a bedroom decorated similar to the bedroom with the nautical theme in one of his dreams. Instead of the wallpaper having the nautical theme, the curtains and bedspread displayed ancient nautical maps, charts, and navigation instruments. The accent colors were tan, gold, and brown, on a background of deep red.

This is it! Not only will I have the house painted, I'll redecorate Andrew's old bedroom. This is great! The bedroom badly needs a new bed, and I can find everything needed at this store. Well, everything but a captain's wheel to hang over the bed. Maybe, I can find one later, or possibly find a substitute.

He was so happy he could hardly contain himself. The only problem was that he didn't know his way around the town, and he thought he might have difficulty finding the store. Ryan snatched up his cell phone and headed for the front porch. He dialed Patsy's number.

"Patsy, this is Ryan; your ex-patient," he began.

"Ryan?" she answered.

She paused, not knowing what to say. She thought she had made things clear to him that morning, and she didn't really expect to hear from him again. Noticing her reaction, Ryan continued.

"Patsy, please listen. I need your help. You are the only one I know in that town, and I need to know how to find a store."

"Find a store?" she asked, as she began to laugh. "I think

I've now heard every line possible."

He explained to her what he was trying to do. He couldn't ask Sally directions, because he wanted to surprise her. Patsy soon sensed the sincerity in his voice, and she gave him the directions. In fact, she became so caught up in the surprise that she asked Ryan to call her back when it was completed to let her know how it all went. In the past, he had been crafty in actions that furthered his career. Now he was being sneaky in an effort to bless a deserving person, and he was having a blast.

ROB WILLIAMS

Chapter 17

RYAN HAD THE WORST SLEEP of his visit. In fact, it was even worse than his imagined stay in the nasty motel room with the screaming couple next door. He would manage to find a comfortable position on the old bed, but within no time he would roll over onto the damaged springs while sleeping. By morning, he was thoroughly convinced he was doing the right thing by purchasing a new bed. He stumbled into the kitchen to find his Aunt Sally making breakfast. Ryan greeted her with a morning hug, and asked if he could help. As she refused, Sally heard trucks drive up in front of the house. Her nephew slipped away from the kitchen. At first, she dismissed the sound of trucks as farm equipment, as the ground in the pasture was not yet ready for planting. However, she changed her mind when she heard Ryan talking to men on the front porch. She turned the bacon down and went to join him on the front porch.

"What is going on?" she asked.

"I'm going to inherit this house one day, and I decided that it needs to be painted," Ryan smugly replied.

Defying her age, and as quick as a cat, she grabbed him by his left ear and pulled him back into the house.

"Young man…" she started.

Releasing his ear, she began to laugh. She couldn't believe what she had just done. She had snatched that ear without even thinking. Still chuckling, she quickly apologized and gave him a sincere hug. Soon both of them came, laughing, out onto the front porch. The paint crew was having a difficult time hiding their amusement. Ryan showed her the selection of shutters, and the gray for the porch and foundation. He assured her that the house would be painted white and told her of his idea of matching the front door to the green shutters. She only insisted the home be painted white, and she said that she trusted his judgment on the rest. Sally thanked him, and suddenly remembered the bacon on the stove. She quickly returned to the kitchen to finish her work.

Standing on the front porch, Ryan still had the ad for the bedding in his hand. As the crew began to remove the peeling paint and prepare the house for the primer, he motioned for the foreman to come over to the porch. Ryan showed him the picture and asked if they would be able to mix a tan color to match that in the bedding. The foreman said that it would not be a problem if he had the picture of the ad. Ryan quickly gave him the dimensions of the room and asked for an estimate to paint it. An agreement was made for $250 to paint the walls tan, and to paint the trim and windows white. He informed the man that he and Sally were to go into the next town for several hours, and that he needed the bedroom to be done while they were away. The foreman said that he would make every effort to finish while they were away, but that he would have to return to the store to mix the custom paint. Ryan quickly signed the addition to the contract, and shoved both it and ad into the foreman's hand just as Sally called him to breakfast.

Sally and Ryan discussed the paint details over breakfast, but he purposefully attempted to steer the talk towards the subject of hunting for something to replace his sedan. He didn't want to give her any hint regarding his plan to have the bedroom painted while they were away looking at new vehicles that morning. Sally became more and more excited about the home being painted. He was having a great time, both in the surprise he had successfully pulled off and in the other that he was putting in motion. All the while, he was also working out a plan in his mind to redecorate the bedroom without her catching on.

Soon they were on their way to the Ford lot. Ryan wasn't sure how the painters would accomplish it. The bedroom was to be painted while Sally and Ryan were away during the morning, and the outside of the house was to be prepared and primed by the end of the day. While all four painters were preparing the house for being primed, the foreman went back to the business to mix the tan paint and pick up the white paint for the trim. When he returned, he found that Sally and Ryan had just left in her car. The foreman assigned two men to paint the bedroom and two men to continue the preparation of the outside of house for painting. The preparation included scrapping the peeling old paint from the home and taping plastic over the glass in the windows. As the two finished this chore on one side of the house, the foreman would come behind them and spray the primer. The actual painting on the outside would have to wait for the following day.

While at the Ford dealership, Ryan settled on a mid-sized SUV. However, before closing the deal he told the salesman that he intended to see what was offered at the GM dealership. He actually was stalling for time, so that the bedroom could be painted before Sally returned. At the GM lot he pretended to be interested, but he had already made up his mind. The Ford salesman became nervous while he was away and called him on his cell phone to offer him an additional $500 off the earlier price. Ryan was pleased with himself. He had lured Sally away and saved money in the process. He was having a great day.

After the purchase, he insisted that he take Sally out for lunch to celebrate. After much coaxing, she agreed to follow him as he drove his new vehicle to a local restaurant. This would give the painters plenty of time to work their magic on the bedroom. However, he didn't want her around when he purchased the bedding and the curtains. After the meal, he told her that he needed to go to the department store to purchase additional clothes. He explained that he originally had not planned to be in Brandon Springs for such an extended length of time, and he needed clothes to cover the two weeks needed for recovery from the concussion. She was a little uncomfortable for him to be driving such a long distance alone since he had so recently left the hospital. At first Ryan had a difficult time convincing Sally not to follow him to the store, but as he talked about the home being painted, she became more and more excited to go back to see how they were progressing. She was hesitant about leaving him on his own, but her desire to see the paint job caused her fears to diminish.

They parted. Ryan drove his new SUV to the store and quickly went inside.

I'm so thankful that Patsy gave me directions. I doubt I would have found this place on my own.

Once inside, he was like a kid on Christmas morning. The first thing he purchased was a queen size bed for $650, and then the advertised bedspread and curtains for $175 and $150. There were also matching sheets and pillowcases in tan and deep red available. Ryan bought a complete set of each for a total of $180. The window already had a curtain rod that would work, so he convinced himself that he could spend a little more. He had noticed that the only rug in the house was a braided oval rug in the living area. Remaining consistent with Sally's taste, he bought two large, braided rugs and two small ones for a total of $700. One matching set of large and small rugs had the colors of his new bedspread woven throughout it. The other matching set had shades of cream, greens and blues.

Between the painting and decorating he was giving his charge card a workout. He instructed the personnel at the store to deliver the items to Sally's house on the following day. Ryan had told Sally that he needed to buy clothes, so he found a clothing store and spent $300 on clothes for himself.

I didn't lie, I do need the clothes. When I arrive back at the house, I'll show her the clothes. The other surprises will wait until tomorrow. This is perfect!

Ryan was pleased as he left the store. However, he was quickly beginning to tire. He was amazed at how easily he became exhausted. As he drove back to Brandon Springs, he became more accustomed with his newly purchased SUV. It handled almost as good as a mid-priced car, and it had the height of a truck. He could easily see the traffic ahead. Ryan had always thought of them as being family vehicles, not something for a single guy. He had enjoyed driving luxury cars and had welcomed comments about them from those more successful than himself. He had wanted to project personal success to those in the corporate world. Ryan's focus had now become family. The longer he drove the SUV the more comfortable he became with his decision to purchase it.

By the time Ryan arrived back at Sally's house the bedroom was painted. All four painters were busy priming the last side of the house. Sally was busy preparing supper as he entered the front door. On the way to the kitchen, he looked in the bedroom to admire the freshly painted room.

"This looks great!" he announced.

From the kitchen he heard Sally's voice call out.

"So, what else are you up too?"

He peered into the kitchen to see Sally pointing a rather large knife at him.

"Well, if you are going to kill me don't do it in the bedroom with the freshly painted walls" he said with a smile. "It would be a shame to splatter blood all over that beautiful paint job."

Sally lowered the knife and continued chopping vegetables.

"I think you still need to be in the hospital," she said. "I think you took a harder blow to the head than the doctors realized."

"Don't you think the bedroom looks good?" he asked.

"It looks beautiful" she said. "You really need to save your money though."

"Sally, I had planned to buy property from you, and you convinced me that would be unwise," he responded. "It's money that I can afford. I plan to come back here to visit you on a regular basis, and I wanted to do something for that bedroom."

"Consider that bedroom to be yours," she answered. "But don't get it in your smashed head to paint my bedroom pink!"

"I won't paint your bedroom," he said. "Andrew's old bedroom looked a bit gloomy. Don't you think it looks better?"

Sally agreed that the room looked very nice, but even with the bedroom window open the paint fumes were strong. By eight o'clock he made the decision to ask Sally if she minded him sleeping on the couch for the night. She approved, but she had a great time kidding him about it over the next half hour. Sally brought Ryan a blanket and one of the pillows from Andrew's bed. She took her evening bath while Ryan prepared the couch. After doing so, he stretched his exhausted body down on it. It very much reminded him of the dream where he and Sally spent the night in Andrew's old house and made plans of fixing it up.

He wondered how long it would be before he remembered new dreams. He thought about Patsy, and imagined what her boyfriend might be like.

I can't imagine her selecting a shallow or cruel person. She's smart; he must be a good man.

As he began to relax, he heard his cell phone. Ryan raced back to the bedroom to retrieve it. He hoped that it might be Patsy, but the voice on the other end was even more remarkable. It was Jonathan Knox, the boy who had just lost his mother. He had asked permission from his father to call Ryan. Sally had given the cell phone number to Mr. Knox in Jonathan's presence. The boy had heard her tell his father that Ryan had lost both of his parents, and they had been murdered.

RYAN AND THE BOY talked for an hour on the call, while Mr. Knox sat reading a book. Jonathan asked many questions and Ryan attempted to give him some of the answers Sally and the pastor had given him. They discussed how much they missed both their mothers. Jonathan told him that he would be spending part of the next day at the funeral home. By the end of the conversation a bond had formed between the two. Ryan was very tired, but he felt a great sense of relief. His days were very full, and his recovery was not yet complete. He prayed for each member of the Knox family, and he thanked God that he was given an opportunity to talk with Jonathan.

Before they retired for the night, Ryan shared with Sally the conversation he had with Jonathan. They sat at the kitchen table and prayed for the Knox family. Whether it was from grief for the Knox children or due to his current state of physical and emotional exhaustion, Ryan wept like a baby as they prayed. They thanked God for each other, and for allowing them to share this time together. He sensed a fullness of life that he had never known.

There have been times for which extended hours worked in the corporate world resulted in accomplishment and exhaustion, but there is a richness in recent experiences that are all-together different. There is something that is earthy, and yet spiritual, about what has been happening.

Later that night, they both enjoyed deep and restful sleep.

A KNOCK ON THE FRONT DOOR by the paint crew foreman stirred Ryan the following morning. At the kitchen table the night before he had noticed how tired Sally had become, and he was concerned that all the activity was beginning to be too much for her. Because of her inner strength, he sometimes forgot her age. The conquest of difficult living had made her strong spiritually, but it had broken her body in ways not apparent to him. He answered the door and told the man to give him a few minutes. Ryan had been right to be concerned, for he didn't see Sally this morning in the kitchen. On other days, she was hard at work preparing breakfast before he woke. He became worried. He stumbled back to her bedroom and gently knocked on the door. He was relieved to hear her sweet voice invite him in. She was still in bed. He became worried.

This isn't like her.

"Are you alright?" he asked.

"It's been a busy week, and I guess it all caught up with me," she answered.

She asked him to sit on the bed beside her. Sally took his hand and gave it that now familiar quick squeeze. She told him how proud she was of him, and that she loved him very much. Ryan kissed her on the forehead and told her that he loved her. He told her that the painters were ready to start and that he had told them to wait while he checked on her. She got up, gathered clothes for the day, and headed for the bathroom to dress. As she entered the bathroom door, she told Ryan to instruct the painters to begin. He took note of her labored short steps.

I guess I've never seen before she's had time to loosen up her stiff aching joints in the morning. I sometimes forget about her age.

Always in degrees of constant pain, Sally had seemed to only be concerned with his. Without saying a word, she was educating him again as to what kind of selfless saint she was. He had seen corporate giants from time to time in the workplace, but he had never witnessed inner greatness like hers. He imagined that in God's eyes, those men would be dwarfed in comparison to her.

When Ryan made it back to the painters, they had already taken the spray equipment off the truck. The foreman told him that they would first spray two coats of the white on the house. Afterwards, they would paint the front door green and hang the shutters. Lastly, they would paint the foundation and porch gray. The foreman estimated that they would be finished by about 3:00 in the afternoon.

Ryan went to the kitchen and began to pull out all the cooking utensils used by Sally to cook breakfast. He had watched her closely as she had prepared breakfast on the previous morning, and everything was laid out by the time she made it to the kitchen.

"You look like you're ready for some breakfast," she said while giving him a wink.

"You bet," he answered.

"OK, you've done enough," she commanded. "Now, get out of my way."

Ryan agreed and went to the bathroom to perform his morning ritual. The timing was perfect, just as he exited the bathroom Sally placed the last plate on the kitchen table. She called to him, and they sat together at the table. They were grateful that the bedroom paint fumes had mostly dissipated, and any faint smell of paint was overcome by the smell of freshly fried bacon. They both talked about how blessed they felt, and while holding hands they thanked God for the food and asked Him to bless the day. There was something special about that morning.

Just as they began to eat, they heard a knock on the door. It was the paint crew foreman. He warned them both to move their vehicles away from the house, as not to catch any of the drift from the sprayed paint. Ryan asked Sally for her keys and moved both vehicles.

When he returned to the table, they discussed the plans for the day. They had both experienced full days during the week, and they agreed that they should spend part of the day resting at the house. They decided to visit the funeral home and pay their respects to the family of the woman killed in the accident. The visit would take place later in the afternoon, but most of the day would be restful.

When breakfast was finished and the kitchen cleaned, they went to the living area to relax. Ryan straightened up the couch where he had slept, and Sally sat in the chair to read a book. After a short time, he went outside to watch the painting of the home. On the previous day they had covered the windows, as not to spray primer or paint on them. Immediately after the second coat of paint was applied to one side of the house, they removed the plastic and tape from that side. He was fascinated at how fast the spraying moved along, but his observation of the work was interrupted within the first thirty minutes. Sally called him from the front porch to tell him that his cell phone was ringing. It had stopped ringing by the time he reached it, but the message left on it was from Jonathan Knox. Ryan immediately pressed the redial, and the voice on the other end was that of Russell Knox.

"This is Ryan Walker; I had a message from Jonathan on my cell phone," he stated.

"Ryan, I will call Jonathan to the phone in just a moment," Mr. Knox explained. "First, I want to thank you for your discussions with him last night. After you two talked, he seemed as if a weight had been lifted from him. He slept through the night for the first time since his mother's death. I overheard him talking with his sister about your conversation, and I want you to know that I have no objection to anything that I heard. Here is Jonathan."

Ryan was relieved by the statements from Mr. Knox, because he had felt he had taken a risk in speaking to Jonathan. Russell Knox was a prominent lawyer, and Ryan wasn't sure whether the man would cause him legal problems because of something stemming from the conversation with the boy.

"Thanks for taking so much time to talk yesterday," said Jonathan. "It really helped. My sister, Christie, is much shyer and quieter than me. She wasn't interested in meeting you. I told her about what we discussed, and I could tell that it also helped her feel better."

"I plan to come by the funeral home sometime during the afternoon," Ryan promised.

The next hour was uneventful. About 10:00 that morning the delivery truck from the department store arrived with Ryan's purchases. Upon hearing the truck, Sally closed her book. She went out onto the front porch and witnessed Ryan signing the delivery slip. The rear door of the truck opened, and she watched as the contents began to be unloaded. Ryan turned from the truck just in time to see her standing on the porch shaking her head. She pointed the book at him, just as she had done with the knife on the previous day, and said, "What am I going to do with you?"

"You told me to consider the Andrew's old room as mine now," he explained.

Sally dropped her head and threw up her hands as if to signify her surrender. Ryan moved onto the front porch and gave her a big hug and a kiss on the forehead. He then went to the bedroom to begin the dismantling of the old bed. Within minutes he had the covers removed, the bed disassembled and the parts leaning against an empty wall of the living area. The workmen quickly set up the new bed and brought in the rest of the goods. Once set up, Ryan placed the red set of sheets in the dresser and the tan set on the bed. He neatly adjusted the spread across the bed and hung the new curtains using the existing curtain rod. Sally watched as he placed everything in its place. After positioning the small red and tan oval braided rug beside the bed and the larger one in front of the dresser, he turned to her and asked her opinion.

She smiled and admitted that the room was beautiful. Sally told him that she had no idea that he had an eye for putting a room together like that. Walking back into the living area, she spotted the other two rugs.

"What are you going to do with these?" she asked.

"Your room has a very barren floor," he said. She said nothing; she only starred at the new rugs. He wasn't sure how she would react to his decorating her room.

"I told you that I wouldn't paint your room pink!" he explained. "I didn't say a word about it needing something on the floor."

It was then that he saw her eyes begin to water. She hugged him and thanked him. She buried her face in his chest and continued to sob. At last, she gave his hand the quick squeeze. She then wiped her face with her hands. They carried the two rugs into her bedroom and spent several minutes admiring them.

The remainder of the morning was uneventful. They enjoyed a peaceful lunch, and from time to time they went outside to evaluate the paint job. They were sitting and talking at the kitchen table when Sally's phone rang. It was an elderly member of her church, Mildred Pickens, requesting help with her wallpaper. Sally told her that she would come over late in the afternoon, after visiting the funeral home. Mildred was a wheelchair bound widow who attended church via the church van. It had a lift to accommodate wheelchairs. Her ancient wallpaper had been hung years before in the home by her and her now deceased husband. From time to time the wallpaper would begin to come loose and droop. It was old wallpaper and Mildred wanted to use an old form of glue made from flour and water to make the repairs. Sally knew exactly what to do, so the crippled woman would call her every couple of years to help put it back up.

"I promised to help Mildred rehang her wallpaper after visiting the funeral home," Sally explained.

"I'll be coming with you to help," insisted Ryan.

"A longer set of arms would be useful in fixing the wallpaper," said Sally. "However, I insist on driving. I know the area and I know exactly how to get to Mildred's rural home. I don't want to have to coach you with directions. It's simpler for me to drive."

"Ok, but I want us to take my new SUV," demanded Ryan.

"No, I don't want to drive an unfamiliar vehicle," Sally said emphatically.

Mimicking what she had earlier done on the porch, Ryan dropped his head and raised his arms in surrender. She promptly swatted him with a magazine and began to laugh.

The estimate of time for painting had been fairly accurate. At 2:45 PM Ryan heard a knock at the rear door. It was the paint crew foreman, letting Ryan know that they had finished.

"The crew is loading the truck with the equipment," said the foreman. "You two should refrain from using the freshly painted front porch until tomorrow."

Ryan called Sally to the rear door, explained the restriction regarding the front porch. He then escorted her outside to inspect the job. They circled the refreshed home twice admiring its new exterior, while the crew finished loading the truck with equipment and material. Sally had never seen the old farmhouse look so good. It had always been painted by

Andrew, and the house had never sported shutters. She was amazed at the difference. She walked around the house inspecting each side again, while Ryan signed the charge to his card. He then gave the foreman and crew another $100 in twenties from his wallet.

"I want to give each of you twenty dollars extra for doing such a great job," he explained. "Supper is on me."

After the crew left, Ryan and Sally spent several minutes standing in front of the place admiring the work. Careful not to spoil the freshly painted front parch, they entered the house through the back door. They again examined the redecorated bedroom and discussed hanging a few pictures or portraits. Ryan told her that he planned to bring new lamps for the end tables on his next visit. Moving to Sally's room, they discussed painting it one of the colors in the new oval rugs. Nothing was decided, but Sally was open to the idea. It wasn't long before they realized that the time to visit the funeral home was drawing near. She advised Ryan to take an additional set of casual clothes in which to do the wallpaper work. Soon they were on their way to the funeral home in Sally's old car.

Chapter 18

SALLY'S DRIVING TOOK RYAN by surprise. Feeling more confident with Ryan's recovery, she no longer focused on his accident. Sally reverted back to her normal driving habits.

Before stepping into the old car with her, he had anticipated having to endure an exercise in patience. Because of his earlier experience of riding with her, he expected the entire ride to be paced at fifteen miles per hour under the speed limit. Concerned with the effects of sudden acceleration on Ryan, during the ride from the hospital she took an incredible amount of time to reach a slow cruising speed. Her turns had been slow and deliberate. He was mistaken in his expectations of the trip to the funeral home.

Now convinced that Ryan was recovering quickly from his injuries, these precautions were no longer pressing Sally's mind. She knew her car, and she went through the gears of the manual three speed transmission like clockwork. He was impressed.

Along the way, Ryan thought about the fact that this was his third day to be in Brandon Springs. He had twice dreamed of being there for three days, but he was now actually experiencing it. As she swiftly covered the country road, he wondered what the fourth day would hold.

It was 3:30 PM when they arrived at the funeral home,

and the parking lot was not yet as crowded as it would soon be. The Knox family was well known. Ryan had spoken to both Russell and Jonathan on the phone, but he had never met them face to face. He and Sally signed the visitation book and proceeded to the parlor where the body of Emily Knox lay. The line leading to the casket consisted of about thirty people. It included people of various ages, and various careers. Standing near foot of the casket, was a man in a dark gray suit with whom several people stopped to greet.

This has to be Russell Knox. Even from this distance I can tell that he carries himself with dignity.

The man appeared to be in his mid-forties, and his hair was beginning to gray. Near the head of the casket was a boy in his early teens; and beside him was a girl who looked to be about ten years old. Ryan could tell that the suit the boy wore was not a new one. The sleeves and pants lengths were a little short. Not so short as to be comical, but just slightly noticeable. Apparently, he was between suits during a period in his life where clothes seemed to constantly shrink before parental eyes.

The girl is wearing a dress that must have been purchased for Easter. Mr. Knox hasn't even considered buying Jonathan a new suit or Christie a darker dress for the occasion. It's obvious that the father isn't interested in putting on a show. His focus isn't having his children present a proper appearance, in order to maintain his image in the community or among his professional peers.

From his observation, Ryan understood that the primary concern for Russell Knox was to make the necessary arrangements for his wife and to concentrate on helping his children deal with their pain during this time of crisis. The attorney occasionally glanced down at his children to see how they were holding up. As if they could feel his attention, they would almost immediately return eye contact to confirm with him their state.

It's obvious that the children draw strength and comfort from their father, for they are never far from him. Children who are not normally close to their parents tend to gravitate to their friends for support during times of personal stress.

Ryan compared this to other funerals for family members of upscale professionals, in which he had taken note that the desire to present a professional image of aristocracy was of primary concern. This really didn't appear to carry any importance with Mr. Knox. There was something that Ryan admired about a man who ignored public perception, but instead immersed himself in concerns for his children's personal well-being.

As the line moved, Ryan wondered if he would ever become a father. If he was to become one, he hoped that he would have his priorities straight when dealing with children.

Within a few minutes Sally reached Russell Knox. He took her hand and whispered something to her. She turned and introduced Ryan. Mr. Knox placed his hand into Ryan's and gave him a firm grip, while thanking him for coming. The eyes of Mr. Knox told of sleepless nights and weariness, but his voice was strong. Within a minute Ryan felt a second hand on his arm. It was Jonathan. He sensed an immediate kinship with the boy, and Ryan told him that a call from him would always be welcome.

"Please never hesitate to call or write me, if you are ever in need," Ryan offered.

Standing beside her brother was a silent girl with swollen eyes. With both hands she held the free hand of her brother. Ryan knelt on one knee so that he would be on eye level with her, and then he told her that he would pray for her each night. Silently she nodded, and then released the hands of her brother to give Ryan a hug. It was at that moment that it seemed that her pain transferred to Ryan. As he stood, he felt as if his heart was about to burst. She gave him a faint smile. The visit was brief because the line behind them was growing by the minute.

Just as he and Sally exited the front door of the funeral home, the tears began to pour down Ryan's face. By the time they reached the car he was sobbing audibly. The grief of losing both his parents revisited him even more than the day of their burial. He thought about how badly the children would miss their mother over the upcoming troublesome teenage years, and he thought about the parental weight that would be on the shoulders of Russell Knox. It was as if the inner pain of the little girl had become his, and it was ravaging his heart.

Before starting the car, Sally asked, "Are you going to be alright?"

"I'll be fine," he replied between sobs. "But that family has been dealt a tremendous blow, and those kids will be at a real disadvantage during trying years."

"That's true," she responded. "Just remember them in your prayers. God is capable of comforting them, and you made it clear to them that they could call on you."

The sky had been clear when the day began. However, clouds gathered like an angry mob as the two made their way to the home of Mildred Pickens. Traces of shadows were gone from the day. As they disappeared, so did the overwhelming shadows of grief that had earlier taken hold of Ryan. He focused on the wallpaper and the immediate duties of helping Mildred. The pain within him dimmed. As the sky grew darker, the brighter the day appeared to him.

They arrived at Mildred's about 4:20 PM, to find her busily preparing the flour paste. She was a tiny woman who couldn't have weighed more than about eighty-five pounds, and her thinning fine white hair sat on her head as puffs of clouds. Her fingers were almost locked by arthritis, and Ryan was amazed at her ability to stir the homemade glue. He could not imagine how she was able to grasp the large spoon, and he watched intently as she let it slide from her grip when laying it down.

Sally gave her a hug and introduced Ryan. After Mildred politely greeted him, she was all business. She told them that they had only a short while before the paste would become too thick to use. She didn't have a ladder, so Ryan volunteered to stand on a chair. With an old paintbrush he painted the back of the drooping paper with the paste, and then he pressed the paper against the wall. Sally handed him a wet towel to wipe the excess paste from the wall. Only two rooms needed the repair, so they were finished by 5:00 PM. Ryan and Sally disposed of the leftover paste and cleaned the pan and brush. Once the job was done, Mildred was much more social. She asked them to stay for supper, but Sally politely refused. She told Mildred that she had planned Ryan's favorite meal.

As they drove away from Mildred's, Ryan asked Sally. "So, you're fixing my favorite meal?"

"Sure," she replied. "What is it?"

Ryan laughed.

Sally explained that Mildred was now poor, and that she barely had enough to feed herself. No one was to know, but the church was giving the old woman financial support during these difficult times. She had not always been in such a state.

"As a teenager she was the homecoming queen while in high school," Sally explained. "I'm sure it's hard for you to picture that in your mind. After graduating, she married the captain of the football team in 1940. The small community considered them a perfect couple, and they sincerely loved each other. It wasn't long before she and her husband were separated by a European war that had come to America. Being an enlisted man during World War II, her husband returned home a hero. He won the Bronze Star and received two Purple Hearts. One of which, cost him his left leg. He is now dead, and most of her friends have passed away. Very few are around who remember him; and most of them are dying in homes for the elderly."

"Except for a few aging pictures about the house, there were little signs of her former life," Ryan said.

"After the war, there were those who were proud just to shake the hand of her husband," stated Sally. "She and Mr. Pickens both enjoyed great respect. He was greeted warmly on street corners, and he never lacked for work. There was a time when the couple was regularly invited to parties, and there were dinners for which her husband had been invited as guest speaker. Though he was not college educated, he was held in high esteem by local politicians and community leaders.

Now she's just a poor crippled old woman living alone.

She has a daughter living in California who pays her yearly visits. The daughter was a member of a peace movement group during the 1960s, and she viewed the actions of her father during the war as a source of personal embarrassment. Mildred's son is a Viet Nam war veteran. He and his wife are members of an RV club, and they spend most of the year traveling with his retired military friends. They drop by twice a year. Mildred's pride never let either of her children know of her financial needs, and because of their polarizing political views the two siblings rarely speak to each other. Outside those three annual visits, and the care sometimes offered by the church, she remains mostly alone."

For the first time in his life Ryan was noticing the lives of the people with whom he came in contact. The lives and souls of others had always been there, but those people had only been part of the scenery. Children and old people were just objects making up the landscape, or sometimes inconveniences that got in his way.

It's amazing how self-absorption, extreme dedication to career, and acquisition of status can blind a man to the reality around him.

As they drove down the country road, the clouds broke open and a cold rain fell. It was brief, but very heavy. Afterwards there was a strong chill in the air. Ryan was amazed at how quickly the temperature dropped. Behind the rain were clear skies, but the sun was quickly retreating behind the horizon.

Ryan considered Mildred's plight, and he thought of all the occasions that he should have visited with Andrew and Sally. He thought about Patsy's care of elderly women, who were not even family members.

Care for the elderly is rarely noted or rewarded, so it usually is entirely a charitable endeavor. It is sometimes not even noticed by family members and is usually only appreciated by the older person receiving the care. Those who work with youth may be remembered by them long after a person's death, and some of the young people possibly may offer a slight amount of appreciative care when those volunteers become old. It is not so for those who care for the elderly.

He thought of the needs of the two Knox children, and even those of the widowed father. He knew that his career was important, but he also realized that jobs come and go. *Family can't be replaced; and once they were gone there is no way of reclaiming precious lost time.*

He considered the fact that sometimes the needs of others were immediate, that the opportunity to fill a gap in the lives of others could vanish very quickly. He determined that he would dedicate a portion of his life to doing something for other people.

Patsy is right. We can't help everyone in need, but we all can help a few.

His thoughts were suddenly interrupted as a deer ran out in front of the car. In an attempt to miss it, Sally swerved. The car's passenger side front wheel dropped off the low shoulder of the road. She tried to quickly compensate, but her aging reflexes were not steady enough to make a smooth correction. Her arthritic hands firmly gripped the steering wheel and she pulled hard to bring the vehicle back onto the roadway. However, this effort was an overcompensation, for the car crossed the center line and headed into the opposite lane. Sally tried to bring it back to the proper side of the highway, but the car suddenly began to slide sideways on the wet pavement. She lost control, and the car slipped off the rural road. It made a partial rotation before striking a large tree on Sally's side of the car. The vehicle then bounced off the huge tree and came to rest on a grassy area in front of a dense forest.

Ryan was dazed. He glanced down and saw that he was strapped tightly by the seat belt. Looking up, he noticed a large crack across the windshield. Even in the moonlight, its edges were apparent. As his eyes followed it from his side of the car to driver side, he noted that it entered an area of several cracks forming a web like pattern. That's when he noticed the still frail form on the other side of the car. Sally was slumped forward with her face against the steering wheel. The glass in the window beside her was gone, and the chilled evening air moving through the opening gingerly stroked her hair. Ryan's head was spinning, and it was difficult for him to get his bearings. It was at the point of dusk, and he had difficulty visually examining Sally's condition. Colors and shapes seemed to blur, and he felt as though he was dreaming. Nothing seemed real.

His vision narrowed, and he felt that he might pass out. Ryan's hands fumbled at the buckle, but he found it impossible to manage the removal of his seat belt.

The air suddenly seemed unusually cold, and he began to shiver from the dampness. Ryan saw movement outside Sally's car door. A full moon was beginning to rise in the clearing night sky; and it enabled him to barely recognize the familiar face of someone standing beside the car.

"It's Jerry," he softly whispered.

Reaching in through the broken window of the car, Jerry's thick and powerful hands carefully and gingerly took hold of Sally. Stunned, Ryan watched him effortlessly remove her from the car through the open window. With her firmly in his arms, Jerry turned to him and said, "She needs my attention right now. You'll be OK."

Ryan's head was spinning, and he watched as Jerry carried her to the edge of the woods. Ryan tried to comfort himself by the fact that the accident had been witnessed.

Jerry saw the accident, and he's now caring for Sally. Soon he'll come back for me, or he'll send someone to the scene.

The moon was now bright, and the light from it revealed a trail leading into the thickly wooded area. It lay right in front of Jerry. The path was wide and clear. Jerry stopped for a moment at the opening in the forest, and lovingly looked down at the small person he was holding. He turned to offer an affirming glance back at Ryan, and then started up the trail with Sally's limp form still in his arms. As he disappeared from sight, Ryan's vision failed, and he collapsed. Everything went black.

Ryan misjudged. Jerry would not return for him that night.

As Jerry carried her up the trail, Sally opened her eyes and began to become aware of the trees moving past her line of sight. At first, they appeared to be just a fluctuating blur, but soon she was able to focus. Still in a mental fog, she asked, "What is going on?"

"You were in an accident, and you need my help," Jerry explained.

"Who are you?" she asked. "You look familiar, but I just can't place you."

Jerry slowed his pace a bit, and answered "I'm Jerry Prescott, and I believe you are Sally Thompson."

Now becoming more coherent, she replied, "I'm Sally Thompson, all right... but..." She stopped in mid-sentence. "You know my nephew, Ryan," she stammered.

"Yes, I know him," Jerry replied.

Sally was beginning to notice the strength in Jerry's arms and legs. Effortlessly, he moved through the forest with her in his arms. The further he carried her up the trail, the better Sally felt. After some distance, she was fully alert and felt stronger.

"You can put me down now," she said. "I would like to try to walk."

Jerry lowered her feet to the ground, but she felt a bit weaker than she expected. Her legs would not completely support her light frame.

"Here, let me help you," he said.

Jerry placed her left arm around his neck, as he placed his right arm around her waist. He pointed to the porch light of a farmhouse just ahead.

"Do you think you can make it there?" he asked.

"I believe so," she replied.

As they neared the house, she became stronger. By the time they went up the steps of the front porch she felt remarkably well. The front porch was clean and neat. It looked to be freshly painted.

"I've driven down the rural road leading to Mildred's home many times, but I've never even noticed this house or the trail in the forest leading to it," she stated.

Most of her trips there had been during the day, and she decided that she might have spotted this porch light if she had driven the road by night. Although this was apparently the house of a stranger, she didn't feel apprehensive to be there. She was remarkably at ease. There was a calming effect in Jerry's presence.

"Well, he isn't a total stranger because he knows Ryan," she reminded herself. *"No wonder he had made such an impression on my young nephew. There's something very special about this fellow."*

She tried to think, but she couldn't remember where Ryan had met him. She couldn't even remember even the smallest details of her nephew's experiences with Jerry, but she decided that it would eventually all come back to her in time. Jerry seemed strangely familiar to her also. She felt no fear as he invited her inside. In her heart, she knew that she needed to be at this house. She had lived many years in her brother's house, but for some strange reason, she felt more at home here than she did in Andrew's old home.

"Everything seems right," she thought. *"Things are as they should be. There was something very special about Jerry, and even more special about this house."*

She was amazed. Sally now felt no effects of the accident. When she had first found herself in Jerry's arms, she had felt intense pain. She had not taken the time to examine herself for blood or broken bones. Sally wasn't even sure what injuries she had sustained in the accident, but she felt sure that she had needed Jerry's assistance in a big way. Sally felt remarkably well to have been involved in such a violent impact. Her fragile frame felt no discomfort, or weariness from years of use.

"Perhaps I'm somewhat numbed by a state of shock," she considered.

She knew the body would sometimes react in that manner in an attempt to help a person suffering adverse conditions. It didn't seem to matter to her. She was alright now.

He opened the door to a warm and cozy living area. To her surprise, she immediately liked the colors of the room and furniture. There, in front of the fireplace, was a couch and two chairs. A man and woman were seated on the couch. They were warmed by the glow of the fire and seemed somewhat familiar. As the couple turned toward the two standing at the door, Sally realized these were Ryan's parents. She glanced back into Jerry face, and the chill of the night air melted into a perfect warmth. Returning her attention to the couple, they stood to greet her. One of the two chairs was empty, but in the other sat her brother Andrew. He rose to stand with Ryan's parents, and she quickly moved to greet them all. As Sally hugged and kissed each one, joy and peace filled her soul. She now understood.

Thoughts of the accident, of the events of the day, and of years of difficulties began to fade. The cares of life were fleeing quickly. As the last remnant of worry was slipping away, she turned back to Jerry and asked, "What about Ryan?"

Jerry smiled.

"There's no need for concern," he said. "Ryan and I won't meet again for a very long time."

About the Author:

Rob Williams, currently residing in Nacogdoches Texas, has served in multiple roles supporting the Christian community. Included in this long list of mentorships was his service as youth director of an inner-city church in Atlanta and working with children in some of the toughest housing projects in that city. Rob worked at a rehabilitation center for five years, where he became acquainted with the homeless. The center helped those on work release from jail and those who were physically and mentally handicapped. He has taught adult Sunday school classes for more than thirty years and led youth in Boy Scouts and Cub Scouts for twenty years. Retired from the high-tech industry in Huntsville Alabama, he writes Christian fiction and science fiction in his free time. Rob is a husband, the father of four, and a grandfather. He is the author of the three novel Brandon Springs Christian fiction series, the dystopian science fiction novel *Sins of Variance*, the Christian fictional crime novel *Gathering of Six*, and Christian mystery *Cabin by the Stream*.